The

Strange

Disappearance

of

Rose

Stone

The
Strange
Disappearance
of
Rose
Stone

J.E. Irvin

***** Whodunit Award Winner 2019

An Imprint of ABSOLUTELY AMAZING eBOOKS

Published by Whiz Bang LLC, 926 Truman Avenue, Key West, Florida 33040, USA.

ISBN 978-1-951150-17-4

For information contact:
Publisher@AbsolutelyAmazingEbooks.com

For all the children
who find their way from the darkness
into the light and to all the adults who offer
a helping hand along the way.
You are doing good things.

The
Strange
Disappearance
of
Rose
Stone

Leslie,
May you enjoy this story
of siblings Peter and Rose.
All Best,
J. E. Irvin

Preface

This is a special book – special in that it is the first place winner in the 2019 Whodunit Mystery Writing Competition.

But also special in that this is the *second* time that author Janet Irvin has won first place in that prestigious writing award. Two separate years. Two separate sets of judges. Both "blind" judging with nobody but me knowing the names of the authors who had submitted three pages of a finished novel for judging. And I didn't tell anybody!

Why only three pages, you might ask? When Absolutely Amazing eBooks began sponsoring this national competition about five or six years ago, we were assisted by noted crime novelist Jeremiah Healy. And the late Jerry Healy had a mantra that we agreed with: That if a book doesn't grab someone within the first three pages, you've lost him or her as a reader!

As Jerry used to say, "First impressions are important."

So writers were invited to send us the first three pages of their book.

As Sandra Balzo – one of the original judges and author of the *Maggy Thorsen Mysteries* – wrote, "I was happy to find that many of the entries did a good job of engaging the reader. Several made me curious enough to want to read the whole book."

As she wrote in a preface to Jan Irvin's original winner, *The Dark End of the Rainbow,* it "grabbed me by the throat and pulled me into its world."

Same can be said about this one.

We're proud to present *The Strange Disappearance of Rose Stone.* We think it will grab you by the throat too!

- Shirrel Rhoades
Publisher, Absolutely Amazing eBooks

Chapter One

Rose's letter arrives ten days after she disappears. The envelope settles in my palm like a wounded bird, the package that accompanies it still nesting inside the mailbox. Neither bears a return address. Seeing my name in my sister's elaborate script rattles free the anxious memories, jars like a random chord on a broken record. We've spoken only sporadically since Kelly and I got married. We used to share many late-night conversations while the world slept and the night whispered dark forebodings, but the bond forged in childhood has frayed. I stopped trying to save her, too busy trying to save myself.

Sensing my unease, Soldier nudges my knee. I reassure him with a pat on the head. The German shepherd tucks his tail and slouches along the sidewalk. A shrapnel scar spans his muzzle like a question mark. Sometimes, when he's sleeping, he twitches the way Kelly says I do, reliving the memories. Except his are all from Afghanistan. Mine go back farther than that.

"I'm okay, buddy." I ruffle the fur on his neck. "So are you."

Rising, he sprints for the porch, leaps the steps, and settles on the welcome mat, but his ears stay perked, his haunches coiled and ready. I scan the street before turning back to the mailbox.

Gathering the package and the rest of Saturday's ad flyers, I run my hand over the swirl of letters forming my name. *Peter Stone*. Even as a kid, Rose couldn't resist the urge to spin the dullest act into gold. Sometimes, when she gazed at the light, or waved her hands in time to music I couldn't hear, she reminded me of a fairy trapped in the mortal world, desperate to find a way back to her true home. Tucking the mail and the package under my arm, I open the envelope, unfold the letter, mouth the words.

Peter,

I can't forgive. I can't forget. I can't let it happen again. Remember when we talked about becoming immortal and famous? Three ways, you said. Marry money. Disappear in grand fashion. Die under mysterious circumstances. I'm shooting for the trifecta. Wish me luck.

P.S. It's your turn to guard the past.

No signature, as if I needed one to tell me who sent it. I stand in the shade of the maple that shadows the front of the house, a solitary man on an impossible mission. Guard the past. Which part, I wonder. When Soldier growls, I whistle him to my side. Together, we trudge up the driveway and enter through the back door. I toss everything on the counter. The package settles next to the article announcing Rose's disappearance, which flutters, slips over the edge, and floats to the floor. Retrieving the page, I smooth the edges and read it again.

April 12, 2008 ... Where Is Rose Stone?

Cleveland, Ohio – Police continue to investigate the disappearance of Rose Stone, whose one-woman sculpture show is scheduled to open at the Winston Gallery July 4th. Stone was last seen one week ago filming a commercial in the Flats district for the Cleveland Arts Commission.

The reclusive artist, 28, a graduate of the New York College of Art and Design, was a relative unknown before winning the prestigious Rodin Competition in 2004. Her signature sculpture, *Kaleidoscope*, a giant, rotating wheel with spokes in the shape of winged children who change colors as the axle turns, is mounted near the Central Park Zoo in New York City. The installation has drawn record crowds since its dedication last September.

Stone is married to Mason Carruthers, lead singer of the band Sweaterz, who was out of the country on tour the day his wife went missing. Upon his return to the States, he issued a statement offering a

$250,000 reward for information on his wife's whereabouts. Police are asking anyone with knowledge of Stone to contact them at the hot line number listed below.

The number provided has a Cleveland area code. I offered our landline. The police declined. But I still put it up on my social media page. I check the antiquated answering machine attached to our phone, used only for emergencies, for messages. No one has called. I liberate my cell from the pocket of my jeans, check for calls. Rose's command intrudes. *Guard the past.* I don't want to start down this path, giving interviews, deflecting insinuations, inviting suspicions. I don't want Kelly caught up in my sister's drama. Kelly. I rub a hand over my face, try to scrub away the tension. My wife has gone to see the doctor. Again. Desperate to solve the riddle of our infertility, she lobbies for the family she wants so badly. I feign enthusiasm, cheerlead our attempts, but in my heart, I harbor ambivalence. Sometimes no family is better than a fractured one.

Standing by the sink, I consider whether to pick up the bucket of soapy water and the roll of paper towels. I know I should stay busy, hurry past the moment, keep my mind on simple tasks. When my wife returns, we can discuss this latest move on the Stone family chessboard. But my body refuses to co-operate. *Stay calm*, my brain urges, *don't panic.* Maybe Rose isn't really gone. Maybe it's all a mistake. I stare at the package I have yet to unwrap, remembering.

"Put your eye to the glass, Peter." Rose pushed the kaleidoscope closer, her little girl voice transformed by the glimpse into the fantasy tube.

The reds and purples shuffled into focus, swirling and settling in new patterns, constructing meaning from abstraction. Our story started there, in between the glass pieces, in the shadows of the shadows, where memory and heartbeat align themselves and color erupts like a blade, ripping past the barriers that time has erected.

Put your eye to the glass, Peter, I tell myself. *Breathe. This is how it began.*

~~~

3

June, 1984

The Saturday we left the mountain I didn't know if we would ever come back. Our car, a station wagon of indeterminate age and patchwork colors, bent its back under the boxes and garbage bags stuffed with our possessions. Wrapped in a tarp that flapped in the wind, Mam's antique desk with its wavy panes of colored glass waited on the porch. Our father's mother had willed it to our mother, who polished and guarded it with the reverence due a family heirloom. Despite its size, she refused to leave it behind.

"We got no room for that, Opal," our father said, his calm inching into anger. Mama beat at his chest, her hands clenched in fury.

"It's got to go with us, Estill. It's all we got left. I'm not leaving it behind."

My father pushed her hands away and spit into the morning wind. "All right. All Right. Shut up now."

His voice tapered off. His shoulders rose and fell, surrendering to her need. From my place next to Rose, I strained to catch the last words.

"We only got room for one big piece, so I can't take my tool bench, is all."

My mother refused to take the bait, to concede to his wish the way she always had in the past. He tied the desk on top of the wagon and finished locking the door, stashing the key under a loose porch floorboard.

The car bucked and rocked as we rattled our way down from Raccoon's Gap. Rose and I huddled together, hemmed in by the clothing and tools that filled the space around us. As we stuttered our way toward the Interstate, Mama turned on the radio. Static punctuated our progress until we reached a reception point. The announcer told the time and the weather. Then he introduced the next song, identifying the voice of John Denver singing about country roads. Rose patted my hand. The trees that hugged the slopes sliced the light into strips of yellow and black. I pushed to my knees to stare out the window, blinking as we crept in and out of shadow, fixing the shifting mountain views into my memory. Just before we sped up the entrance ramp to the interstate, I spotted my

4

father's face in the rearview mirror. Loss plowed furrows across his forehead.

We spent the first night at a rest stop, cuddled in worm-like tangles, our dreams night-crawling around the inside of the car. We'd almost reached the Ohio River when the shaking started. I grabbed the back of the seat and touched my father's shoulder. He didn't speak, but somehow in the clench of his muscles and the angle of his body I knew this decision he'd made to point us toward the Dayton factories, this humbling of his pride, had carved out an empty place inside him that would never be filled again. The car lurched along, humping the berm, my father cursing and my mother praying, for eighty more miles.

The clutch cable snapped just as we cruised to the curb in front of the Belmont Art Theater. My mother's hair had frizzed out around her head like a dandelion gone to seed. My father stepped out of the car, kicked a tire, and leaned, with a heaviness born of despair, on the hood.

"Estill," my mother said, pointing at a poster mounted in the window of the theater's ticket booth, "what day is today?"

My father rubbed his head with one hand. "Saturday, I guess. June 23?"

She looked around, her mouth cocked at an angle, at the shuttered store windows. Sawhorses blocked off the ends of several streets. She turned back to the poster.

"Well, we're not going any farther tonight," she said. "Might as well go to the street fair."

I shuffled closer to Rose. Her not-quite-four-year old feistiness had faded as the miles dragged on. Whenever she was certain our parents couldn't see her, she sucked her thumb. At mom's words, she stood straighter, smoothed her red and white-checked sundress, and wiped the drool off her chin. "What's a street fair?" she asked.

I knew my father was frustrated with this forced detour. He had intended to reach Englewood and our aunt Pearl's house before it got dark, but that plan was now a bust.

"We can't pay for a tow," he said, turning his back on the poster.

5

"Big Butch'll come get us. You call and tell Pearl and he'll come," Mama said. She opened the door and pointed at us. Rose and I clambered over the metal box that held my father's tools. Mama, distracted, lifted Rose out. "Peter," she barked. I stretched out my hand and she jerked me to the sidewalk, scraping my knee on the corner of the box. Blood from the cut left two red spots on the concrete.

"Mama," Rose whispered, "I have to go to the bathroom."

"They'll have potties down there, baby girl." Mama swept her hand in the direction of the sawhorses. I lifted my head and noticed, above the roofs of the buildings, a crescent moon riding the early evening sky. I stumbled and the thin fingernail of light sliced back and forth like a scythe. My father shrugged. He checked the ropes binding Mam's desk to the roof. His eyes scanned the street, taking in the weary houses sharing space with the storefronts, everything stone-faced and silent beyond the hum of traffic.

"I got a feeling," he said.

"We won't be gone all that long, will we?" Mama touched his arm, her voice a mix of plead and cajole. "And Pearl and Butch, they'll help."

Reluctant to abandon the car, my father stopped every two feet to twist his head and look back. "I hate to be beholden to anybody."

My mother smoothed the sleeve of his t-shirt. "Butch and Pearl are family," she said.

"Don't matter." His voice carried claws sharp enough to graze my heart. "I'm my own man."

I didn't know, that midsummer's eve, that we had stumbled on the annual Appalachian Homespun Festival sponsored by Immaculate Conception Church. The festival embraced all the displaced hill people from Kentucky and Tennessee and other places south, all the ex-patriots from Boone County and Jellico and the towns hidden in the folds of the mountains. The migrants had adjusted to the city, grown accustomed to the loud nights, and welcomed the paychecks GM's 'generous motors' plant provided. But in their hearts, those stolid beating red chunks at the center of their chests, there rested unease and the sharp melancholy of loss.

We strolled by the main cluster of tents and tables. When a fiddler took the stage, my father stopped, stood still as a rabbit in a field. Then he began to hum. The music swelled. Tapping her foot, my mother kept an eye out as my father listened to the mountains calling. His eyes grew shiny and wet in the beam of a streetlight. His hand shook when my mother passed him a beer in a white plastic cup.

"You'll find work here, Estill, I know it," she said, sipping from her own drink. Rose and I hovered at the edge of their conversation. We had heard those lines before. We moved off through the crowd, my father trailing behind. Mama held Rose by the hand, shaking it every few minutes to assure herself my sister was still attached. She leaned against my father as they walked, whispering something I couldn't hear. Rose watched me, imitating my careful passage through the crowd. We were tall for our ages, already showing promise of the rangy, athletic bodies that would allow us to see over other people's heads. Later, when trouble came to call, our height would give us time to run.

I allowed myself a moment to study our surroundings. Festival booths crowded the curbs and sidewalks. Laughter echoed around us, the sounds of *y'all* and *I declare* mingling with the flatter accents of the northern crowd. A large group of junior high schoolers bubbled toward us, their bodies and their mouths out of control. My mother flattened herself against the window of a local realty office until the preteens passed. Then she turned to read the list of featured available homes.

"Estill, there's a house, just two bedrooms, but look, it's not all that expensive. Maybe we could?" She glanced up at him. The sound of "Rocky Top" carried from the performer's stage, and my father, half-smiling, slapped his leg. Placing his beer on the ground, he took my mother in his arms and danced in a tight circle. She followed him easily. Rose and I crouched, forgotten, on the sidewalk. She reached for my hand and we waited there, watching, alert for danger. Happy could go sad in half a beat.

There was a pause in their movement. They stood still, their eyes locked together, and then my father spoke. "If I can find work, we'll stay." Rose and I let out the breath we'd been holding. Neither of us moved. They must remember us without our help. That's how it worked.

"C'mon, then, let's see what else this fair has to offer." My father took my hand, his work-callused palm unyielding and rough, and we walked along the street. My mother stayed behind, scrabbling in her purse for paper and a pencil, writing down the information about the house.

At the end of the church parking lot, flat up against a police barricade, a broad shelf of a woman stood behind a table covered in black velvet and decorated with stars. Although I didn't know what they were called until she told me, a display of kaleidoscopes beckoned. I skipped over to take a closer look. My father nodded once and I lifted one of the slender tubes. Rose, less cautious, snatched up a bigger one, twisting it between her fingers.

"Well, I bet you never seen one of these before, did ya now?" The woman bent toward us, her face a full moon of dark cheer. She pried the kaleidoscope out of Rose's hands, placed it to my sister's eye and turned the barrel. Rose laughed and clapped. Then the woman handed it to me.

"Hold it up to your eye, dat's de way," the woman urged, her island voice a caress. "Here, young sister, have a second look."

She handed Rose a different tube. Rose lifted it and sighed, entranced by the shifting patterns inside the carved wooden barrel. While we stood motionless, lost in the swirling colors, my father snorted impatiently. Mama joined us at the table. Seeing him coming undone, she filled the moment with her own anger and waved the woman off.

"We haven't got money for such foolishness."

The old woman handed one of the kaleidoscopes to my father.

"Beauty ain't a foolish thing. Here, sir. Might be you see something of your other world in the glass. I know I do, see my islands shining, and when I turn the barrel, I remember the sun and the shadows of my home. Could be you will, too." Her words caught my father's attention. He settled the eyepiece next to his cheek and stared into the tube.

"These be the best there is, children. Don't want no cheap kaleidoscope, no sirree. Them cheap ones lead you on, then repeat the same pattern they started with. Quality, now, quality, gives you a new pattern every time you turn the barrel." The woman lifted Rose's chin. Pushing my sister's hair off her forehead, the woman looked into her eyes. Then she did the same to me, nodding her head and shaking mine in rhythm with her own. She spoke again, staring straight at my mother. "Uh-huh, quality don't repeat the same patterns."

"How much?" my father grunted, his hand already scrabbling in the pocket of his jeans.

"For you, fine sir, a special deal." I could see her sizing us up, looking at my mended shirt and Rose's faded dress. When she named the price, my father didn't hesitate. He pulled five dollars from the three remaining bills in his pocket and handed the kaleidoscope to me.

"You take care with this now, you hear? Anything happens to it, you're responsible."

I wanted him to say my name, to pat my shoulder, but he didn't. Unbuttoning my shirt, I settled the kaleidoscope next to my ribs, hugging it to me as we moved away from the table. When I looked back, the old woman was watching us, one hand on her chest, the other making the sign of the cross.

My father spent the next-to-last of our money on hot dogs from a vendor's stand. We huddled together, chewing with slow, careful movements. Rose tried to catch my eye, but I ignored her. I wanted to stay here, where the smells of frying and chocolate and popcorn warmed the cold, lost corner of my heart. I hugged my arms closer to my body and imagined our mountain sleeping under the blanket of night, our family safe in its embrace. The kaleidoscope poked at me, a star-filled barrel aiming straight at my heart.

At the very end of the street, we found a gas station. Inside, a pay phone hung on the wall in the space between a soda machine and doors marked *Men* and *Women*. Mama pointed at the phone and took Rose into the restroom. I listened while my father dialed Aunt Pearl's number and waited through the ringing. He hung up before Big Butch

9

could answer. When he remembered me, my father frowned and pressed one finger to his lips.

Five minutes passed, ten, before Mama hustled out, Rose in tow. A piece of toilet paper clung to her shoe. "Did you get ahold of Pearl?" she asked. "Is Big Butch on his way?"

"No answer," my father said, turning his back on her anxious face. "Guess we'll have to hold off until tomorrow." He cocked his head and waited to see if I would contradict him. I felt the shifting of a lock, the closing of a connection. We were conspirators now, uneasy allies in a game of fool-my-mother.

"I have to go to the bathroom, too," I said. Before my father could object, I disappeared into the men's room. My head ached.

We wandered the fair until it closed, strolling past the same booths over and over again. After the fireworks, we returned to the car. Only one of the houses had lights on. The stores brooded, a buzzard's roost of decaying commerce. Long before we reached our parking space, I realized that Mam's desk was gone.

"Damnation!" My father pounded the side of the car. Flecks of spit dappled his chin. He picked up the ropes, rubbed his thumb over the ends where a knife had sliced through and tossed the pieces into the gutter. "That's it then."

My mother didn't flinch, but I could see her shadow, a pool of shivering blackness cast by a streetlight halfway down the block.

"Call the police," she said, her words punctuated by sobs.

"No damn police," my father answered. "No damn past. And no workbench neither. Get in the car."

We piled in, Rose and I curling up on the quilts my mother also refused to part with. I lay awake, cradling the kaleidoscope in my arms, wondering what new pattern had been put in play.

10

Chapter Two

To call or not to call? The cop in me pushes against the wall of the past, trying to free Peter Stone the man from the snares of his personal history. Soldier laps at his water dish, yawns, and flops down on my shoes. Crouching, I give him a good ear rub before sending him into the living room. When he circles back, I order him to stay. Then I fill his food bowl, sweep up stray bits of dog food, and pick up the package. The ink is smudged. Beneath the smear, I decipher a stamp. New York City. What was Rose doing in New York? How did she get there? Gnawing on that conundrum, I rattle the package, listen for the slip of stones. Sure enough, I hear a swoosh as I turn the box over. The rush of memory threatens to knock me over. My sister always knew what to do to unnerve the people around her, especially me. I scratch at the postmark, searching for a date and find one. April 5. The day after Rose disappeared. It took the post office a while to find me at our new address. Ten days ago, Rose Stone was alive. Closing my eyes, I turn the timeline over in my head, heart skipping beats, fingers gripped tight around the proof that my sister didn't bury the past we both tried to outrun.

~~~

We spent that first night crammed into the crowded car. The next morning Daddy finally called Aunt Pearl, but that didn't solve all our problems. After Uncle Butch found him a part-time job, after the fight with one of their neighbors, after the police came, we had to move out of Aunt Pearl's spare bedroom. We spent two more nights sleeping in the car before Mama got up the courage to call the realtor. When the man said the place was still available, she arranged to see the house. Rose and I burrowed into the nest of belongings in the back seat and tried not to make a sound.

All twelve of the homes on Dream Street sat close to the curb, except for the farmhouse that commanded a larger piece of land. Mama said that the owner probably sold off the smaller lots to pay the taxes. I rolled down the window and stared. The street was a dead-end that ran smack into a dented guardrail bearing paint smears from careless drivers. On the far side of the rail, the land sloped down toward a creek. Beyond the stream lay a field ringed by stands of hardwoods, maples, oaks, willows and poplars and, every hundred yards or so, a clump of pines. The bungalow we had come to see faced the farmhouse. The covered front porch, graced by two dying ferns, was just big enough for two chairs and a small table. Mama ordered us out of the car. Standing on the sidewalk, I checked out the other homes. Most were modest, one-story dwellings with faded paint and crumbling walks, no two alike. When I looked at the old farmhouse, I saw someone in the window looking back at me.

"You kids stay here. Don't even think about moving." My mother, anxious to make a good impression, twisted the hem of her dress until it hung like a rope around her knees. When the realtor got out of his car, Mama smoothed down her hair and held out her hand, then followed him into the house. They weren't gone long. Whatever she said to the man, he believed her. I watched him pat her back as they came down the front steps. Behind him, the dark, carved wood of the door resembled an etching I saw once in a book of Grimm's fairy tales.

"Well, all our furniture's in storage. And payday's not until Friday. Can my husband bring round a check for the month's rent first thing Saturday morning?" Her voice sounded convincing. One small lie lay hidden beneath the words, but only Rose and I could tell. When the man hesitated, Rose sidled up next to him.

"Is this going to be our house, Mama?" She spoke to our mother, but she looked up at the man's face. I shuffled my feet. The kaleidoscope tucked inside my shirt rubbed against my skin. The man's eyes glided over me and settled on Rose. I knew what he saw, the perfect face, the graceful body. I watched him covet her, just like all the men she would ever know. Because she was still a child, the instinct to protect her kicked in, and he spoke from that need.

"It sure is, little girl. What's your name?"

Rose jabbered at him, Mama's hands on her shoulders, until the man handed over the key, got back in his car, and drove away. My mother winked at me and we went inside.

While Mama explored the kitchen, writing out a list of things we needed, Rose and I explored the bedrooms. There were only two, just like the advertisement said. Mama and Daddy would take the largest one. Rose and I would have to share. The air pulsed with dust. We traced our names on the wood floor and blew at the motes floating in the rays of sun. Rose sneezed.

"You kids all right in there?" Mama called. We covered our mouths to keep our laughter from spilling too far from our hearts. We took turns squinting into the kaleidoscope, using the light from the window as a backdrop. I was tired from our fitful nights in the car, but every time I closed my eyes, I felt disconnected, lost. We had all left our true selves on the mountain, but right now this house felt safe. Perhaps here we would find those selves again. Stretching over the floor, I stared at the ceiling, imagining a life in this empty room. Just before I drifted off, I made a wish.

When I woke, the afternoon light was already fading. Mama was still rattling around in the kitchen. Rose knelt beside the bedroom door, humming. I heard a sound like claws scrabbling over stone. I opened my eyes and gasped. The kaleidoscope lay in two sections. The colored glass pieces that filled the interior were arranged in piles across the floor. With great concentration, Rose rolled the stones from pile to pile, counting and sorting the pieces. Rearranging the colors to suit herself, she filled part of the tube and shook it.

"Rose!" I tried to snatch the toy away, but she shifted out of reach. "You broke it."

"No, Peter. Here." She handed the kaleidoscope over. "You'll see. It's all new now."

"Daddy's going to be mad." I swallowed hard. Fear crabbed my gut.

Shaking her head, Rose nudged me. "Put it back together. Make a new pattern."

Dropping the remaining stones into the divided tube, I tried to screw the ends back on. It took three tries before I managed to seal it up. I balanced the kaleidoscope in my hands, waiting for the chips to shift into place.

"Put your eye to the glass, Peter," Rose ordered. "Tell me what you see."

Lifting the kaleidoscope to the light, I waited for the new pattern to emerge. I held my breath as the bits of glass tracked from one section to the next. Like shadows moving across the mountain. Like light winking between the trees. Like the glass panes in Mam's old desk, now reflecting patterns in someone else's life.

Chapter Three

*J*uggling the package, I debate the wisdom of calling the station, of requesting additional time off to deal with my sister's disappearance. I'm still caught in the bob and weave of memory. If the note reads true, Rose hasn't been kidnapped or killed. Instead, she has chosen to run away, expecting me to figure out where she has gone and why. Quality makes a new pattern, the island woman said. Quality, or fear? I finger the note lying on the table. Damn you, Rose, always tearing things apart, expecting me to put the pieces back together, to decode the new design for your life, and for mine. Leaving the package on the table, I retrieve my phone from my jacket and dial Mason's private number. *Don't go to voice mail*, I plead with the universe. Some communication god must hear me. After twelve rings, my brother-in-law picks up.

"Mason? Where are you?"

"Pete?" Rose's husband, one of rock music's bad-boy front men, fumbles the phone. I wonder if he's using again.

"Did you hear from Rose?" His voice recedes.

"Mason? I can barely hear you."

Guitar chords clang. There's a thump as he puts the instrument down. "Can I talk to Rose?"

"No, man. She's not here."

"Then why are you calling me?"

I take a deep breath. "I need your help. I need you to tell me something."

"I already told the cops everything I know."

"So you say. Humor me and tell this cop. When's the last time you talked to her?"

If you could hear someone thinking, this is what it would sound like, Mason sighing, scratching his stubbled chin, snorting into the receiver. I hold my breath until he speaks again.

"The night before she disappeared. I called her from London."

17

"And told her what? You were leaving her?"

"Go to hell, Stone. I love Rose."

"Maybe, in the beginning. But you wouldn't stay home long enough to give her a child."

"You're one to talk."

"This isn't about me, Mason."

"Oh, it's so about you. It's always been about you and all those Stone skeletons rattling around in your head."

"Just tell me what you know, Mase, and I'll let you be." I count to ten while he takes a long drink.

"The night before she left." He chokes back a sob. The guy's hurting, and I'm adding to his pain. Nice going, Peter. I can be a real shit, sometimes. "The night before, Rose said something about checking the Internet news feeds. She had us subscribed to newspapers all over the state."

I almost drop the phone. I thought she stopped searching years ago.

"Did you? Check the feed?"

"Yeah. It was all about the primary elections and some escaped convict and the number of possible hurricanes this year. Lots of local stuff. Nothing connected to either of us."

"Can you send me the links?"

"If I do, will you promise not to call again until you have real news?"

"Hey, I want to find her as much as you do."

"I doubt that, Pete. I think you'd be just as happy if you never saw her again." He hangs up. I stare at the phone, awash in guilt and grief, paralyzed by the thought that maybe Mason has it right. Do I want to be rid of Rose and all her drama? Shaking off that poison dart of truth, I head downstairs. The dog pads after me, his desire to protect overriding the command to stay. I wait for him to catch up.

The unfinished basement is crammed with boxes from our recent move. Shoving aside the ones Kelly has identified as wedding gifts, good china, and household, I free the carton marked *Peter's things*. Kel asked if I wanted to throw away all those faded scraps of my life before, but I couldn't make up my mind. So she wrapped each scuffed toy and brittle certificate in tissue paper before tucking them inside, inking the contents on the box in permanent marker, and stashing my past in the trunk of our car.

Rubbing a knuckle across my forehead, I kneel, slit the tape with a box cutter, and remove the packing. The only photo album my mother ever assembled stares up at me, its spine cracked, the plastic cover curling at the bottom edge. I skip over the school pictures with their toothless grins and stiffened poses. Mine resemble mug shots, marked by the embarrassed scowl of a boy wearing threadbare t-shirts and untrimmed hair. Rose always smiled in pictures. That wild beauty she wore like a crown could not be dimmed no matter how ragged her clothes.

When I reach them, the handful of black and whites of the old house on Dream Street, I catch my breath. Still startling in their clarity, each picture captures one unguarded moment in the life of the people we met there. Their faces peer out from the celluloid film, smiling, sneering, turning away. All the ones who hurt us, the ones who saved us, and the one who gave birth to a monster.

~~~

October, 1984

With the cellar door closed, the hot water tank belched before cycling down for the day. In the shadowed corners, mice skittered, rustling through the mounds of old magazines and newspaper. Ignoring their whiskery greetings, Lacey Webster counted the boxes. Squaring up the edges, she numbered them aloud. Twenty, no more, no less, in each stack by the stationary tub. The most recent pile was one box short. Pausing to straighten the bottle of sodium bicarbonate that had misaligned itself among the others – carbonate, chloride and sulfate – on the shelf above the laundry sink, Lacey shivered. Something was missing. Maybe she should check on the children. Even though he sat with them, he couldn't be trusted. He didn't want them, after all. But it was getting late, and time gnawed at her. With a shake of her head, she postponed desire. Hope would have to do. Then an idea occurred: a nanny. That would solve all her problems. She would find a woman to look after the babies during the hours when she couldn't be at their side. Settled now on a course of action, Lacey stomped the newest box, a discarded juice container, with her sturdy brown walking shoe, and balanced the flattened carton on the pyramid of cardboard. Satisfied, she wove her way through the horde of trash and up the stairs to the kitchen.

On the counter, Queen Nefertiti blinked at her from the cover of the library book. Lacey stuffed the book into her purse along with the lime green grocery sack. Slinging both bags over her shoulder, she tiptoed past the sleeping tabby. Four striped kittens rippled like flags as they settled closer to their mother's teats. At the front door Lacey paused, head cocked, but no sound drifted down from upstairs. Best not to disturb the quiet of naptime. Sighing, she unlocked the deadbolt and the key lock and unhooked the chain. Once outside, amid the bags of old clothes and tattered blankets, the jumbled chairs and second-hand tables, she relocked the deadbolt and the key lock. It worried her that she couldn't refasten the chain. For a full minute she chewed on her thumb, but it couldn't be helped. *Time for work, Lacey, time for work.* She recited the words five times, an incantation against the chaos of the unexpected. Her breath puffed out white in the cold air.

By midmorning the washers at the Patterson Laundromat were churning and the dryers hummed their swish-thump. Lacey swept the floor with small, careful strokes. After each load was done and the dryers abandoned, she collected the lint from the traps, folding the soft balls of hair and string and tiny pellets of dried up tissue into the growing bulge in the mesh sack. She had just cleared the final trap when Bettina Cowhee rushed in, her two grandchildren scrabbling at her legs like minnows. She plopped a laundry basket onto one of the orange plastic chairs.

"Lacey," Bettina puffed out the words around the cigarette dangling from her mouth, "can you wash these for me? I'll be back."

Without waiting for an answer, she hoisted the snot-faced little boy to her hip, gathered the girl under her arm, and stomped toward the door. Lacey glanced at Bettina's plump behind and sturdy legs. She could be the nanny. But the grandchildren pulled at the woman's sleeves, whining about suckers and lunch. Lacey thought about the difficulty of separating Bettina from the demands of family, of luring her to Dream Street. Before she finished thinking, the woman and her charges had gone.

By the time her shift ended at three, Lacey had collected enough lint to fill a small pillow, the perfect size for Deirdre's head. A dryer buzzed. Bettina's clothes waited, subdued and patient in their latticed basket, but the woman had not returned. Shrugging away her disappointment, Lacey stacked the basket on top of a washer, tucked an empty soapbox under her arm, and headed home.

The cool morning had fled. A warm breeze wrapped its arms around her, tugging a few more drops of sweat from her forehead. Lifting the heavy frizz of hair off her shoulders, she held it above her head, then let it fall. The movement pulled the faded jumper tight across her full breasts and taut, round belly. Lacey patted her stomach and smiled. Outside the library, she lifted the handle of the book return. *Nefertiti and the Age of Mummies* slid down the chute.

Two blocks from the Laundromat, Lacey passed Norman Loveless Memorial Park. She didn't know who Norman Loveless was, but she thought he could be the man who had waited for her on spring Fridays and summer Tuesdays and gloomy days when the weather prevented him from completing his park chores. Today marked another Tuesday.

Squinting, Lacey searched the picnic shelter for his bulk, picturing the dark green overalls with the word *Maintenance* stitched above the breast pocket, the straps that slipped down so quickly, revealing his soft, hairy chest and belly and the thing that he asked her to hold and stroke, that he buried inside her mouth and her other, secret place.

In the time it took Lacey to walk past the swing sets, she recalled Norm unlocking the door marked *Storage*, leading her by the hand into the shadowed depths, only one window high up and sometimes the rain beating against the rippled glass. He slipped his hands under her clothing, lifted her breasts to his mouth and her hips to his hunger. It only hurt, really, the first time.

21

Norman never said the words *I love you, Lacey*, but she hoped, until he started to give her the pills, when he touched her stomach in the fall of the year, and the leaves whispered in warning, and he felt the swelling. Then he told her *this will make you feel better*, and he kissed her neck greedily, sucked in the hollow above her collarbone. The next morning her skin wore a bruise. The next month the swelling was gone.

But no, Lacey remembered. Norm was gone. He wouldn't be back. *Just me today, alone but not alone.* She rubbed her fingers in slow circles over her belly as she walked.

Now the park was behind her and the cemetery loomed. Lacey tried to cross the street, but the traffic rushed by, too many cars to risk a dash, so she walked faster, her eyes cast down, and repeated the ritual words. *Time to go home, Lacey, time to go home.*

Past the wrought iron fence, the sign above the arched entrance read *Cairo Baptist*. The rows of tiny crosses and the sarcophagi with names like Foster and King reminded her that this was where families go when they die. But not all families. Lacey touched her belly again. *It will be all right, this time.*

When she reached the corner of Dream Street, a group of small boys, the ones who inhabited the neighborhood like cats, stared as she hurried past.

"Hey, bag lady," the tallest one called, "I have something for you." He pushed forward a smaller boy holding a shoebox with size 13 printed on the end. Lacey paused, calculating. There might be room for that box in her cellar stack, but the shouting boy was grinning like a sphinx. He had a secret. Perhaps the box hid a frog or a snake. Lacey shook her head. She moved beyond the scrum of dirty faces for two strides more, before the need overtook her.

Twisting to face them, Lacey lashed out like a whip, snatching the box from the boy's outstretched hand. Startled, he reared back, stumbled, and fell hard onto the sidewalk. The others laughed, calling him names like stupid and bigfoot, but one voice, a girl's, rang like the tinkling of bells.

"Are you all right, Peter?"

"Peter?" Lacey rolled the name on her tongue. "The one who betrayed Jesus."

"You leave him alone." The girl sang out.

The command vibrated in Lacey's chest like an oracle of doom. She searched for the owner, but the pack closed in, teeth bared, hands fisted at their sides. She swept the box out in front of her, threatening until they stopped moving. Sediment spilled from the end of the carton, showering down on the seated boy. He scrambled back. The pack retreated.

Lacey hurried now, down the block and into her house, dead last on the left, almost but not quite concealed by the maples that stood, one on each side of the porch, her own private sentinels, guardians of the tomb. The screen door sagged when she flung it back, the curtained windows yawned. Juggling boxes and bags, Lacey unlocked and unlocked, thrust herself through the opening, and slammed the door behind her. With the bolt clicked into place and the chain secured, she released the breath she'd been holding.

"Norman," she called, one hand on the newel post, "I'm home."

In the dim early evening light, it was challenging to walk the labyrinth that defined the living room. A foot-wide path wound among the magazines and stacks of china, the bags of empty Coke cans, and the containers empty of shampoo or mustard or milk. But Lacey knew the way. She shut her eyes, envisioned the trail, and moved through it. She scarcely noticed the smell.

In the kitchen, more bags stuffed with used paper towels, rubber bands, and string jostled for space in the corners. Now she relaxed, threading her way to the garbage bin where she stored the lint. Relieved of the day's collections, she carried the detergent box and the shoe carton down the basement stairs, stepping carefully around the socks and folded cleaning rags. She counted the items in the stack, flattened the box from the Laundromat, and set it on top. Then she recounted. Twenty. She circled the stack, the shoebox large and sturdy and heavy in her hands. Now she had one too many. Glancing at the shelf above, Lacey decided it was time to hide the chemicals. Placing the bottles in the shoe box, she closed the lid. Something skittered past the basement window.

Heart jumping, she reached for the string dangling from the ceiling. When the light switched on, she croaked at the sudden illumination. For one blink, then two, she saw the basement as it really was, a giant garbage dump, a dead end, like Dream Street, for every small piece of her life. Her mother used to say, "There's nothing wrong with Lacey, she just likes to collect things." What would Mother say now? She shivered off the glimpse of reality, hugging to her the comfort of the boxes and the cardboard and the string. *My talismans*, Lacey whispered, *to prevent the unknown from striking when I am unaware.*

Upstairs, Lacey stowed the shoebox in the broom closet, poured a cup of dry food into a bowl and bent to feed the cat. One of the kittens, the smallest of the litter, had died. Lifting the stiffening body, she stroked it twice with her index finger before stuffing it into the pocket of her jumper.

Her stomach growled. She warmed a can of soup, tore off the label, and pressed it into the drawer that held a hundred others. Out front, the porch boards rattled. She stopped, holding the empty can in her hands and her breath in her lungs. Was that a shadow moving across the window? Gulping air, she listened harder. In the stillness she felt a wing beat deep within her. The moment expanded, her heart loud and hammering. The baby was alive. The doorbell chimed. Lacey dropped the can. It rolled sideways, catching on the bottom of the stove. Was the shadow at her door?

One hand on her belly, the other in front of her in a warding gesture, Lacey retraced the passage to the front of the house. The bell rang a second time. Hovering between fear and curiosity, she unlocked the door and opened it just wide enough to peek out. Then she reached behind her. From the rack beside the light switch, she lifted a hammer, the claw still wearing a tuft of brown hair. A woman in her twenties dressed in a raincoat and open-toed sandals had already turned away, preparing to step off the porch. Two doors away, a white van idled.

"May I help you?" Lacey imitated a voice she'd heard on the American Movie Classics channel. The soft, cultured tones invited the visitor to turn around.

24

The woman's face brightened. She extended her hand, offering Lacey a standard business card with black lettering. It looked like a funeral invitation.

"I'm sorry to bother you, but I represent the Good News Army." Lacey didn't respond. Stepping closer, the woman pointed in the direction of the house up the street. "My colleague and I collect clothing and furniture items for the needy in our community. We're canvassing your street today, and your neighbor, a Mrs. Stone, suggested you might have something to donate."

"Oh, I don't have anything I could spare." Lacey toyed with the chain on the door. Nanny. The idea formed in the dimming light.

The woman's eyes swept over the bags and chairs and small tables piled on the porch. One eyebrow lifted.

"I was really hoping you could help us out."

Lacey calculated the force necessary to confuse and overpower. Her mouth was dry, but her hand stayed steady. She opened the door a little wider. "Perhaps I can help after all. Would you like a cup of tea?"

The woman rocked back and forth, her eyes darting from Lacey's face to the chaos filling the space beyond. She took a step back, then another. The van pulled into the Stone's driveway, backed out, and drove to Lacey's place. The window on the driver's side rolled down.

"Caroline, are you ready?" Another young woman, wearing an identical raincoat, climbed out to stand by the curb. Lacey teased the idea around. Handmaidens, two, to accompany the children.

"You get anything from the bag lady?" Leaning against the van, the driver stared at Lacey's house, her lips curled in a small knot of distaste.

Lacey scowled. She banged the hammer against her thigh before flinging it into the debris filling the room, where it buried itself among a collection of old socks.

"Ma'am, can you help us? Even a small donation would be welcome." The woman slumped at Lacey's frown.

"I'm sure I cannot now." When the woman began to speak again, Lacey cut her off. Slamming the door, she locked and relocked it. Then she peered through the curtains, watching the woman shrug as she moved down the steps and joined her companion.

Turning, Lacey surveyed her home, stared at the accumulated trash. The close encounter with strangers left her trembling and perturbed. Why couldn't she part with anything? She threw her arms out to encompass the clutter and shouted. "Maybe I don't need you anymore."

The butterfly in her womb beat its wings, reminding her to check on the children. Digging out a candle, Lacey mounted it in a holder fashioned from a piece of cardboard and lit the wick. She lifted her skirt as she climbed the narrow staircase leading to the second floor.

Above, two rooms opened off the landing. In her bedroom, Lacey checked to see that no one had disturbed the rose-patterned comforter, the cluttered dresser. She rested a hand on the baby clothes from the Laundromat, filched from clients, now washed and waiting for a future use. She willed herself to remain still while the memory of Norman filled the space, his body stretched out across her bed, a solid presence in the dark corners of midnight. His breath blew across her naked shoulder as he struggled against the rope bindings and she touched him as he had touched her, deaf to his pleading. Oh, she had been scared at Norman Loveless Park, but in this room, she commanded. In the dark, his name remained a curse and a prayer. Lacey whispered it aloud. *Norman.* The room shuddered with the sound of it, clearing the confusion from her heart.

Possibility layered over Lacey. She could make an offering that would draw him to her while she dreamed. Placing the candle in one of the candlesticks on the dresser, she clomped down the stairs, hurried to the door, undid the locks.

The porch light was still on. Lacey hesitated, flickers of doubt blurring the edges of her control. Then she picked up a bag and dragged it to the curb. After the bags, she carried the chairs, one at a time, unstacking and restacking them in the chilly air. At last she was done. The empty space of the porch mocked her, but Lacey squeezed her eyes shut, went inside, and turned off the light. Her palms were sweaty. Her dress, a wet rag, clung to her back.

Up the stairs again and into the second, smaller bedroom. The smell of incense enveloped her, masking a thicker, earthy, metallic odor and the pungent chemical scent. Here there were no boxes, no bags, only a single bed and a low pressboard bookstand where the joss sticks rested next to a ceramic candy dish. A threadbare ottoman and a rocker occupied the corner under the eave. The bed was tented with an old shower curtain. Lacey lifted the plastic, which crackled as she folded it back.

They were lined up, Deirdre, Titi, Nila, each tiny skull wrapped in linen strips. Featureless, their bodies remained small lumps beneath the one-piece christening gowns. The odor of dust and decomposition rose to greet her. Circled around the babies were the skeletal remains of birds, several mice, a dog. Taking the dead kitten out of her pocket, Lacey nudged it in place next to the largest of the bodies.

"I've brought you another playmate." Her words hissed around the room. The dark curtains that blocked the single window swallowed her voice. She moved from the bed to the armchair, caressing the sealed canopic jars resting on the floor. Each bore a label identifying the body part contained within. She pulled up the afghan that had slipped off Norman's sunken chest, checked the ropes that fastened his arm bones to the chair. One of the skull bindings had slipped loose. It trailed down the back of the chair, the end curling upward. His jawbone sagged.

In the candlelight, the room flickered in and out of shadow. Lacey settled in the rocker, cradling her belly in her arms. For a moment she imagined the woman from the porch here, swaddled and calm, a dependable companion for her babies. Then she discarded the image, battered it like the boxes, and set it aside. The child within flipped as she chanted names. Cleo or Nexus for another girl. Kohl for a boy. Cole. Coal. A fit name for the dark promise that glided with her as the chair creaked back and forth. A sigh escaped Norman's corpse, and the baby in Lacey's womb rolled again.

Chapter Four

I flick a nail against the photograph, trace the roofline and the frame of the window tucked under the eave, count the porch steps of the Webster house, the one place Rose and I avoided, even when we had nowhere else to go. I refuse to look at the foundation, refuse to acknowledge that one narrow pane of wavy glass yawning at me from beneath the overgrown junipers. From the cavern of the porch, Lacey frowns at the camera, baby Coal on her hip. Trash bags fill the space around her, their black bulges serving as ballast for a woman lost in her own endless sea.

Closing the album, I tuck it under my arm and return to the kitchen. Soldier trails after me, his presence a solid comfort. Too bad Rose and I never had a pet. Maybe a dog would have protected us from the worst of it. Upstairs, I pour myself a soda, set the album on top of the refrigerator, stall for time. The package waits on the table, daring me to open it. When the phone rings, I check the number, swipe the screen, and wait for Tuck Cornell to speak. My partner in solving all things crime-related has great timing. Not. While he hails someone in the background, I pick at a corner of the brown wrapping paper until I expose one corner of the package. Detergent, the drawing screams, Laundromat inked beneath it in Rose's perfect hand.

"Pete?" Tuck coughs twice before repeating my name. "Duty officer says you're not coming in today."

"I'm taking some personal time, T. I need to clear my head."

"Understood." Covering the phone, Tuck shouts to someone in the room. When he comes back, he's command-boy Tuck, all in charge and serious. "Pickle and I will be over at seven. I'll bring the beer."

"No, Tuck, I—" Before I can finish my protest, the line goes dead. Part of me wants to be alone, but a larger part accepts his offer to help me bear the burden of my sister's

29

disappearance. This is what it means to have friends. My hand closes around the note. *Poor Rose. You never had the chance to find them.*

~~~

July, 1985

I blinked, and Rose disappeared. I thought the trees lining the alley behind our house had swallowed her whole. One moment she was skipping ahead, blonde curls jiggling. The next she was gone.

I glanced back. Against the window in the back door, the curtains hung limp and stained from water that leaked through the cracked caulking whenever a storm blew in from the east. The kitchen was dark. No one moved there. Stumbling off the concrete slab that served as a patio, I almost stepped on one of the crows.

The birds lay with their feet in the air. Their dead bodies looked smaller than when they were alive, diminished and free of malice. Perhaps now that the threat had been removed, my father wouldn't cut down the oak that spread its limbs over the back half of our yard. Jumping over the chain saw resting against the rusted toolbox, I followed my sister into the woods.

The muffled traffic sounds from Grandview Road reminded me of the world of men and work, of cold words and granite voices, but here, under the canopy of sycamore and sweet gum and birch, I could pretend I lived in a fairytale where all fathers were kind and children were safe from their anger. Up ahead, my sister's head popped out from behind a scrum of honeysuckle crowding the path. I hurried to catch up.

Looking over her shoulder, Rose smiled, raised an arm to wave me on. Her yellow sundress swayed like a brush, swishing away our father's words uttered just before we edged out the back door. "Don't you be wandering off now, you hear?"

I tracked her along the narrow lane, kicking at the wildflowers that grew in fits and starts, punctuating the dirt with bursts of color. The violets had flowered and died, but bluebells winked at me and, in patches of sunlight, purple loosestrife waved. I knew what they were because of the book

I stole from the library, the one that listed the plants by name and illustrated each page with a picture.

A garter snake wriggled across the path, reminding me that we weren't alone, that more than humans inhabited this fantasy world. I picked up a stick and beat at the underbrush, trying to spot more flowers. I liked knowing the names of things, like the constellation Orion in the winter sky, and the lake called Titicaca in the far away country of Peru. Someday I planned to have a dog and give it a name of its own. The weight of all the things I wanted to know pressed on me. I felt small and empty, like the crows.

A distant siren cut the stillness into before and after. Ahead, I glimpsed Rose dropping down the embankment that led to the creek. We were forbidden to come here, which made it all the more exciting and dangerous. I felt vulnerable again, and wary. Checking the path behind me, I stood rock-silent, listening for footsteps. Under the trees, the heat had dissipated. I sighed, grateful Rose and I had escaped the charged and stuffy air inside the house. There was only one fan, and it blew across the bed in our parents' room.

When I was certain there was no movement behind me, I walked on. A crow cawed above me. When I looked up, I tripped over a tree root. From the bottom of the ditch, Rose called my name.

"Peter, come. Look at the claws on this one."

I hurried to the end of the path and, sliding down the dirt bank, stepped to the edge of the water carving a channel through the clay soil as it tumbled from the main road all the way to the pond behind Piedmont Elementary. Farther downstream, the eddy dubbed Drowned Man's Curve appeared, thick ribbons of rainwater trickling into it from a concrete catch basin that sloped gently down. Here, at the bottom of Dream Street, the drop-off stood five feet high, not easily navigated by neighborhood children. The stream harbored tadpoles and skipper bugs and, in a deeper pool created by a spray of flat, angled rocks, crawdads.

Crouching, I stared at the rocks. Layered and stacked, they resembled ribs. Squinting, I focused on the swirl of deep water, imagining the heart of the world beating in the twists and burbles of the stream.

Rose poked at the crawdad she had plucked from the creek.

"Be careful, Rosie. They hurt when they catch your finger." I pestered the waving claws with my stick.

"I'm not afraid. If they bite me, I'll just bite them back." My sister bared her teeth. Her small, serious face wore a scowl of determination. She shoved the crawdad toward me.

"Here, you take it."

"I don't want it." I backed away, my seven-year old body overruling my desire to show her I wasn't afraid. Raising my stick, I whacked it against the trunk of a willow and remembered what afraid felt like, this morning, after breakfast, when my mother took my father's twenty-two and, swearing, took aim at first one black bird, then another.

"Hell, woman, they're just protecting their youngins." My father wrapped his fingers around my neck, his words as brittle as the false promise they offered.

"So am I, Estill." Her voice skittered out, like tires on gravel. My father's hand tightened. I didn't move. His grip didn't ease. I held my breath, heart leaping and kicking in my chest, while my parents stared at each other. Beside me, Rose repeated the words our mother spoke. They swished around in her mouth like tiny bubbles.

"Hellfire, woman. You just don't want any more bird shit in your hair." Turning, my father dragged me with him into the house.

Rose crouched down beside the creek, her dress bubbling out around her skinny legs. Holding the crawdad in one hand, she used the other to draw a stick figure in the mud. When she finished, she lined the drawing with small stones and placed a larger one, smooth and blue and heart-shaped, in the center. I heard her mumbling but I couldn't make out the words. Then she stood and ground her foot over the heart-shaped stone.

"Be careful." My shout interrupted her concentration. "You'll cut yourself."

"Stone against stone." She giggled. Balancing on one leg, she examined the sole of her foot. "I'm not hurt. See?"

"We better go back." I nodded in the direction of the house.

Rose stared at me a long time before she answered.

"Don't worry, Peter. I won't let him do it again." She flung the crawdad into the water. It twisted itself in the sluggish current before squeezing beneath a rock. Wiping her hands on a clump of moss, she reached into the pockets of her dress.

"Want to see something?" Her words puffed out, breathless and quieter than usual. She lifted her hands and opened them, palms up. "Look."

"They're just pebbles, stupid little white pebbles." I laced my voice with scorn. "They're too little to even build with."

"It doesn't matter how small they are." Rose rolled them from one hand to the other, her voice shifting into solemnity. "They're magic. I found them over there."

"Where?"

She pointed to a tumble of the stones covering the opposite bank of the creek. Lifting the treasure closer to her face, she whispered, "Aren't they wonderful?"

Before I could reply, I heard the whistle, the one that meant come home now. Rose shoved the stones back into her pockets and held each one closed with her dirt-stained hands. Then we ran toward the house, the sound of our feet against the dirt a flapping of wings.

Chapter Five

I lift a fist to my mouth, trying to cram that ugly genie back in the bottle. No. I do not want to revisit that day again. Two deep breaths, three. Setting the photo album next to the package, I move to the window. Outside, the ankle-high grass is rustling. I should have mowed the lawn last night. The new leaves on the poplar turn upside down in the gusts of wind sweeping through the yard. I check my phone for a weather warning and sure enough, the announcement scrolls into view. Severe thunder-storm approaching. Flood warning for Montgomery, Warren, Greene, and Butler counties. I finger the package, sweat trickling its way down my spine, then peel loose another thumbnail's worth of wrapping. No more clues scribbled in Rose's hand, just the box and whatever it contains. When I shake it again, the contents shift and roll. Maybe it's not what I think it is, not glass, not stones. Maybe it's just a secret shredding its way out of the box. If it's a gift, I want it to be amnesia, but, like air escaping from a balloon, there is no way to stuff the memory back in my head. Fighting the urge to huddle in the corner, I let myself out the back door. Soldier whines to come, too, but I make him stay inside. As I tie down the umbrella over the picnic table, the past resurfaces, swimming up from the bottom of the creek, its claws aimed straight for my heart.

~~~

I dried the dishes and covered the leftovers with tin foil before I noticed my father standing in the doorway. Beside me, Rose danced with the dishtowel, waving it like a flag and talking in her singsong voice, the one she used when she was pretending to be somewhere else. The stones in her pockets rattled each time she hopped from one foot to the next.

"Stop that, Rose." My father's voice, loose, husky, the voice of whiskey and too many cigarettes thundered around us. I folded the dishrag and draped it over the faucet.

"Come here, son." His arm slid around my shoulders. He pulled me tight against his body, the roughness of his jeans scraping my cheek. "I haven't seen you since breakfast. Tell me, where were you and Rose this afternoon?"

"Nowhere." Slipping free, I backed away, cut my eyes to the door, wondering if I could make it out in time. But it was too late. In this house there were no stones to shimmy under, no rocky ribs to hide behind.

"Don't you lie to me, son." His hand landed on his belt buckle, picked at the leather. I backpedaled down the hall toward the bedroom Rose and I shared. As my father turned to follow, my sister lowered the towel and blinked very slowly.

"We were just in the alley," Rose said, moving up behind him and pulling on his pantleg. He shrugged her off and kept coming.

As I stepped through the doorway, I glanced at the window, measuring my chances of escaping that way. The lights were on all over the Wentworth house. Drawn by the pool of artificial suns, I stared across the yards, desperate to erase the sound of my father's heavy footsteps. Firecrackers pop-pop-popped. Mr. Wentworth must be having a party to celebrate the Fourth of July. There weren't many parties on Dream Street. In a fairy tale, Rose and I could walk over later or just watch the show out the window. But our story wasn't a fantasy. I cowered away from my father's advance. His slap slammed my head against the wall.

"Listen to me when I talk to you. Where'd you go today, huh? Didn't I tell you to stay close to home?" He swiped a hand over his head and inhaled sharply, the noise like a giant gear grinding into place.

When I didn't answer, he pushed out the breath coiled inside and raised his voice. "Is this the thanks I get for putting food in your belly, shoes on your feet?"

I recognized the speech. My father was working over all his complaints, rehashing the lines of his favorite rant. A glob of spit formed in the corner of his mouth. It wouldn't be long before he took off his belt. From the room down the hall, my mother shouted.

"Shut up, Estill, shut the hell up." I heard the whir as the fan started blowing, the noise muffling when she closed the door.

Shaking now and captive, I sank into the corner opposite the bunk beds. My father turned his back to the window, muttering to himself as he loosened his buckle. Unnoticed, my sister crept into the room. Dropping to her knees, she crawled along the wall beside the beds. Her dress dragged, weighed down by the stones. She headed for the shoebox where she stashed her special treasures. The lid canted at an angle, pushed up by an oversize piece of pink quartz she'd found imbedded in the mud of the creek wall after the last heavy rain.

Fascinated by her progress, I forgot to watch my father. The sting of the belt across my shoulder and face caused me to cry out. A trickle of blood oozed from my nose, dripped from my lip. I lifted my arms to ward off the next blow. Raising her head, Rose looked at me through the space created by our father's outspread legs.

Without turning my head, I imagined myself twisting away, scurrying to hide, nameless and unharmed, under the bed. The whine of a bottle rocket punctuated the moment. I huddled deeper in the corner. Rose crept closer to the bed. Watching her, I pictured us on some future Sunday morning, lying in the dirt, sticklike and frozen, our crow legs twisted and stiff. My heart stuttered, pounded again, and turned to stone. When the belt cracked a second time, I grabbed for it, latched on, and tugged it toward me. Looking up, I saw panic on my father's face. I jerked the strap harder. My father lunged toward me, his hands like talons stretching for my heart.

"No, don't." Rose hugged our father's leg to pull him away. The stones spilled from her pockets and scattered across the floor. Like a bird in freefall, my father stumbled backward, arms flailing. I released the belt. It flew from his hand and slapped against the dresser. Rose let go of his leg.

Pinwheeling, our father fell, shoulders framed in the window, the firecrackers from Wentworth's party raying out around his silhouette. His head hit the sash, bounced, and rocked back, knocking against the stick propping the window up. The stick rattled once, twice, popped free, and fell forward onto the floor. The window crashed down, slamming with a thud against his forehead. I held my breath, but my father didn't move again.

Gathering the stones, Rose placed each one carefully back into her pockets. She lifted the lid on the keepsake box and stared at the quartz rock within.

"No, Rose." I laid my hand over hers and pressed down. She closed the lid. Grabbing the green Army blanket from my bed, I took my sister by the hand and led her down the darkened hallway. In the backyard, we stopped to watch the fireworks exploding above Mr. Wentworth's roof.

Smoke and the smell of explosives drifted through the yard, collecting around us like mist. Party voices carried in the night. The fan in the window of our parents' bedroom labored at full speed, sending out a spray of heat. Standing beneath it, Rose and I let the hot air spill over us. When the fireworks ended, I wrapped the blanket around our shoulders as we moved toward the trees.

At the creek, I squatted near the water, filling my hands and rinsing my face to wash away the blood. Wiping my nose with the sleeve of my t-shirt, I rested my head on my knees. My heartbeat slowed. I wasn't afraid any more. I stared at the spot where the mud man guarded the approach to the stream, its talisman heart rock steady and unyielding. Where, I wondered, did the real heart of the world live?

Beside me, Rose patted the back of my neck with one small hand. With the other, she caressed the stones in her pocket. Then she leaned over and whispered in my ear.

"I told you they were magic stones."

Chapter Six

I shake Rose's package. Maybe she sent her lucky stones back to me. I close my eyes, rub my tongue over the words she spoke. Magical, my sister's belief in talismans, like the fireworks blossoming above the Wentworth house that long ago night. Wentworth. The name coaxes a host of memories from the box where I store the past. I re-open the album and page through the photographs. When a fist pounds at the front door, I jerk like a windsock.

"Pete? You in there?" Tuck Cornell's drawl reaches through the cut glass and oak surround, sliding into the living room of the craftsman-style home Kelly and I fell in love with, despite the maintenance issues. I didn't have to tell her how it reminded me, in the most elemental way, of her father's house. She felt it, too, that sense of belonging. The cove ceilings, the wide baseboards, the walnut-stained floors, the smell of lemon polish lovingly applied to tabletops and cabinets. A home where love thrived. So different from where Rose and I grew up. Except for the front entrance to our house on Dream Street. That old door. Carved into flowers and vines and angel faces around the stained-glass window. The only other thing of beauty in the whole damn house. My sister was the first, the light that shone in the deepest shadow. Maybe that door taught Rose how to sculpt her life.

I stash the box with the album by the back door, fling a dish towel over the package, and hurry to let Tuck and Hannah in. Hannah, whom he calls Pickle for reasons I do not understand. Hannah, who doesn't like to be kept waiting. Tuck's the newest forensics tech in the Sinclair Police Department. Over the past six months, we've worked together on a number of cases, developed a bromance of sorts. He envies my military stint. I respect his thoroughness. I might even like doing his job someday. If I stay in the job. Hopewell, like most of the smaller suburban towns in the area, isn't large enough to have a lab of its own. Even Kettering, where Kelly and I live, sends all the important evidence to the Miami Valley Crime Lab. But T. C.'s smart enough to do most of the crime scene chores: dust for prints, collect trace evidence, warn us off touching the deadly mixes of opioids that pass for street drugs these days. He knows about blood spatter and trajectories. Yeah, Tuck's a smart guy, but not as smart as Hannah, who chairs the criminal justice department at Sinclair Community College. That woman can sniff out lies faster than a bloodhound.

When I step aside, Tuck hustles in, dragging a case of our favorite IPA, a bag of snacks, and a ton of raindrops.

"Where's Pickle?"

My partner shakes like a dog. Water sprays over the floor, speckles the furniture. Kelly won't be happy about that. "Something came up. Said she'd be by later."

He works hard not to catch my eye. He's evading the question, but I don't know how to address the problem. Pickle's a complicated woman, maybe too much for Tuck, but he's so stupid crazy about her, he doesn't see her flaws. If they worked on the same force, they'd make a great but volatile team. Whatever sparks fly between them, they've somehow made it work so far. Even Kelly agrees, and she's known them both longer than I have. She and Hannah were in undergrad school together, and Kelly and Tuck dated for a while. Yeah, it's complicated.

Shrugging out of his jacket, Tuck tosses it over the recliner as he slips off his shoes. "Stone," he says, "you need a little R and R."

"What?" I grab the bag of chips, hoist the case, and motion him to follow me to the kitchen.

"Not what you think, Pete." Tuck claps me on the back. "Reconnaissance and rumination are my way of saying I'm here to help. Sorry to hear about your sister."

I shake my head. "Thanks, T. Not much we can do from here."

Maybe Tuck hears the hesitation in my reply. Maybe he notices the package peeking from beneath the dish towel or spots the box of albums. His forehead creases as he scrubs the rain from his hair, then lifts the towel.

"You gonna tell me about it, Pete, or do I have to play twenty questions?"

I set the snacks out on the counter and shove the carton into the fridge. "I'm not in the mood for shop talk."

"Neither am I. Not local cases. But we are going to take a look at yours." Tuck holds up a hand to forestall my argument.

"Beer?" I shuffle through the refrigerator and select two IPAs, hand one to him. He examines the label, then takes a long swallow before dropping into a chair. Soldier pads over to demand a head pet, sniffs Tuck's ankles, and trots back to the living room.

"Solving puzzles is what I do best, Pete. If you want my help, I'm in."

I lean on the counter, debating. Do I want to open myself to Tuck's scrutiny, reveal all the old ugliness and heartache? Because going back, revisiting the whole sorry tale of how Rose and I survived our childhood feels like open-heart surgery without a by-pass over the damaged parts. Despite all my efforts to overcome that past, it rears at me, cobra-like and poisonous. And my sister is gone again, perhaps for good. Picking up the note, I stare at her words.

I can't forgive. I can't forget. I can't let it happen again.

"I know about the disappearance." Tuck looks at the card in my hand, taps the package. "I don't know about this."

I take another swallow, stalling. The grandfather clock in the hall whirs as the hands tick forward.

"At some point," he says, "you'll have to talk about it. I know it's a long shot, but maybe we can help you find her before they do."

"We?"

He cracks his jaw, flexes his fingers. "Me and Hannah, if...if she decides she wants to."

"What's going on, Tuck?"

"Later, man, I'll explain later."

When he doesn't offer more, we stare at walls and drink until I make up my mind. Handing over the note, I retrieve the photo album and rap it with my knuckles. "Wentworth."

"Kelly's dad?" Cradling a beer, Tuck leans his forearms on his knees, cocks one eyebrow, and waits for me to go on.

41

"Yeah," I acknowledge his surprise. Opening the cover, I shuffle through until I find the right picture. Rose and I posing with Fox, the baseball gloves he bought us raised in triumph. "Fox Wentworth. After my dad died, all that really mattered began with him."

~~~

January, 1986

Inside the darkened bedroom Fox Wentworth listened to the snow, the soft slide of flakes against the shingles, the stutters and growls as the wind climbed the fence post and banked up the side of the house. Although the walls kept silent, each creak of the roof provoked a crescendo of memory. This was where the lie had tossed him, the silky words of betrayal muffling protest, erasing the bare, bald truth with the whiteness of deceit. He drifted in the king-size bed, covering his tracks with a broom made of animal pelts and a length of blue velvet ribbon.

When the radio alarm clicked on, Fox depressed the off button before the peppy voice of the morning DJ could announce the next song. Shuffling to the window, he lifted the sagging slats of the blinds. He watched the snow whirl around the lamppost at the end of the driveway. The flakes pasted themselves to the front of the home he and Jill bought ten years ago, the house she left him when she walked away from his apologies, taking Kelly and the dog with her.

Scrubbing at his face, Fox considered crawling back under the comforter, but the manic voice of conscience reminded him that he mustn't be late again. It would take at least half an hour to shovel the drive.

Peering through the window again, Fox guesstimated four inches had fallen since midnight. He wondered if his truck, old and cranky, could plow through the accumulated drifts but dismissed the idea. The tires were too close to bald. He didn't feel like taking the chance. Still, that inner voice, the one he tried to ignore, teased: *It's a long shot from the garage to the street but a straight one. Go for it.* Shivering in the chilled air, he pulled on jeans over his long johns.

The garage door stuck when Fox tried to pull it up. He kicked at the bottom panel until the ice released its grip. The door sprang upward, wrenching his arm but arresting its momentum. Settling the rusty blade of the shovel into the edge of the snow, he started to push.

"Push. Harder." Fox buries his shoulder in the couch arm and yells at Jill again. They are moving into their first house, the jumping off point of their dream life together, the one they planned during football games and study dates at the library. Now here they are, sweaty from carrying furniture and boxes on the hottest day of July, excited and irritated and desperate to get on with it.

The phone rings and the answering machine they just hooked up clicks on. In a minute, Hillbilly's voice drawls hello, mentions the football fantasy pool is forming and hopes they're not doing it in their new home yet. Fox makes a note to self to call his best friend back later. Jill gives him one of those looks, a frosty reminder that things are different now, and they return to their work.

Fox shoveled the snow, following a pattern only he could discern. He walked the blade a few feet, lifted, tossed the heavy load to the side, pushed on. Two long furrows marked the path his tires would follow in case he ran out of energy before he ran out of snow. By the time he cleared the first section, the muffler he used to close the gaps around the collar of his old navy pea coat hung from a branch of the crabapple in the side yard. His snowcap kept slipping over his eyes. He pushed it up with his wrist each time he deposited another shovelful of white stuff. The driveway began to resemble a tunnel.

Panting from his exertions, Fox leaned on the shovel to catch his breath, air pluming out of his mouth like a geyser. He looked at the bushes that lined the front walk, admiring the ice cream smoothness of their covering of fallen snow. Wind had swirled the yard into a confection of small dunes, ridging the sides like contour lines on a map.

Jill, newly pregnant leans over the Atlas spread out on the kitchen table as she traces the roads from their house on Dream Street to Las Vegas, Nevada. They are planning their first vacation, a trip to see Fox's uncle who works as a dealer at the Stardust Casino, and the budget is tight. Jill wants to stop at historical markers and outlet malls. Fox is studying a brochure on how to win at blackjack.

"We're going to set a limit on how much we play each day, okay, Fox? I want to see the dam and there's a park, Red Rock, I think it's called, where we can hike." Fox murmurs his agreement. He's working out a system, just like the book says. He re-reads the advice on when to stay and when to hit. Jill's admonition is the first rumble of the avalanche that will bury him.

"Fox? You understand, don't you? We have to be smart about this."

"I promise I won't do anything foolish, hon." It isn't a lie, not really, Fox thinks. He won't do anything foolish, just try to win them a little security. He feels the bulge of yesterday's pay riding comfortably in his hip pocket. "Can I have some of that frosty root beer you brought home from the store?"

The wind picked up a little, driving ice crystals into the hollows of his cheeks. Fox licked his lips, reached into his coat pocket for the Chapstick he bought yesterday. He gazed at the path he had cleared, but newly fallen snow covered it like a lace curtain. He squinted his eyes against the tiny pellets and tilted his head. The sky glowered at him, dealing faster than he could clear. Old man winter just upped the ante, Fox thought, still stuck on his old way of sizing up a situation.

"Fox, we have a situation here." Fox's boss leans back in his chair and fiddles with a pencil on the desk. "The accounts don't seem to balance, and you were the only one working the register yesterday. Got any explanation for the discrepancy?"

Fox looks at the ring of keys clustered at his belt. The small silver one that opens Jill's jewelry box is gone. "How much is missing, Mr. Glover?"

"Oh, about twenty dollars, just the amount a man might need to place a bet on tomorrow's game."

"Come on, Mr. Glover, you know I don't do that anymore. I maybe play a little scratch and win at the Eagles, but I gave up those sports bets." Fox rubs his hands on his knees, the

chinos chafing his palms. Mr. Glover nods, and Fox knows he is dismissed.

When the promotion he was expecting doesn't happen, Fox explores other options. Three months later he gets the call for an interview at Lebanon Correctional.

Fox wiped his nose on his sleeve. Thinking about the prison, he tossed another shovelful of snow on the mountain growing beside the house. He should have bumped up a pay grade last month, but the warden claimed there was a moratorium on raises due to budget cuts. "Bullshit," Fox said out loud. He reviewed his shift for the week, reminded himself to check on his insurance coverage, and thought about the rumor of layoffs he'd stumbled into in the break room yesterday.

The sound of an engine pulled his head up. Two doors down, a battered, salt-streaked truck with a plow on the front bumper backed into the street and yelled at Peter Stone to get in. Fox recognized the boy's uncle, Butch Tepe, hanging out the driver's side, breath streaming as he gestured the boy along. Squinting against the swirl of snow, Fox could just make out a figure in the window that faced his house, Pete's sister Rose. She and Kelly were friends. Last summer they wore their hair tied up in ribbons and played in the sprinkler every hot day. The memory stalled Fox's efforts for a moment. He picked up the shovel and twirled it in his hands.

The door at the front of the Stone house opened and Mrs. Stone, who reminded him of a witch from one of those Disney movies, thumped her way to the car. She tapped on the passenger side window. When Peter rolled it down, she handed him a backpack and jabbed her finger into the boy's shoulder.

"Mind your uncle now, you hear?" Her words echoed up the street.

As the truck skidded and chugged past, the plow kicked up clots of snow, mounding it at the bottom of Fox's driveway. The boy pressed his face against the glass and waved. Standing on the porch, the Stone woman took a long pull on her cigarette and turned to stare. Fox felt her eyes boring into him, daring him to judge her. He turned away.

When he reached the end of the concrete slope, Fox decided he was too cold and too tired to clear more than a cursory path through the apron. He pushed his boots back along the furrows, kicking at the white crust beginning to cover his tracks. Like a whole heap of little white lies, a soft layer hiding the ice underneath. He spit into the wind and ducked.

Back inside, the windows had steamed over and the coffee pot purred. Fox treated himself to an extra spoonful of sugar, gulped down the brew, and headed for the bedroom. He shook his newly laundered uniform out of the plastic bag and slipped into the starched white shirt and blue pants. When he opened the dresser drawer for his belt, he spotted the revolver he'd bought for Jill. Lifting it, he weighed it in his hand. The gun shifted like a live animal, knocking over the last picture he took of Jill and Kelly, the one in Washington under the cherry trees. All around their heads the pink and white petals floated, a cloud of springtime flakes.

The deepest despair Fox had ever known drifted onto his shoulders, worked its way past his heart, and settled in his gut. A sob bolted its way out of his mouth, and a voice he did not recognize told him to do something about it. He glanced at his watch, saw that it was already after eight. He'd better hurry. Placing the gun in the drawer, he covered it with an old t-shirt, ran down the stairs, and banged out the back door. Once in the truck, Fox gave himself to the job. Prison guards who brought their troubles to work didn't last very long.

By the time Fox's shift ended, the winter twilight had come and gone. Snow had fallen all day. He groaned with the thought of the shoveling ahead of him. *There's no way I'll get the truck up the driveway if I don't clear it.* He pulled a cigarette out of the pack he kept in the glove compartment. Just one, he told himself, and the little voice that never left him alone whispered, *I've heard that before.*

The stoplight at Patterson and Grandview wasn't working. Traffic had backed up half a block. Fox waited in line, while the lights from Carl's Bar flashed on and off in invitation. *What the hell.* Pulling out, he crossed the tread-churned road

46

and bumped his way over the moguls that ridged the parking lot next to the bar.

Crowded with factory workers and city staffers smoking and joking and complaining about the weather, the tavern welcomed him in. Fox nodded to a few familiar faces but didn't stop to talk. At the bar he claimed an abandoned stool and ordered a draft. Carl himself was serving tonight, drops of sweat rolling down his pudgy, bearded face. He nodded to Fox but didn't speak either, too busy with drink orders to ask about Fox's day. The mirror behind the bar reflected the clientele. Fox looked at his reflection – receding hairline, long nose, sad eyes. *I wouldn't want to meet me either*, he thought, surveying the few women who had ventured out tonight. *They're either with someone or looking to get laid.* That reminded Fox of something Hillbilly might have said. He almost smiled, but the grin lodged itself in the ache of loneliness and disappeared. After three beers and a half pack of cigarettes, Fox was ready to go home. The guy next to him turned when Fox bumped against him getting off the stool.

"Hey, you wanna get in the pool?" The man swigged down a few swallows of beer and wiped his mouth on his sleeve. "We're taking bets on the number of inches it snowed today. Final tally won't be until midnight. Got a measuring stick out on Carl's back deck." Seeing Fox hesitate, the man increased his pitch. "Only cost you twenty. Whadda you say?" He held out his hand, waiting for the money.

The itch grew and the voice nagged him on, but Fox moved away.

"Maybe next time," he said.

"Old lady got you on a budget, eh?" The guy gave him one of those we're-in-this-together grins and slapped him on the back. Tears stung his eyes. Fox blamed it on the smoke.

The wipers scratched at the windshield as he eased the truck around the corner and headed home. If the city plows had passed through, they must have come earlier in the day. He inched forward along the now-invisible tracks. The crunch and grind of the tires as they caught, then slid toward the curb competed with the lurching of his heart. Fox stopped in the middle of the street in front of his house, left the lights on, and trudged to the garage. Without bothering to remove his uniform, he struggled to clear a new path.

Snow had crusted up around the mailbox, preventing him from checking for bills or perhaps a letter from Kelly. He watched the beam from his headlights poking through the shimmer of falling flakes. By the time he had paths for the tires, his fingers were numb, his pants soaked to the knees.

Back in the truck, Fox gunned the engine, wheeled through a skid just enough to get a running start, and barreled up the drive. He barely avoided smashing into the left side of the garage door. "Betcha thought I'd never make it," he crowed to the air.

In the bedroom, he switched on the radio. The weatherman announced a blizzard warning, school closings, an additional five to ten inches. Wandering around the room, he touched the shelf where Jill kept the photo albums, ran his hand over the painting they bought together to celebrate their fifth anniversary. She left that behind, too. The press of memories drove him to the dresser.

Opening the drawer, Fox uncovered the revolver and drew it out. He took a single bullet from the box of ammunition, loaded it in a chamber, and snapped the gun shut. He crossed to the rocking chair in the corner and sat staring into the dark face of yesterday. The morning sob returned. He listened to the wall clock ticking in the hall, the one that stopped making bird sounds the day Jill and Kelly left.

Resting the gun in his lap, Fox surrendered to the animal noises that tore through him. Tears ran down his face, dripped onto the sleeves of his shirt, rolled into the hand cradling the gun. He lifted the gun to his mouth.

When the telephone rang with the sharpness of an alarm, Fox sat suspended, waiting for the machine to reveal the voice of the caller, waiting for a choice to make itself clear. He was betting on something, but he couldn't decide what. Roulette was for gamblers and fools. The phone kept ringing. The clock ticked away. The answering machine picked up. Fox held still through the greeting, the cold barrel pressing against his tongue, the slickness of his tears making his hand slip a little.

In the pause after the recording, he heard the caller clear her throat.

"Hello, Mr. Wentworth? This is Rose, Rose Stone. I live down the street. I'm sorry to bother you so late." The girl's voice faltered, dropping into shyness just like Kelly's used to. "Um, Mr. Wentworth, there's no school tomorrow, because of the snow, and I saw your light on, and I'm up late too so I guess it's all right. I was wondering if you could give me Kelly's phone number. I miss her. Well, I'll call back tomorrow then."

Fox could no longer hear the clock. The hand slapped down in the space between him and the gun. Five-card stud, nothing wild, double or nothing. The invisible dealer smiled, shuffled, grinned again. Time to ante up, Fox, or fold.

He lowered the gun to his lap. The tears returned, huge, racking sobs that pulled him over and tore at his chest. Unloading the gun, he placed the bullet back in the box, shoved both in the drawer. Then he stood by the answering machine, rested his hand on the receiver, and murmured a thank you to Rose Stone.

In the morning, the city had cleared most of the street, depositing thick blocks of crusted ice once more across the bottom of the drive. Fox returned to shoveling. This time he sliced up huge chunks of good packing snow and heaved them to the side. Maybe he'd make an igloo when he finished.

He had almost reached the street when the blade dug up a length of ribbon buried at the edge of the drive. Fox cleaned off the snow, lifted the blue velvet to his lips, then jammed it into a pocket of his coat. Movement down the street made him pause. Through the mounded drifts, Rose's slight figure approached. When she reached him, he fished in his other pocket for the paper on which he had printed Kelly's address and phone number. Rose thanked him and, folding the note, she tucked it into her mitten. Then she looked at the wind-sculpted hills that framed his driveway.

"What are you doing, Mr. Wentworth?"

"Oh, I'm working off a bet, Rose. Just working off a bet."

"You're a nice man, Mr. Wentworth." Stepping out of his way, Rose tugged the hood of her coat tighter, then raised a mittened hand to wave goodbye. "A good father. Kelly's lucky to have you."

Lucky, Fox mouthed. Lifting his hand in reply, he bent his back to the snow.

Chapter Seven

Leaning against the kitchen counter, I flip a bottle cap between my fingers. Rain shivers down the window behind me, turning the glass into a Rothko print. "Kelly's dad is the closest thing to a father Rose and I had. He stepped up, filled the hole in our lives."

"You lived with him?" Tuck gets up to fetch another beer.

I shake my head. "No, that was never an option. At least, not when we were young. But he seemed to know when we were hurting, when we needed a break from the drama at home. Feels silly saying it, but if we'd been a normal family, Fox Wentworth wouldn't have been more than an occasional presence in our lives. If my father had survived, we wouldn't have had the same kind of relationship."

"Whoa, wait a minute," Tuck says. "What's your definition of normal?"

Folding myself into a chair, I wave my beer in his direction. "Well, you, and Hannah. Your families. I mean, two parents, siblings, a house you own, no addictions, no craziness. Normal."

Tuck puts a hand on my knee. "I grew up in my grandmother's house, Pete, while my parents chased their get rich schemes. Most of the time it was just me and her and a shitload of money problems. I never really knew my parents, still don't. They chose each other over me. When I was five, they took off following some wild ass dream of striking it rich in Alaska. The next year it was a Hollywood movie career. Every spring brought a new plan. Only reason I made something of myself is thanks to Grandma. Hannah, if she were here, would say the same about her family."

"She was raised by her grandmother?"

Tuck laughs and wipes his hands on his jeans, one at a time, examining each palm when he's through. "No, she had the traditional two parent upbringing. But she'd say it was anything but normal. She's got a queer sister, an uncle who raises and sells marijuana, and two cousins who ran cons using other people's credit cards. Even robbed a bank in Goshen. Both are currently doing time in prison."

"Still, her parents weren't criminals or junkies."

"True, but they spent a lot of emotional coin on the extended family problems. Not exactly normal. In fact, there's no such thing as normal. Everybody's got weirdness in their backgrounds. So, don't expect sympathy, Stone. Just understanding. Now, I'm gonna order a pizza, contemplate switching to root beer, and you, my friend," he taps me on the head with the empty bottle, "are going to tell me all we need to know about Wentworth and Rose and anyone else who might figure into this strange case of the missing sister."

When I look up, he offers me a smile so sincere, I forgive the flippant tone. Tuck rummages around in the refrigerator before wandering into the living room.

"Hey, Pete," he calls, "this from your wedding?"

Giving Rose's package a final glance, I follow him to the fireplace. He picks up a picture of me and Kelly and the wedding party and hands it over.

"Kelly claims it was a perfect day," I say, rubbing my thumb over the glass.

"What do you think?"

"I agree." I set the picture back in its place of honor. Reaching over my shoulder, Tuck points at one of the bridesmaids.

"Is that who I think it is?"

"Yeah." I clear my throat around the lump that rises. "That's Rose."

"Holy shit, Pete." Tuck lets out a low whistle and knocks back half his drink. "She's beyond beautiful. Like drop-dead gorgeous."

"Yep. It is, as they say, her greatest blessing, and her greatest curse."

"You mean she had to fight off unwanted attention." Tuck purses his lips. "Easy to see why."

"All the time, right from the beginning. Men always wanted to touch her. Women, they hated her before they even knew her. Beauty like hers is rare, ethereal, makes people covet. Fox was the only one who never looked at her that way, the only one who realized what she had to deal with. What we were both going through. He taught me how to make the hard choices."

"And your sister? Did he teach her, too?"

I look down, into that startling, focused gaze, and shake my head. "No," I tell him, "he didn't have to. Rose already knew."

Linking arms, Tuck guides me back to the kitchen. "Pizza's on its way. We got plenty of beer, and the drive-thru's open twenty-four seven. Now, tell me, Pete, what you think I need to know."

"It's gonna take a while."

"We got all night, bro." Tuck swings a chair around so he can straddle it, settles his arms across the back. Soldier pads in and flops down, his muzzle planted on my partner's shoes. "Tell me about those hard choices."

~~~

April, 1987

Fox hadn't intended to kill anything that Saturday morning. He planned to be a good father, to take Kelly and Rose Stone, who lived two doors down, to the mall to buy Easter baskets. His schedule included selling a baseball card or two at the hobby shop over on Patterson. To cover the water bill. Then Jill called.

"Kelly has a fever," Jill rasped, her voice an indication that the cold had originated with her. "She's not coming over."

Fox chewed on the fact that his ex-wife had spent the night at her girlfriend Carleen's, a habit she'd picked up sometime before she filed for divorce. And she'd taken Kelly with her. Carleen's place, the exact opposite of tidy, had served as a halfway house in the months before she cured herself of her addiction to him. Spending nights away from home turned out to be symptom number fucking one of a marriage about to disintegrate. Fox, an old hand at laying odds, considered that a sure bet. Today, besides being sick, his ex-wife was angry. She'd have to stay home with Kelly, and somehow it would be his fault.

"I can take care of her." Fox forced the words through his clenched teeth. Shouting would only make things worse. "I'm a good father."

"Uh huh."

He counted the slats in the window blind to keep from swearing. "This makes the third weekend you've kept her away," he said.

"I know you have to watch the game," Jill said. Not want or like. Have to. Like he had an incurable disease. Fox recognized the unvoiced accusation, the painful dig she couldn't resist.

"I'm not betting on it," Fox told her. "I'm not betting on anything anymore." An awkwardness he couldn't climb over straddled the line connecting them.

Jill paused to cough twice. "When a child's sick," she said, "she needs her mother."

"That's not fair!" The words exploded out of him, crackling with fury and pain. Jill called him a bastard and hung up.

The day, empty now of breakfast banter and the pleasant chatter of his daughter playing with her dolls, stretched out like extra innings. He could pretend nothing happened, but sooner or later the sadness would snap back and sting his ass unless he kept moving. *Idle hands are the devil's playground.* His mother's words, but they sure as hell rang true sometimes. The bitter weight of Jill's distrust refused to lift. He had asked for full custody when she left. He'd argued that his salary and his job security counted more than her call center position, her unorthodox lifestyle. She was in love with Carleen, for Christ's sake. But the judge didn't buy it. And the child wars dragged on. Staring at the phone in his hand, he wished he could take back the bitterness, wished he could turn his world back to before. Finally, when the static from the broken connection reached annoying, he made up his mind to find one good thing to do.

Somewhere up on Grandview Avenue, a boom like an explosion. Fox flew to the front window. Ever since that mini-riot caused a lockdown at the correctional facility where he worked, he found himself twitching at every loud bang. He stared up and down Dream Street. Nothing moved. He waited five minutes. Ten. No repeat, no explanation. He rubbed one hand over his face, over his head. The burr cut was growing out. Jill used to cut his hair for him. Her eyes flashed mischief as she circled his body, rubbing herself against his back, running the clippers over his neck, each move a promise of another, better one to come. And there'd be Kelly, bouncing in her swing, cooing at mommy and daddy, her small body proof they had loved each other once. Damn! What time was it? He glanced at the clock. Eight thirty-five. A.M. Fox checked the TV guide. The Reds game didn't start till three. Six and a half hours left until the first pitch. Too much time to think.

Jill's words tossed back and forth in his head, like a pitch hitting a catcher's mitt. Wait for the signal, juggle, windup, whap. Anxious and angry because she had to change her plans, she blamed him for everything wrong with her life. Scrubbing at his front teeth with a thumb, he stared at the dead tree stump in the front corner of the yard. He'd sheared off a few of the weakened branches last week, but the base, some eight feet high, was leaning a little more than it had yesterday. If he didn't take care of it soon, grumpy old Mrs. Robinson would sure as hell sue him for the bark shredding all over her yard.

The screen door banged as Fox padded out, coffee mug in hand, to pick up the morning paper from the bottom of the steps. His bare feet slapped against the doormat, the green *welcome friends* letters all but faded away. He tucked the paper under one arm, hitched up his blue jeans, and rubbed his hand across the front of his faded t-shirt. He was developing a gut. Maybe he should take advantage of that wellness program they offered at the prison. Sipping from the rainbow-colored mug Kelly gave him last Christmas, he noticed his hand shaking. He put that down to the mid-April chill in the air. He thought again about the empty day peeking at him through the rent in the cloud cover and sighed. Glancing across the street, he glimpsed Ralph Krueger shuffling through the living room.

Krueger, whose place claimed title as the original farmhouse for all the acreage now occupied by early '50s bungalows and patched-together one-stories designed on the build-as-you need-it plan, used to do all right, but lately Fox thought the old man might be slipping. Ralph chose to come outside just then. Embarrassed to be caught staring, Fox waved.

"Gut morning." Ralph's voice, pitched to carry over the whine of tractor motors and diesel-powered grain trucks, which he no longer drove, still carried the inflection of his native Austria. The greeting boomed in the quiet air. Fox winced, afraid they might disturb the neighbors. Of course, Mrs. Robinson couldn't hear anything. But he was certain those two big Dobermans she kept penned up behind her chain link fence could sense even a change in air pressure. He didn't know the guy who lived right next door to Krueger, just that he owned a flower shop, kept to himself, and dressed kind of fruity. The Stones lived between Mrs. Robinson, and that creepy woman with the baby, Lacey Webster, who owned the place on the other side of the empty lot next to the Stone house.

"Good morning, Ralph." Fox strolled toward the curb. "Nice day for a walk."

"Bah, what's good about it?" Krueger batted his hand at the air. He headed for his garage, zipping up his jacket as he walked. "No time for exercise today. I'm needing to renew my driver's license."

"Well, good luck then." Fox turned away. He had almost reached the house when Krueger's voice assaulted him again.

"Have to take the good with the bad, Fox, I'm thinking. The bad with the good."

Back inside, Fox poured the rest of his coffee down the drain and placed the cup in the sink. Krueger's words kept repeating themselves in his head. For some reason they put him in mind of those other neighbors, the Stones. Their girl Rose was the same age as Kelly. The two had played together five days out of six before Jill left. Whenever Kelly stayed over, she invited the girl to play. His ex-wife might object, but who was he to stand in the way of friendship? So she could use a bath and someone to de-tangle her hair. She spoke politely, cleaned up after they played, and always thanked him before she left. Her brother Peter took care of her. The boy seemed like a bright kid. His mother was way hard on him, father had been, too, until he died, what, two years ago. Fox felt sorry for the kids, growing up with that witch for a mother. *Stop it*, he reminded himself. *If you can't be Kelly's father, you're not caring for anyone else's kids.*

Out in the garage, Fox moved Kelly's bike out of the way as he rooted for the tools he needed. Dragging the shovel out of its hiding place behind the stack of window screens, Fox placed it in the wheelbarrow along with the pickaxe, a pair of garden gloves and a six-pack of beer in a small red cooler. *Might as well partake of a little liquid refreshment while I work.* He wheeled everything down to the stump. Using the axe, he edged out a ring in the grass and started digging. Every ten strokes he came up for a swallow. The mountain stream on the can reminded him of the time he and Jill traveled to Vegas, his goal of striking it rich blazing in the back of his mind. They came home more than empty-handed. He'd lost his pay the same night they checked in to the hotel, the Stardust, it was, and they had to ask Jill's parents to wire them cash to finish out the holiday. Jill demanded he never set foot in a casino again. Not his finest hour. No, Fox mused, just the middle of the end.

"Hi, Mr. Wentworth."

Pulled from his memories by the cautious voice of Peter Stone, Fox bumped the shovel against his shin. "Damn it to hell!" The words whipped out of his mouth before he could restrain them.

Flinching, the boy took two steps back and shoved his hands in the pockets of his shorts. "I'm sorry, Mr. Wentworth. I didn't mean to scare you."

Fox took another sip and looked up. "Fox."

"Sorry?" Peter said.

"You can call me Fox." Fox waved his hand in the direction of his leg. "No harm, no foul."

The boy hesitated, shuffling forward and back along the sidewalk. "Mama says we have to call grownups by their grownup names."

"Suit yourself." Tossing the empty can onto the grass, Fox worked the shovel under another stubborn tree root. "But you can call me Fox." He lifted his head to see the boy frown, his hands clasped behind his back, his right foot kicking at the dirt Fox had piled on the driveway. He waited while Peter made up his mind.

Finally, the boy took his hands out of his pockets and leaned closer. "What're you doing?"

"Need to get this stump out before it falls and knocks down Mrs. Robinson's fence. Wouldn't want to let those dogs of hers out now, would we?" He winked. Peter glanced over his shoulder at Mrs. Robinson's yard. The dogs were still inside the tiny house. But they'd be outside soon enough.

"No, sir, we wouldn't." He watched Fox's face, read the scowl, and started over. "No, Fox, we wouldn't."

The boy's shy correction caused Fox to grin. Damn kids! They had a way of melting the blackest of hearts. Made him wonder how those psychopaths at the penitentiary could ever harm a child. Shaking off that thought, he set the shovel aside and lifted out another clod of grass and dirt. Peter stood still, hesitant and eager. Fox surrendered.

"Want to help?" he said.

"Yes, sir. I mean, yes, Fox, I do." Peter's frown lifted. Fox felt guilty for not inviting him sooner. He looked closer at the boy. A quiet observer, and tall, taller than Fox would have expected for a kid about nine or ten. He'd grown since his father died. Maybe he had to.

"Go in the garage and bring out that other shovel hanging on the wall. You'll see it pretty easy." Fox wiped his forehead with his sleeve. The temperature had risen since he'd started. Squaring his shoulders, he removed his shirt. The tee underneath stuck to his belly, highlighting the gut blooming over the waistband of his jeans.

Peter scurried up the driveway. When he returned, he removed his own faded shirt and hung it over the porch railing. Working together, they circled the stump, rocking the roots back and forth to loosen their hold on the earth. Though they didn't speak, they fell into a rhythm, taking turns digging and shoveling. Fox began to hum one of those catchy tunes Kelly liked.

"My dad used to sing when he worked. Sometimes." Once again Peter's words pulled Fox into the present. He leaned against the shovel, listening to the boy. "When he wasn't yelling."

Fox grunted. What was there to say? He'd heard the man often enough when the windows were open and his shouts carried across the distance between their houses. "This sure is one stubborn tree," Fox said. "Right, Pete?"

The boy didn't say anything, just nodded and kept digging.

It took two hours with Fox using the axe and the boy pulling on the exposed roots to chop through all the surface feeders. The taproot remained tangled and hidden beneath the ground. They pushed and rocked at it until finally the stump leaned toward the street. It reminded Fox of a picture he'd seen of some tower in Italy, Pisa maybe. Too bad he didn't have a camera. He could take a snapshot of the boy pretending to hold up the tree. But that might be dangerous.

"Stand back, Peter," he cautioned as he pressed his back against the bark and shoved the tree once more toward the street. An object, brownish-red and solid, flew out from the top of the stump, landing with a thump on the blacktop.

"Fox!" Dropping the shovel, Peter ran to the street. He leaned over and poked at the still form. "It's a squirrel. I think it's dead."

A breeze ruffled the boy's hair, stirred the sweat on Fox's chest. It lifted the fur along the squirrel's back. Then Fox heard the mewling. He groaned.

"What's that?" Peter said.

Fox didn't answer, just scuffed his way back to the garage and dragged out his uncle's old wooden ladder. He spread it open beside the leaning stump, climbed up, and looked into the hollowed-out top. How could he have failed to see it when he trimmed the upper branches just a few weeks before? The nest, hidden from street view, had been laid under the bark covering of the hollow wood. Three newborn kits, bereft of their mother's protection, wriggled in the sun.

59

"Damn it to hell!" Fox said.

Peter stood at the foot of the ladder, one hand resting on the lowest rung. "What is it? What's wrong?"

Fox climbed back down.

"Babies," he said, the word squeaking past his regret. He rubbed his hands together, thinking. "Peter, I need you to bring me a bucket of water. Then I want you to take the mother squirrel behind the garage and bury her." He examined the boy's face, searching for reluctance or revulsion. "You think you can do that?"

Before Fox finished speaking, the boy started for the garage. "You don't have to worry about me, Fox," he said. "I've seen death before."

Fox climbed back up the ladder. He lifted the kittens out of the nest and carried them down. He couldn't think how to do what he had to do without crying in front of the boy, but already Peter, hands wrapped around the handle, struggled to bring the heavy bucket to the curb. When he reached Fox, he set the bucket down. Water sloshed over his tennis shoes, wetting his socks and splashing the cuffs of his shorts.

"My feet got wet then, too," Peter said, staring at the dark puddle in the dirt. He avoided looking at the squirrels.

"Take the mother now, son, and bury her."

"I mean, when my dad died, Rose and I ran away, to the creek. We hid by the water." Peter pointed at the metal barrier that blocked off the end of the road, the railing that prevented motorists from driving down the embankment and into the stream bed at the end of Dream Street.

Fox sighted down Peter's arm, squinting as he picked out the line of trees that marked the watercourse and hid the field beyond. The horizon fuzzed in and out of focus. *I must need glasses.* He blinked and tried again. This time he spotted Lacey Webster, the nut bag recluse who occupied the last house on the street, standing on her porch, her arms crossed, her body squeezed tight up against one of the tall trees that appeared to stand guard over her property. Her three-year old son Coal had climbed onto the railing and balanced there, staring at Fox and Peter. Even without glasses Fox could tell the boy was scowling. He turned back to Peter.

60

"That was a bad time," Fox said.

Picking up his shovel, Peter wiggled it under the squirrel's body until the dead animal balanced on the blade.

"Do you think some things are meant to die?" Peter stared at Fox, his arms trembling under the burden he carried. "Some people?"

Fox recalled the last prisoner sent away to death row, how the thirty-year old serial killer had begged to die. "Kill me now. I can't stand being in this hellhole any longer," he'd shouted over and over until he was too far away for Fox to hear. Peter didn't move, just kept searching Fox's face. *I don't want to be anybody else's father*, Fox thought, but his heart had other ideas. He placed his hand on the boy's shoulder.

"I think," Fox said, feeling his way through the words, searching for ones that might help, "that's a question only God can answer."

"Do you think people sometimes do what God can't?" Peter didn't move.

Fox thought truth might be better than some fancy adult rationalization. "Maybe," he said. "Maybe they do. Now, go bury that squirrel. And, Peter, leave room for the babies."

The boy looked at the blind kits squirming in the grass beside the bucket. Then he started for the back yard. He'd only taken three steps before he stopped and, without turning, asked one more question. "Fox," Peter said, "do you believe in God?"

Fox Wentworth, bitter from a divorce he didn't want, bitten by the teeth of a gambling itch, anxious to be a good father to his only child, hesitated. What could he tell this boy that would be true for both of them? *The only thing you can,* his conscience whispered. "I don't know, Peter," Fox said. "I really don't know."

Above his head, a vee of geese disturbed by the rush of cars along Grandview Avenue grumbled and honked. Fox pulled his watch out of his pocket and checked the time. One o'clock. God, he was starving.

"Hey, Peter," he yelled. The boy swung around, the shovel swiveling with him, the sun glinting off the bloody fur of the dead squirrel. "You hungry?"

Peter lifted his head and looked toward his house. "I need to fix lunch for my sister." Fox sighted down the street. In the window of the room that served as Peter and Rose's bedroom, Peter's sister watched them through the glass. *I don't want to be anyone else's father.* The thought clashed against the yearning inside. Drowned out by the need to make up for this day's work. To do one good thing.

"Have Rose come, too," Fox said. "We'll eat tuna salad sandwiches. And then we'll watch the Reds. You like baseball, don't you?"

Later, after the kids fell asleep on his couch, dusk sifting over their sleeping forms, Fox slipped outside. The squirrels were barely moving now, their newborn slickness dried to a sticky paste on their unprotected bodies. He could think of no way to save them. He lifted his head toward the house. The image of Peter and Rose huddled warm and safe inside flickered before him in the darkening air. Lifting the first of the kits, he placed it in the bucket and pressed its head down with the shovel. Ignoring the tears running down his cheeks, he repeated the action until the three tiny forms lay soaked and still, lined up on the grass. When Peter spoke, Fox jerked like a piece of kindling suddenly torched into fire.

"I'm ready now," the boy said, his face shiny in the reflected light of Dream Street's single lamppost. He patted Fox's arm, his palm gentle and warm. Bending down, the boy loaded his own shovel with the remaining two kits.

"It was a hard thing to do," Fox whispered. "A very hard thing."

"I know," Peter answered, his shadow preceding him as he carried his burden to the grave behind the garage. His voice floated behind. "Did we do a good thing today, Mr. Wentworth?"

Fox rubbed his chin to hide a sob. *One good thing*, he whispered, just as Lacey Webster pushed past the house and the boy, leaning forward in his seat, pointed toward the shovel.

"Look, Mama. Dead. Can I have one?"

Chapter Eight

"Bite me." Tuck reared back in his chair. "Did the kid really say that?"

Nodding, I massage my chest with the heel of my hand. The ache eases. "Beer." I clear my throat. "I need more beer."

Tuck visits the refrigerator. Rain drums against the roof.

"So, Kelly's father," Tuck says, handing me a bottle, "he took you and Rose under his wing?"

"Something like that." I hesitate. Fox did more and less than that. He never overstepped whatever boundary he'd set between us, but he was there for those years of uncertainty and loss. "He taught me how to do so many things. Especially how to man up, choose the right course. But I always hated making those tough choices."

"You keep mentioning that." Tuck raps his knuckles on the table.

"Shit. I didn't think I said that out loud."

Tuck snorts. "Before you open that door, the one you obviously don't want to go through, tell me what you know about Rose's disappearance."

Rising, I cross to the roll top desk tucked into the corner of the dining room, pull out the printouts from the Internet news outlets and toss them next to the package on the table. While Tuck reads through the pages, I set out plates and napkins, wondering where Kelly is, when she'll be home. The thought of her driving through rain-soaked streets on almost-bald tires makes me nervous. She insisted on going to this last appointment alone, and she isn't good at navigating in the dark. No sooner does she cross my mind then my phone pings. Outside, the storm has dropped an ebon cape over the street.

P, going to visit Dad. Want me to get something for dinner?

I text her back. **Tuck's here. No hurry. No worries. Ordered pizza. Drive safe, K.**

Tuck looks up from his reading. "Kel on her way home?"

I shake my head. "Says she's going to see her dad. Dismissed as coincidence?"

Tuck laughs at our insider joke, initiated by a vintage ad from TV about UFO's and ESP and other weird occurrences. "Rose?" he prods.

"Here's the five-minute bio. After she graduated from Wright State University, my sister studied in New York, then traveled to Paris. She took summer classes at the Sorbonne and accepted a teaching job at an American school over there. She continued to work on her statues. The artsy crowd noticed her pretty quick, but she wasn't selling much to the big spenders when this rock star, Mason Carruthers, shows up at one of her shows. Strange, really, but the dude was into art and liked to collect up-and-coming work. God knows, he had money enough to do that. So, immediately, he's all interested in her sculptures. He buys two pieces, comes back the next day, hangs around until she agrees to go out with him. Rose claimed she didn't even know he was famous until a month into the relationship. By then, her cred had begun to rise. She was nominated for several prestigious prizes. She never talked to me about returning to the States, but the next thing I know, she shows up at Kelly's bridal shower sporting an obscenely large diamond and announces that she and Mason tied the knot in Giverny."

"You didn't expect that?" Tuck shoots me a speculative look.

"No, I ..." I stare at the wall, see my sister at seven stamping her foot and swearing she was never getting married, never, ever, and asking, at thirteen, in the saddest voice I ever heard, "I don't have to, do I, Peter?"

"She always said she didn't need a husband. After seeing our parents fight and Fox so saddened by his divorce, she wanted to avoid that kind of pain."

"Well, kids grow up." Tuck shrugs. "Things change."

Shifting to face him, I pound the surface of the table with my index finger. "You don't know Rose. Once she makes up her mind, she doesn't change it. Not ever.'

"But she did."

When I don't reply, he nudges me with his elbow. I shuffle through the articles and go on.

"So, after our wedding, Rose and Mason bought property in New York, a big mansion on Lake Ontario. They also leased a loft near the Rock Hall of Fame in Cleveland. Rose spent most of her time there. And her career grew wings." I pause, snared by the struggle between fight and flight and the memory of those terrible choices.

~~~

May, 1991

Raindrops in exact proportion to the heaviness in Peter's heart splattered against the window and collected in puddles on the ledge. Missing its screen, the poorly insulated casing whistled as the wind sneaked in around the panes. He lifted the string tied to the top of his prototype and watched the plane twirl. The undercarriage sagged from the weight of the rubber band strips that guarded its cargo.

It will never fly. Snatching the plane from the string, Peter twisted it apart and hurled it with all the rage coiled inside his thirteen-year old chest. The experimental craft bounced across the top bunk and wedged itself between the bed frame and the wall. The egg broke apart. A yellow smear leaked down the wall.

The instruction sheet Mrs. Patterson had handed out six weeks ago lay hidden beneath his backpack. Rose's box of magic stones nestled beside it. Teasing the paper free, he re-read the instructions. ***Design a package that will safely fly an egg from the top of the steps outside Lincoln Intermediate School to the sidewalk below***. The sentence ruled the space below the heading of Science Fair Requirements. There was a rectangular box where each student was supposed to sketch their design. The edges of the page, smudged with fingerprints and erasure marks, were curled and torn. The assignment, bearing all the hope he could muster, weighed a ton. Releasing his grip, Peter watched the sheet float to the floor.

"What am I going to do?" His voice sent shockwaves down the hall. No one answered.

The science fair counted as more than a classroom project. It was a brass ring, the tantalizing prize a coveted slot in the magnet school's advanced science and math program. The ring dangled just out of reach above Peter's head. He stalked the room, almost tripping over his sister's solar system project. Lacking funds to purchase foam balls at the craft store, Rose had used clay from the creek bed. Now the planets with coat hanger wires protruding from their polar caps sat drying on newspaper spread in front of the sagging closet door.

Peter was tempted to kick Uranus into oblivion. He contemplated stomping on Jupiter and Mars until they were reduced to rubble just like the plane. When they dried, the forms would be too heavy to pick up anyway. He wondered how Rose intended to carry them all the way to school.

Scuffling sounds in the hallway warned that Mom, stirred from sleep by his yell, was closing in. Her slippers scratched a warning across the wood floor. Snatches of song punctuated her journey. He recognized "Fly Me to the Moon," an old Sinatra tune she must have picked up on one of her visits to Carl's Bar. At least most of the time she was a quiet drunk. Snatching up the instruction paper, he stuffed it into his back pocket. Then he pushed away the hair that had fallen over his forehead and straightened the rumpled bedcover. There was no time to clean the wall.

"Talkin' to yo'self again, Petey?" The words oozed like squashed bananas, slippery and queasy sweet. His mother lifted a cigarette in greeting and leaned her bathrobe-swaddled body against the doorjamb. Peter didn't respond. She moved on. "Where's Rose? I tol' that brat to fix me some soup."

Beyond the bulkhead of his mother's shoulders, Peter spied his sister's toweled head through the half-opened bathroom door. Her face, when she peeked out, was streaked with tears. His mother swiveled to follow his glance, pawing with her free hand at the glasses in the front pocket of her robe.

"Mr. Wentworth asked her to go with Kelly to the library, Mom. She'll be back at four." Peter's words pulled his mother's

66

eyes back to his face. Rose mouthed a thank you and eased the door closed.

"Wentworth." His mother spit out the name. Several tobacco leaves clung to her tongue as she licked at her lower lip. Her head bobbed twice, then bounced up. She stared at Peter. He lowered his eyes and counterattacked.

"Don't you have to go to work soon? I'll fix your soup."

He waited for her to start in on how the neighbors were always interfering with her family, but she just coughed. "You're a good boy, Petey, a good boy. I think I'll just lay down a while longer."

Peter watched as she shuffled away. He clenched his fists and considered punching the wall. *I'm not a good boy, Mom. I'm selfish, just like you.*

Picking up the scattered remnants of the plane, Peter salvaged as much as he could. Then he gathered his schoolbooks. If she didn't go to work, how would they pay next month's rent? Rose needed shoes. Examining the frayed cuffs of his jeans, now almost two inches above his ankles, he chewed on the offer of a stock boy's job at Tallman's Grocery.

The grocery remained the last neighborhood link to the old days, Fox Wentworth said. Mr. Haloub, the new owner, bought out Tallman's interest ten months ago but kept the name. Now he was looking to hire someone to sweep the stockroom and wait on customers. He liked Peter, said he had an honest face. *Yeah, right, that's me, Honest Abe Stone.* Peter separated the pack of stolen typing paper from the books and weighed it in his hand. He should take it back. The longer he looked at it, the heavier it got. Stuffing it under his mattress, he headed for the kitchen.

Late afternoon light, a brief window in the cloud cover, angled through the grimy kitchen window, slicing up the pages of his history book. Peter reached to close the curtain just as Rose grabbed his sleeve.

"Leave it, Pete." She glanced over her shoulder, listening for a sign that their mother was on the move. "You can sit over here. I like to watch the dust floaties."

Peter shifted his books out of the sunlight and bent his head. He had to finish the chapter on the Wright brothers before he could tackle algebra. But the countdown had begun. The student who designed the best egg-carrying vehicle won a scholarship to the Kettering Magnet School for Science and Engineering. Peter could study trigonometry and calculus and design space vehicles. If he did well, maybe he could learn to fly someday. He pulled out the instruction sheet, smoothed it with the palm of his hand, and laid his head on the table.

"Tell me, Pete." Rose slipped her slender fingers under his chin and forced him to face her. The tear streaks were gone, replaced with her usual serious look. "Tell me, and then we need to go to the store. I started my period."

Rose's words sounded matter-of-fact, but Peter didn't miss the panic skittering beneath. He tallied up the years. Only eleven and no longer a girl. He felt an urge to protect his sister as she moved beyond childhood. The world shifted, rearranging their roles, creating a new tension to replace the old familiar stress. The sun disappeared. Rain clawed against the window.

"I only have three dollars," Peter mumbled. The materials to construct another plane cost twice that much. Rose stood beside him for a moment, then shrugged and turned on the overhead light.

They worked at the kitchen table until six, their books stacked around them like a stockade. Their mother wandered in and out every fifteen minutes until she called in sick to work. Then, shuffling methodically between the front and back of the house, she locked the doors.

"Don't neither of you leave." She glared at them, her cigarette weaving a trail like a plane streaking through the evening sky. "I'll hear it if you do." Satisfied, she took a long pull on her cigarette and disappeared. They waited ten minutes before moving to the bedroom.

"Is it safe?" Rose rested her hands on the windowsill and hoisted herself up. Already outside, Peter reached for her. The rain had downgraded to a fine mist, obscuring the corners of the faded clapboards that framed the small bungalow.

"Hurry, Rose, before Mr. Wentworth sees us." Peter glanced over the chain link fence that corralled Mrs. Robinson's Dobermans to the house beyond. Wentworth's blinds were drawn, the porch light already on. Strobes of light from the TV flickered beyond the living room window. Through the drizzle, Peter couldn't see any sign of Fox or Kelly.

"Is it safe?" Rose asked again.

He nodded. His sister swung out and down in one precise movement.

Shoulders hunched against the rain, they scurried up the alley that ran behind the houses on Dream Street. Three blocks east the sign announcing the grocery beckoned, its watery yellow glare mournful and wavering in the dying light. Peter trudged ahead, his sodden clothes increasing the drag. When they reached the corner, Rose tugged on his shirt.

"Maybe I should stay here." She blew on her hands to warm them, then shoved them into the pockets of her shorts. Grabbing her elbow, he nudged her through the front entrance. The door whispered shut behind them.

"Peter." Mr. Haloub finished sweeping, wiped his hands on his apron, and moved behind the counter. "Do you come to tell me you will take the job?"

"I'm not sure yet, Mr. Haloub. My mother..."

Mr. Haloub stopped smiling. He rocked back and forth twice and stared at a spot just above Peter's head.

"Your mother...yes, a son must always take care of his mother. So, Peter, Rose," Haloub nodded at the girl, "what can I do for you?"

Peter blushed. He looked toward the window at the front of the store, watched the traffic pass in the growing dark. The reflection of his face stared back at him. If he squinted, he could just make out the green eyes that stared from beneath the untidy brush of dark hair. Then Rose stepped forward, her figure gliding across the counter. The perfect oval of her face betrayed no misgiving, no uncertainty. She wore her beauty like a shield and spoke into the silence with a voice as clear and honest as the wind. When Mr. Haloub returned from filling her request, Peter gulped down his embarrassment and handed over his last three dollars. He was glad there was no one else in the store.

69

The streetlights had all popped on when Peter and Rose left Tallman's. Rose stuffed the sanitary pads into her waistband and waited. Pulling up the collar of his jacket to keep the rain from dribbling down his back, Peter headed for the alley. His sister followed, her footsteps a quiet echo behind him. When he reached the first set of garbage cans, Peter looked around before lifting one of the lids.

"There are only five days left, Rose. I have to do this."

The occupants of the houses on the streets parallel to Dream Street kept their trash lined up and hidden behind their garages. Most were dented metal containers with crumpled lids, the result of windy days and garbage men too harried to pick them up. Peter tried not to breathe too deeply as he examined their contents.

One of the houses had thrown out a sturdy box with *Big Screen TV* written on the side of it. Peter ordered Rose to wait halfway down the alley, in case they had to run. People were touchy about their trash. He waited a full five minutes before he approached the box. By the time he had cannibalized the contents, the drizzle had segued into a downpour. Peter removed his jacket and wrapped it around his treasures. Then he and Rose sprinted toward the house, their long legs flying, their feet spraying gravel and mud. In the dark he imagined wings sprouting between his shoulder blades, imagined the lift and thrust as the wind carried him into the sky. Before they reached the window, the pull of wet clothes tethered his daydream. He was only Peter Stone after all, earthbound and heavier than air.

While Rose fixed another can of soup in the kitchen, Peter spread the results of his trash-picking adventure over the worn comforter that covered the bottom bunk. He eyed the thin squares of packing foam and the yards of bubble wrap.

"Can I help?" Pale but composed, his sister handed him a mug and a spoon.

"No, you better work on your project."

"Mine has no possibilities. But yours does." Rose stared at him, her eyes shining with love and something else, a belief in him so unwavering that, shaken, he had to take a step back. Hair rising in a cloud, eyes sparking, his sister shone like a fierce and fiery angel. Her support was an offering he dared not refuse, even if she deserved the scholarship more than he did. She was light years ahead of her class, but their mother refused to allow her to enter the gifted program. "She's never goin' to college, be lucky to graduate without gettin' pregnant. Just teach her the basics," their mother told the teacher.

By midnight Peter had all the foam tiles cut into quarter-inch squares. He gathered all the pieces, packed them into an empty cigarette pack and eased into bed. Above him, Rose slept, her soft breathing a counterpoint to the rain that had started up once again. Closing his eyes, he pictured the moon frowning down on the cloud cover, the constellations beyond whirling in the spring sky, and himself flying, like Icarus, with brand-new wings.

~~ ~

The lobby of Lincoln Intermediate was empty at six-thirty in the morning. Through the pebbled glass of the door marked OFFICE Peter waited for the silhouette of the secretary to move across the room. After she turned her back, he carried one of the visitor chairs from the waiting area and planted it below the plaque. From his book bag, he extracted a single sheet of paper and a charcoal stick he'd borrowed from the art room. Balancing on the chair, he placed the paper over the bronze relief and rubbed the stick across the page. At first the etching appeared faint and unclear. Slow steady strokes revealed the date – 1903, then the figure of a young boy running over the dunes beside the Wright Flyer.

"Mr. Stone!" The whipcord voice of Mrs. Patterson, the science teacher, cracked at him.

Startled, Peter rocked backward. The charcoal hit the marble floor, broke apart, and skidded across the lobby. The paper floated on a draft. Reaching out, Mrs. Patterson used one hand to steady Peter and the other to corral the falling sketch. She looked at it carefully, avoiding his face until his anger and embarrassment faded. Climbing down from the chair, he noticed, for the first time, that he was taller than her.

"You have a good use for this, I suppose?" She extended the paper toward him but held on to one edge.

Grasping the drawing, he tugged hard, anxious to leave before the other students arrived. Mrs. Patterson wouldn't let go.

"Are you going to finish your project in time?" She didn't wait for an answer. Leaning forward, her brown eyes staring at him through the lenses of her tortoiseshell frames, Mrs. Patterson spoke in a whisper. "I have already recommended you, you know. It's where you belong." Releasing her hold on the drawing, she moved away, shoes tapping loudly down the hall.

Peter glanced at the paper. Next to the boy's raised leg he noticed a delicate smudge, a fingerprint face, a perfect oval. It reminded him of Rose. Placing the paper inside his notebook, he headed toward his locker.

Wind gusted around the corner of the building as Peter carried his project to the second-floor landing. He unveiled the plane, careful not to dislodge the foam that coated the underbelly of the aircraft. Bubble wrap, cut to fit, lined the inside, cradling the egg that nestled within the cockpit. Four miniature batteries culled from the refuse bin of Radio Shack balanced the weight evenly from nose to tail. Wingtip to wingtip, the craft measured two feet. Peter wondered if Orville and Wilbur felt this nervous at Kitty Hawk. He wished he could have been there.

The gusts diminished as more of the participants crowded onto the landing. While Mrs. Patterson gave the class final instructions, a reporter from the local newspaper snapped photographs. Students from gym class and study hall jostled each other to get a better view, while other classes watched from the doorways. When his name was called, Peter stepped forward to launch his plane. He glimpsed his sister among the students gathered below.

A breeze lifted Rose's hair, fanning it out around her face. All the older boys turned to watch as she, oblivious to their attention, raised her hand. The long, slender bud of her body pulled the boys closer, the promise of great beauty a fire in which they were already eager to burn. He waved back, raised the plane above his head, and set it free.

The wings caught the wind, dipped, and rose on an updraft. The craft circled and climbed. It hung for a moment above the crowd, then spun down in long, slow swoops. Something lifted from Peter's shoulders, joined with the plane, and soared above the crowd. Light flickered across the figure decorating the nose as the boy appeared to run, one leg lifted, joy spilling from his outstretched hands.

The craft coasted to a stop inches from his sister, the egg still intact among the bubbles. Peter closed his eyes, imagining the way it would be at the magnet school, the smell of new books, the lectures and the drawings and the labs, each day filled with new possibilities. When he opened his eyes, Rose had gone back to class. He looked at Mrs. Patterson, her face beaming as she clapped for his success, then turned to press his way through the cheering classmates. Tomorrow he would accept the job at Tallman's.

Chapter Nine

"Damn, Pete." Tuck finishes the last of the IPAs from the refrigerator and sets the bottle in the sink. Then he cracks open a can from the case he brought. Twisting the tab, he tosses it on the table.

"I thought you were switching to root beer."

Tuck scratches his chin. "Best laid plans, my friend, best laid plans."

"Didn't take you for a poetry buff." I lean back in the chair, contemplate what might have been.

"Sometimes, a poem says it better than I ever could."

I sense in his hesitancy the need to offer more, but before he can say anything, the doorbell rings. At the same time, the backdoor whooshes open. Yelling, "I got this," he pulls out his wallet and sprints toward the front of the house.

"Kel?" I scoot around the table to take the grocery bags from my wife. Water drips from her raincoat, forming small puddles around her sandaled feet.

"Hey, Kel!" Tuck yells from the living room. "You're just in time for supper. Want a beer?"

Grabbing a clean towel from the linen closet, I wrap it around my wife, kissing the tip of her nose, then her mouth, holding her close as I breathe in the scent of rain and lilacs and essence of Kelly, afraid to let go in case she, too, disappears. She hugs me back, then pushes away.

"No news?" I murmur.

"Later, babe." Her words whisper, her shoulders sag, her eyes stare at me through the film of a childless future. When she spots the package and the scrum of newspaper articles about Rose splayed out across the table, she shrugs off her coat and drapes it over the sink. Rubbing the towel over her hair, she returns to stare at the mailing.

I touch her arm, tentative, uncertain. How much is too much to ask? "I thought you were going to see Fox."

Still toweling, she shakes her head. "The house was dark. I rang the bell a dozen times. He wasn't home. I decided to go to the store."

"Weird. It's not like him to be gone on game night." The Reds were playing in St. Louis. WLTV was broadcasting the series.

"You don't have a key?" Tuck strolls in, arms filled with pizza boxes, and gives us that lidded look that means he's sizing up the clues and preparing a hypothesis.

"Hey, Tuckerman, back off." I punch his arm, try to draw away his scrutiny. Kelly shivers, but she doesn't back down.

"I do, but my dad's, you know, a private person. I never go inside when he's not home."

"What if something happened to him?" Tuck says.

Kelly shrugs off his question. As do I. Best to keep some secrets buried. I lift the lid off the pepperoni pizza. The room fills with the aroma of sauce and cheese.

"Nothing bad is ever going to happen to Wentworth," I say. "He's tough" I force myself to believe my own words. Kelly catches me clenching my fist. Reaching over, she grabs my hand, uncurls my fingers Then she looks at the table again.

"You finally heard from Rose." It's not a question.

"Save the explanations for later," Tuck says, slinging plates and napkins on the table. "Let's eat first. Dinner is served."

We seat ourselves around the evidence of Rose's disappearance, suddenly quiet. In the stillness, only Tuck moves, grabbing our plates to dish up slices of cheese and pepperoni or onion and mushrooms. Unfolding her napkin, Kelly angles it across her knees and picks at the quilted edge.

"I'm not really very hungry. Can someone get me a beer?"

Tuck reacts quicker than I do. Resentment flushes through me. Like I said, it's complicated. He knows her in ways I do not, this woman we both love. When he sets a can and a glass beside her plate, she takes a long swallow, belches daintily, and sighs.

"Just pretend I'm not here," she says, her gaze locked on some inner space.

I reach for her but she arches away. "Just keep talking," she says. "I'm curious what our Rosie's up to now."

Rehashing what I've already told Tuck, I pause to stuff more pizza in my mouth and take a drink. "Rose always deserved better, you know? Our mother dismissed every dream my sister had, bought in to all the old stereotypes, that Rose was just a girl and therefore stuck in the way Mom believed all women were stuck. My sister fought that every day. Finally, she decided to make her own good luck."

"Where were you then, Pete?' Tuck asks. Arrested by the pain in my wife's eyes and my own guilt, I almost miss the question. Kelly nudges my shoulder.

"It's all right, Pete. Go ahead. Tell him."

We exchange one of those wordless married-people glances. I want to tell Tuck to shove off so I can spend the night comforting my wife, but Kelly doesn't want that. Whatever she found out has pulled the fight right out of her. Maybe the love, too. She blinks slowly and turns to stare at the package. I look at Tuck, who's chewing his lip trying not to say something he shouldn't. I hunch over my plate and go on.

"I was training, running every chance I could, working on my escape route, while Rose carved her own way out."

~~~

September, 1995

Rose waited beneath the open kitchen window, the permission slip clutched tight to her chest. A fist of wind rounded the corner of the redwood frame house and punched at the hem of her jean skirt. Her mother's voice escaped in brief snatches, like static from a long-distance phone call.

"I ... told ... never ... listen ... bitch."

Leaning her head against the siding, Rose strained to decipher the words that rode the faint scent of Chantilly, Aunt Pearl's favorite perfume. She must have stopped by after her shift at Delco ended. Rose wondered where she'd parked the truck. Sniffing again, she identified the tell-tale aroma of tomatoes. Her mother was preparing sauce for tomorrow's lunch at the high school cafeteria, spaghetti a la Opal and the kids all teasing about how her mother wore a hairnet and smelled like grease. Embarrassed, Rose glanced at her shoes, the laces re-tied where they had broken, the heels in need of repair. She gazed down the stretch of driveway, counting the trees that shaded the empty lot next door and those that hid the Webster house at the end of the street. Thirteen. She found no refuge in numbers.

Afraid to interrupt her mother's conversation with Aunt Pearl, afraid not to, Rose remained in place, pinned like one of the insects in her biology project. She tapped her feet to keep her mind from the reasons, this time, she must not fail. The moment spun out, a spider's web where she hung, stranded and alone.

Cramming the permission slip into the pocket of her skirt, she inched her way around the corner of the house. A stronger gust of wind pushed her forward. Goosebumps traced a line down her back. She glanced over her shoulder to see if anyone was watching. Her skirt caught on a branch of the climbing rose that snaked up through a crack in the pavement. Bending to unhook the fabric, she lost her balance and fell forward, burying her nose in a cluster of blooms that crowded the trellis anchored to the back of the house. Startled, a scatter of bees lifted from the red blossoms and buzzed in angry circles around her head. Against all odds, the bush had flowered again in late September, the petals like bloodstains against the dingy white of the clapboards.

The screen door banged and Aunt Pearl, blonde hair caught in a ponytail, cigarette dangling from the fingers of her right hand, grabbed at the railing and started down the three concrete block steps.

"Don't pay no mind to what you just heard, honey."

When Rose shook her head, Pearl took a puff of her filtered menthol and blew smoke into the space between them. "Don't matter none. I know you was listening. I did the same when I was fifteen."

"Really?" Rose smiled at her aunt's toothy grin.

"I softened her up for you. You kin go in now." Her aunt puffed again, flicking the ashes into a crack of the driveway before navigating the remaining two steps. She hugged Rose to her ample chest and patted her back.

78

Rose hugged back, willing her aunt to stay just a few moments longer, but she knew Pearl had no time to waste. Saucy and little Butch were waiting to be picked up from school and Big Butch would be hollering for his supper in another half hour.

"What did you say to her?"

"I didn't say anything. I just fixed her up with my boss is all. Your momma's going on a date." Pearl winked at Rose.

"When?"

"All day Saturday to the company picnic and half the night at the country music concert out at Indian Lake. We can't go." Pearl paused for breath and a drag. "Big Butch knows the homecoming is this weekend, and you know he never misses a football game. That man. The dance is Saturday, right?"

"But, where'd you park, Aunt Pearl? I didn't see your truck."

Pearl gestured toward the alley. "Back where that weird kid can't see it. You know he keyed the side panel one day when I told him to get out of the driveway. Put a five-inch gash in the rocker panel. He's a delinquent, for certain sure."

Planting a kiss on Rose's cheek, her aunt moved off like a semi taking the ramp to the expressway.

The door repeated itself behind Rose as she entered the kitchen. Her mother, shoulders hunched, was washing pantyhose in the sink, swaying back and forth to music only she could hear. On the stove, the aluminum kettle rocked, burbling out globs of tomato sauce. A few spattered onto the floor.

Her mother had lost weight. Her pants sagged at the hips, her frame now a smaller version of her younger sister, bony where Pearl was soft. Her mother's hair was still her best feature, a thick fall of blonde and brown harried by gray intruders. Already Rose stood taller than both of them, but she and her mother shared the same face, except for the frown lines at the corners of her mother's eyes and the hard set of her mouth. Waving a soapy hand at Rose, Opal coughed. Suds arced out from her fingertips and splashed over the countertop, frosting the over-sized shot glass that was her constant companion.

"Damn." Her mother swiped at the soap, took a drink, and pushed her hands into the water again. She didn't turn around. "Didja see Pearl?"

Rose didn't reply. Her mother's back loomed between them, a wall she couldn't climb. The note in her pocket crackled as she stepped past the overflowing trash bin and onto the faded linoleum. She placed her hand against the paper and slipped around the kitchen table. When she gained the hallway, Rose stiffened, waiting to be recalled, but her mother stood frozen, staring out the window. For the moment there would be no interrogation. Rose tiptoed along the hardwood until she reached the smaller of the two bedrooms. Once there, she slung all her books onto the bottom bunk and opened the window.

A blast of garbled sound shocked Rose to attention. Her mother had turned on the radio, some oldies station. Another crackle of unintelligible noise and Rose heard a man's voice announcing The Brothers Four. Her mother cranked up the volume. Song lyrics spun their way down the hall, the title matching the opening lines: *"Try to remember..."* Rose pushed at the door, which only closed part way.

At the small desk, the one that used to hug the corner but now stood centered beneath the window, she doodled in the margin of her English essay on "To an Athlete Dying Young." *Rose Marin Stone. Mrs. Rose Campion. Mrs. Rocky Campion. Mr. And Mrs. Rocco Campion.* She turned to the page where Rocky had scribbled an invitation and read it aloud for the twentieth time: *Saturday...the homecoming dance... dinner at Gino's. Say yes.*

Rose shivered. Thorns of desire pricked their way under her skin. The feeling pleased her. Alien and unexpected, the fire coiling at her core remained a secret thing to be handled with care, alone, in the shadow minutes between waking and sleep. Rose clutched the notebook to her, mindful of her mother stirring and drinking in the other room, stewing about their life, about what Rose was up to. She didn't want to share Rocky with Opal. She didn't want to hear the demands and accusations: *you're too young to date* and *girls are nothing*

80

but trouble and *no daughter of mine is getting pregnant before she's married.*

Reading the note one last time, Rose turned the page, and reached for her English book. In her pocket, the permission slip rasped with her movement. The permission slip. She pulled out the square of paper and skimmed the details. Art class field trip, leaving at 9:15 a.m., returning at 3 p.m.. It seemed a simple correlation. Isn't that what she learned in geometry class? Point A permission slip, point B parent signature? However, the shortest distance between two points in her house didn't always equal a straight line. Rose set the Rocky problem and the permission aside and concentrated on her essay. One of the floorboards creaked. Something hard banged against the doorjamb.

Rose looked up. Her mother balanced herself in the doorway, a spatula in one hand, a glass of her favorite gin in the other. Pearl's surprise arrangement of a blind date had almost wiped out the frown she wore every time she talked to Rose face to face.

"Where's your brother?"

Rose shrugged. "He has track practice, and then he has to work."

"Yeah, I bet he does." The sucking sound of an inhale hovered between them.

"Peter's a good boy, Mama," Rose whispered. "Leave him alone."

"I'm going away Saturday." As usual, there was no preamble to her mother's statement, no how was your day or I'm glad to see you doing your homework. No agreement where her brother was concerned. Just that one sentence barked out like a warning. She set the glass on the dresser and wrapped her arms around her waist, waiting, but Rose, lost in the distance between them, swept the pages of her notebook to a blank section. A loose sheet slid out. Her mother snatched it, her face lighting with anticipation. On the paper Rose had inked a sketch of Rocky. His dark hair, cropped short for football season, framed oval eyes and a square jaw. A small scar creased his chin and the hint of a beard hovered around his mouth, which turned up at one corner into a lopsided grin.

Rocky's eyes stared straight out from the page, daring the artist to come closer.

"Someone I should know about?" Her mother stepped closer, then hesitated. "He looks like your father." Her eyes moved beyond Rose, to the window sash. Whatever she saw there caused her to shiver. She hiccupped once, closed her eyes, and whispered, "Now where did I put my drink?"

Rose didn't take her eyes off her mother. Moving carefully, she dislodged the sketch from her mother's hand and smoothed it out on top of her book. Time to speak.

"It's just an art assignment." Rose's voice carried just the right blend of appeasement and bravado. "Do you like it?"

Her mother coughed around the cigarette. Sensing her hesitancy, Rose grabbed the advantage. "The teacher says I have a gift for it. She likes my sculptures, too." Now came the moment to ask for permission, but the set of her mother's jaw stopped her.

"This is nothing but doodling, you hear me, Rose? You can tell the teacher I said so. Best learn something you can make a living at." She stabbed her finger at the sketch, but Rose moved faster. She tucked the sketch into the notebook and rearranged her books. Then she looked directly into her mother's half-lidded eyes.

"Where are you going Saturday?"

The question spoke to her mother's ego. Opal responded with an eagerness Rose had never seen. "Well, your Aunt Pearl fixed me up with her boss. Your mother," she touched a hand to her hair, picked up her glass and moved into the hall, "has a date."

When Rose was certain her mother had retreated to her bedroom, she pulled out the permission slip and tore it into smaller and smaller pieces until no one could tell what it was for.

~~~

"Hey, Stoner!"

Rose turned to the squealing voice and returned the greeting.

"Hey, Marinade." She smiled at Cindra Martin and Cindra's black dreads, caught up in a high pigtail, and the

82

three strands of hemp and beadwork circling her neck. "Love your necklace."

"You going to the dance with Rocky?" Cindra waited, hands on hips, for Rose to reply.

"It's complicated." Rose touched a hand to her forehead, then picked at the spiral binding of her notebook. She thought of the dance and the sculpture competition and her mother standing in the doorway with a drink in her hand. "I don't have anything to wear."

"So, let me help you. That's what friends do, right?" Cindra grabbed Rose's arm and tugged her closer, but Rose pulled away.

"We'll talk later. I need to see Miss Salvatore before class. She won't like it if I blow her off." The lie slipped free as easy as a leaf drifting from a tree. Turning before she could see Cindra frown, Rose headed toward B hallway.

In the art room, Rose's statue, draped with a linen towel to keep it moist, waited. Lifting one corner, she inspected the slump of the shoulders, the droop of the head. The woman's body, sagging and ill-kempt but with an essential dignity untouched by her burdens, struggled to lift her feet out of the mud at the base of the sculpture. Rose wondered if her mother would ever notice the resemblance.

Placing her books on the floor, Rose removed the cover. She used her thumb to smooth the drape of the woman's blouse, creased the brow with an edge of her fingernail. When Miss Salvatore spoke, the sound cracked like a gunshot in the empty room.

"It's an extraordinary piece, Rose, and I really like the title. Earthbound. Whatever made you think of that?"

Rose raised her gaze to the art teacher's plain face, eyes lively behind tortoiseshell glasses on a rhinestone chain. "I'd like to work on it some more, Miss Salvatore. Can I come in during study hall?"

Miss Salvatore waved her hand and nodded in assent to Rose's request. Her mind was centered on the statue. "I want to enter this in the Rookwood competition, Rose. Oh, I know it's supposed to be for upperclassmen, but this work is exceptional. The judges like to meet the artists, you know, it makes an impression, and there'll be some college reps there, too. So, I need your mother to sign that slip. Do you have it?"

For the second time in less than a day, Rose felt a moment expand itself around her like a net. She shook her head.

Miss Salvatore fidgeted with the bracelet on her wrist. "If I don't have it by the end of seventh period, Rose, I'm afraid it will be too late."

The net tightened. Placing the towel over the sculpture, she picked up her books.

"I lost it, ma'am. I'm sorry. If you give me another one, I'll get it signed. I promise." Then she held her breath, waiting.

Miss Salvatore didn't berate her for losing the note. She didn't ask how Rose would get a parent signature before the end of the day. Instead, she crossed to her desk, pulled out a new slip, and held it out. Accepting the replacement, Rose creased it between the pages of her lit book. By the time the warning bell rang for third period, she had run halfway home.

The living room was dark, shrouded by the curtains covering the grimy windows, forcing Rose to squint as she crept across the carpet and reached for her mother.

"What are you doing home?" The voice hissed at Rose. Her mother's hand, the one not holding the bottle, clicked tight around her wrist.

"I forgot something. Can you help me find it?" Rose allowed a note of pleading to escape as she bent closer. She could smell it now, the sweet whiskey odor and something else, fear, like a vapor spreading out between them. Her mother's eyes snapped open and she stared at Rose for a full minute. Something shifted, hissed like a needle scratching against a record. When Opal spoke again, Rose didn't recognize the clear, happy voice.

"He was somethin' else, your father. He wasn't always angry, you know. In the beginning, before he brought me here, there was some good times. We had fun. I don't know why things changed." Rose waited, captured by the wistfulness, as her mother raised the bottle and shook it. "Well, maybe I do."

"Mom..."

"Don't interrupt. Don't you ever interrupt your mother, Rose."

Rose arched backward, but she didn't pull her hand from her mother's grasp.

"Something here turned him mean, changed his spirit. I just couldn't make him stop, the beatings, you know, the beatings." Her mother was losing focus. It was time to act.

"Mom." She leaned in closer and pulled the permission slip out. "Mom, I found it and I need you to sign it or you'll be in trouble with the school people. Can you do that? Just sign your name?"

Wriggling free of her mother's grip, she laid the paper on top of her notebook, pressed a pen into her mother's hand, and guided it to the line that read *Parent signature*. By the time she reached the back door, her mother was singing, the words low and scratchy in the morning stillness. "*Deep in December, la-la,la,la,la-la...*"

The door squeaked as Rose eased it open. The singing stopped. She stood very still.

"Rose, what did I just sign?" Her mother crept through the archway separating the living room from the kitchen. Her eyes shone black and dangerous in the dimness of the light filtering through the window above the sink.

"Mama, did you ever have a dream?" Rose shivered, ashamed of the capitulation in her voice. She hadn't called Opal mama since the second grade. It felt like surrender to go back to the old way. Only babies needed a mama.

"Dreams ain't worth nothing without the money to pay for them. What did I sign, Rose?" Shuffling closer, her mother set the bottle on the table that separated them.

"It's permission to enter my statue in a competition, to go with the class to the judging."

"You been keeping that a secret from me, Rose? What else you keeping from me?"

In the moment it cost to look at her mother, Rose decided. She flung her books on the table and grabbed the edge to steady herself.

Her mother imitated Rose's gesture. "Tell me," she said.

"I'm going to the homecoming dance Saturday." Rose folded her arms to stop the trembling. She examined her mother's face, cheeks blotchy from drink and anger, her hands shaking as they fumbled a cigarette out of the pack on the counter.

"I knew it would come to this, I knew it. You always was a handful. Willful like, and mouthy." Her mother paused, wiping a slow hand across her face. "Pearl knew all about it already, said I should let you go."

Rose watched her mother tamp the cigarette against the table, hold it close to her mouth, and light the end with shaking hands. Across the gulf that the years and the booze had created, her mother straightened her shoulders, tossed her head back, inhaled change in a long, slow pull of smoke.

"I have a right to grow up, Opal, to live my own way."

"What if your way's wrong, Rose? Didja ever think of that?"

"If it's wrong, I'll pay for it then, won't I."

"We all pay, baby girl, some of us sooner than others." Her mother backed away from the table, pounding her chest around the coughing. "What's the statue look like, Rose?"

"You, mama. It's a statue of you."

Gathering her books, Rose stepped out the back door. She listened to the traffic moving along Grandview Avenue, heard the buzzing from the grasshoppers hiding in the tall grass along the side of the garage. Inside her, a faint chord hummed. She hugged her books to her chest and looked up. Perfume from the rose bush enveloped her. A bumblebee rose from one of the buds, its body poised for battle, and swirled in angry warning around her head.

Chapter Ten

Kelly tightens the scrunchie holding back her hair, swipes at her cheeks with a napkin. I lean over to pull her chair closer to mine. She pushes my arm away. When she looks up, the past rears between us.

"I never knew all that happened," she says. "Rose never told me. Why didn't she tell me?"

"You had your own problems to deal with. I think she didn't want to upset you, Kel. And she was distracted by Rocky, and Coal."

"Isn't that the day after I found –?" Glancing at Tuck, she purses her lips, trying to take back those last words.

I catch her eye, blink twice, slowly, then start to cough. Rising, Kelly pounds me on the back. I pat her hand, willing us both to erase Fox's suicide note from our minds before Tuck receives a telepathic clue. Don't laugh. It's happened before. The guy has a knack for sniffing out secrets.

"The day after what?" Tuck leans across the table.

Giving my back a final thump, Kelly sits down, fists her hands on the table. "The day I found out I had to go live permanently with my mother, which was wrong more ways than I can count. I should have been there for Rose that whole school year. For her, for Dad, for all of you."

Before I can reassure her, Tuck tacks his way back to the story. He rests his chin on the back of the chair and pokes me in the chest.

"Who," he says, "is Cole?"

"Coal," Kelly says. "C-O-A-L. A perfect name for him."

"Why?" Tuck thinks she's going to tell him a funny story. He tips the chair back, preparing to be amused.

"Because," she blows her nose in the napkin and tosses it at the sink, "that's what he was, a mass of tinder and dark energy, waiting to ignite. Combustible, insidious. Rocky never had a chance."

~~~

87

September, 1995

Straddling his bike, Coal Webster swallowed his gum, extended his arms through the pine branches that screened him from view, and depressed the button of his new point-and-shoot. Holding the camera steady, he snapped a second photo before Rose Stone, denim skirt swaying, red tee clinging to her slender chest, disappeared around the corner of the house. Coal shifted his weight from one foot to the other, his cumbersome body overpowering the small dirt bike. In the past two years, his legs and arms had outstripped his twelve years. He looked like a man, except for his eyes, which still bore the desperation of an untamed child. The baseball bat he carried knocked against his chest. He laid it across the handlebars, tightening the Velcro straps to hold it in place.

"Coal?" His mother's voice floated at him from the porch, petulant, whiny. He ignored her. Shoving the camera into a pocket of his cargo shorts, he counted to twenty, the length of time it took Rose to pass from the kitchen to her bedroom. Pedaling down the alley, he eased through the fence separating the Stone house from the neighboring bungalow and waited for her to reappear beyond the glass, first her shadow, then her shiny blonde hair, finally the curve of her long and graceful body. Patience, Coal believed, brought rewards, especially to a boy waiting in the shadows.

"Coal! Come home now," Lacey Webster called, her words a veiled menace. "Boys who disobey their mothers are bad. Bad boys will be punished. "

Coal didn't care about his mother's threats. He was bigger than her now. She couldn't lock him in the upstairs room anymore. He checked the sky. The sun had moved farther down in the west, its light climbing Rose's bedroom wall as he circled closer. He leaned his bike to set the kickstand. One of the handlebars thumped against the siding. Rose's voice drifted through the open window.

"Go home, Coal. Stop eavesdropping."

"What's that mean?" He adjusted his weight on the bike seat and the bat handle banged against the metal. Standing on the pedals, he lifted his head above the sash, bobbing up like an apple in a bucket of water. His dark hair stuck out around the oval of his pale face, his flushed cheeks and violet eyes a match for a cherub in a Botticelli painting.

"It means you shouldn't be listening at people's windows. Go away."

Adjusting his eyes from the brightness of the outdoors to the dim bedroom interior, he noted the outline of Rose's body as she moved to shut the window. He reached forward, hoisted himself halfway onto the ledge, and hung there staring at her. Lifting weights in the basement had strengthened him. His biceps bulged under his white cotton t-shirt that screamed *No Pain No Gain* in black letters tinged with flames. On his left arm, just below the sleeve, the tattoo he'd inked displayed a row of thorns with the letters r-o-s-e entwined among them.

"I miss you," Coal said. "Come out and talk to me."

"We've had this conversation before, Coal. Just because we live on the same street doesn't make us friends." She stared at him, her eyes slanted with disdain, and lifted one eyebrow. He flushed a deeper red.

"I'll be an eighth grader next year. Lots of freshman date younger boys."

"I'll be a sophomore next year. I skipped a grade just like you did, remember? And I won't." Prying his fingers from the window, she pushed him off. "I. Won't. Date. You. End of discussion. Go away."

Lunging forward, Coal grabbed her wrists. Yanking her forward, he settled back onto the bike seat. Rose fell through the opening, the front half of her body balanced over the sill. She grunted as her stomach slammed against the wood. Her hair fanned over his face. The smell of lavender and honey washed over him, a current of shampoo and deodorant and her own fragrant girl smell. Her nearness pulled at him. Tugging her closer, he licked her cheek. He breathed deeper, once, twice, capturing as much of her as he could. When she struggled against him, he let her go.

The quickness of the release startled Rose. She fought her panic, twisting to look up at the window hanging in its frame above her outstretched body, remembering her father's accident ten years ago. Paralyzed by the memory, she stopped struggling. Coal recognized the fear and guilt in her eyes. He could almost see the scene himself, every image as eerie as his mother's description, delivered in a weekly sermon meant to inspire him to goodness.

"My mother told me about your father, Rose, how he died right here. She told me all about bad men, how they get what they deserve." Coal rocked back and forth, imitating his mother's lecture. "She saw him, your father, laid out below the window, his head almost severed from his shoulders. They didn't want to let her see, but she waited until they turned their backs, and then she tiptoed in. Saw his arms like wilted branches against the bedroom wall. Served him right, my mother says. Bad men always get what they deserve."

Recovering her balance, Rose pushed herself back through the window and turned toward Coal. She lashed out, scoring his face in four long scratches from forehead to chin. With a cry, he tumbled backward off the bike. When Rose slammed the window, the wall shuddered. Outside, sprawled across the dandelions and crab grass, Coal scowled before checking the pocket of his pants. Satisfied that his camera was intact, he touched his face. Blood smeared the palm of his hand. He tasted it. Looking up, he squeezed his eyes into tiny slits.

The following morning, Coal waited behind the pines that screened his house from Dream Street and the Stone property. He had lied to his mother, skipped school yet again. He didn't mind missing that assigned speech in English class. What I did on my summer vacation. Stupid, and besides, he didn't have anything to share. They never went anywhere. His mother feared a break-in, worried that an intruder would disturb her trash, uncover all her secrets. Coal scowled. He had secrets, too. After his mother left for work, he doubled back down the alley and rehearsed his plan. He still carried an old note, one he'd been saving for the right opportunity.

Please xcuse my son Coal I didn't feel well and needed him to stay home with me.

Signed l. webster

He'd erase the date and use it next week. His mother had trouble remembering what day it was. She'd never know if she'd written it or not. Thrilled at the deception, Coal unlocked the back door and went in to find his camera.

Four exposures remained on the roll from yesterday, four more chances to catch Rose unguarded. He was eager to finish it off. Perhaps today Mrs. Stone would forget to leave the back door unlocked, she did that sometimes. Then Rose, unable to get in, would sit on the front steps, waiting for her brother, or sneak behind the house and smoke cigarettes until her mother came home. He could use the zoom and get a close-up of her.

Legs crossed, sitting in the shade of the hedge behind the wild yarrow and thistles that screened his home from the Stone house, Coal poked at the chipmunk in the small wire cage. It hadn't taken long to capture, and it would make a good trophy. The animal chattered at him, retreating to the farthest corner, but Coal's stick was long and pointed, and he had five hours until the high school let out. When his stomach growled, he unwrapped a peanut butter and jam sandwich, spread a handful of potato chips over the wax paper, and cut the sandwich into exactly as many pieces as chips. He counted them twice to be sure they were even. Then he began to eat. When he finished, he folded the paper into a square and stowed it in his pocket. His mother would ask for it later.

The morning wore on. Bored, Coal jabbed at the chipmunk until he heard it, the complaint of a rusty hinge. He checked his watch. Only ten-thirty. Peering through the pine needles, Coal saw Rose enter her house. Odd, her being here in the early morning. Maybe she was sick. Perhaps she wouldn't come out again. But he could go over there, comfort her. No, her old lady hadn't gone to work yet. Probably too sloshed to get out of bed. Damn it. Coal chewed on the lost opportunity. Or maybe she had only forgotten something. He could walk her back to school. Best to be prepared.

Throwing a scrap of cloth over the cage to quiet the captive rodent, Coal turned the camera on and slipped along the weave of trees that lined the empty lot between his house and Rose's. Using the weeds along the alley for cover, he positioned himself in sight of her back door and waited. He would give her one hour. Ten minutes passed. Fifteen. Thirty. Then the screen door banged against the side of the house.

When Rose came out, she paused by the rosebush that tangled its way up the corner of the house. She was smiling. Coal raised the camera and adjusted the lens. The short, sharp click echoed across the yard. Rose raised her eyes, spotted him, and crossed her arms. The smile vanished.

"What are you doing here?" One arm cradling her books, the other making a fist, she pushed her way through the weeds to reach his hiding place.

Lifting his hand, Coal waved the camera. "Just finishing my project for art class."

"You took pictures of me?" Rose studied him. He shifted his weight to stop his legs from trembling. Unless Mrs. Stone was inside the house, the neighborhood was empty. He and Rose were alone.

"My teacher said to pick the most beautiful thing we owned and take pictures of it," Coal blurted out, sidling closer, his hand brushing the tops of the foxtails that waved around him.

"You don't own me, Coal Webster. I'm warning you. Leave me alone." Rose backed away, moving swift and sure as an arrow onto the safety of her porch.

The screen door creaked again, banging into the back of Rose's legs as her mother peered out. The strong odor of liquor enveloped them.

"Who you talking to, Rose?" Stepping next to her daughter, Opal put a hand on Rose's shoulder. "Oh. If it isn't the hell boy."

Even though he knew Mrs. Stone couldn't reach him, Coal took a step backward.

"Aren't you s'posed to be in school?" Mrs. Stone spewed out a fresh cloud of alcoholic breath.

Coal owed her no explanation. He should just turn and leave, but some force tied him there, rooted his feet in the still damp, weed-choked grass. He shuffled his choices, picked one, slammed the card down.

"Still sitting in the dark sucking on a bottle, Miz Stone?"

Opal recoiled, her head snapping back like she'd been slapped. Rose glared, but Coal stood his ground. He raised the camera and took a picture of the two of them framed by the rosebush. Putting her arm around Rose, Mrs. Stone spoke out across the space between them.

"I've known you, Coal Webster, and I've known your loon of a mother for twelve years now. I don't want you near my Rose. If you don't leave, I'm calling the police. Go on now. Get out. And stay off our property."

Raising his middle finger, he pumped it twice. Rose took a step toward him.

"You better do as she says," Rose said. "She has a gun, and she knows how to use it."

Turning his back, Coal trudged the alley back to his house. All the way he muttered to himself, a litany of laters to feed his anger. Later, he would follow Rose and that dipshit boyfriend she hung around with, spy on their make-out session. He checked the pocket watch his mother had brought home from the laundry. Three hours and then he'd show them. When he reached his yard, the wind had blown the cover off the cage and the chipmunk, frantic to free itself, had bloodied its claws against the metal bars. Ignoring the chattering, Coal picked up the cage. He knew exactly what to do to pass the time, and exactly where to do it. But first, he intended to find out what chipmunk hearts looked like.

~~~

The path, rutted and strewn with gravel, snaked down to the quarry. Parking their bikes at the top of the hill next to a '65 GTO, Rocky Campion and Rose skidded their way down the slope, laughing and swearing as the stones tore at their shorts. Their tennis shoes slipped, kicking up small puffs of dust. It hadn't rained for a month, and the level of the excavated pit had dropped about two feet, exposing the sharp, sedimentary layers of rock that lined the edges.

From his spot atop the bluff, Coal could see and hear without being seen. Usually the place slept, silent and empty, his own private refuge. But others had found the lake today, the unseasonable heat drawing them to the cold water. Coal recognized most of the guys from the high school football team: John Ashburn, Kurt Mahrer, Junior Moss, the owner of the GTO, and Casey Stahl. The linemen looked huge and flabby in their cutoff jean shorts. The receivers, Ashburn and

Moss, appeared leaner, more muscled. Coal planned to be like them, hard and handsome, and king of the world. He leaned on his elbows, watching as they dunked each other, shouting expletives each time they went under. When Rose and Rocky reached the bottom, Moss waved them in. The others hooted and teased as they splashed their way toward shore.

"Hey, Campion," Stahl called, lunging out of the shallows, "you here to get hosed?" He stuck his thumbs in the waistband of his shorts and did a bump and grind.

Face burning, Rose slipped behind Rocky.

"Can it, Stahl." Rocky squeezed Rose's hand. "There's a lady present."

"Yeah," Moss said, pushing Stahl's head under the water as he leered at Rose from beneath the wet crop of bleached blonde hair that covered his forehead. "Let's give them some privacy. Race you to the other side."

Up on the ridge, Coal scowled. He reached for his camera and the binoculars he had lifted from the sporting goods section of Mendelson's Hardware. The chipmunk's flayed body lay spread out on the ground in front of him. His baseball bat waited there, too.

The late afternoon heat shimmered over the land. Coal adjusted the field glasses until he could see the small beads of sweat that lined Rocky's forehead. When he and Rose reached the water's edge, Rose pulled back.

"It stinks here." Rose's voice, strong and musical, drifted up to Coal's hiding place.

"What's it smell like?" Rocky grabbed Rose's hand and pulled her toward the water. She resisted.

"Oil. Or the inside of a cistern. I don't like it."

Coal focused on Rose, looking around as she did. The willows that had grown up along the far shore of the pit drooped, unstirred by even a hint of a breeze. On this side of the quarry only bare earth reigned, the land scraped and pawed by the dirt bikes and 4x4s that used the shore as a dragstrip.

"Aren't you coming in?" Rocky grinned as he wrestled his jersey over his head. His shorts had slipped down, exposing the waistband of his briefs. He grabbed her hand and ran it down his chest before hugging her body to his. Twisting free, she backed away. "Ah, c'mon, Rose. You know you want to. Please. For me."

Wading backward into the water, Rocky held out his hand. Rose remained on the shore. Suddenly, the shelf of rock where Rocky stood crumbled, pitching him backward into the dark water. Rose cried out. Rocky regained his footing, slapping at his wet chest and laughing at her fear.

"No worries," he said, holding out his hand again. "I'll race you to the other side." Rocky dove under, came up gasping from the cold, and dogpaddled his way out from shore. The other boys had headed for the far side of the quarry, their strong strokes carrying them beyond Rocky's reach.

Coal flung down the binoculars and picked up his bat. He scrabbled in the dirt for a handful of rocks. Throwing them up into the air one at a time, he launched them at the water. At first, the small pebbles drew no attention. Raining down in short bursts from the outcrop of rock, they fell to ground just short of the quarry's edge. Coal stopped swinging. He gathered larger rocks. Below, Rose lifted her head. After a pause, she heard a series of cracks. A flock of stones flared out above the bluff, arcing against the cloud-streaked sky like a murder of crows. Each stone plopped heavily into the water, its entrance marked with ripples that spread across the surface. Protests rose, muffled oaths, threats as the swimmers kicked free of the reach of the missiles. Coal put down the bat and picked up the binoculars again, focusing first on Rocky's face, then on Rose's. He hated the way she kept checking back with Rocky, the way she held out her hand as though she could prevent the stones from falling. Stepping closer to the edge of the bluff, Coal moved into their line of sight.

"Rocky!" Rose shouted. "Get out of the water. Now!"

Rocky lifted his head to follow the curve of Rose's arm. Up to the top of the hill. Straight to Coal's hiding place. And Coal watched him, watched Rocky tread water, saw recognition transform his face.

"Get back, Rose," Rocky yelled.

Coal lifted the bat and flexed his arms, the need to punish Rose a burning he couldn't extinguish. Picking up a stone the

95

size of a softball, jagged and crusted with bits of gravel, he tossed it above his head. As it fell, he swung one final time, sending the stone flying through the heated air to land on Rocky Campion's forehead.

"Rocky?" Rose's voice carried over the water. She screamed, turned to look back at Coal, then shouted to the group. "John! Moss! Find Rocky."

The guys turned back, swimming hard to reach the spot where Rocky had gone under. They dove, surfaced for air, dove again. Gasping with cold and panic, Moss yelled for Rose.

"Rose! Take my car," Junior called. "The keys are in my shorts. Get help. "

Panic drove Rose forward. She raced along the shoreline, stopped to rummage through the shorts along the shore. When she found the keys, she staggered toward the path, fell to her knees.

"I can't drive." She gasped out the words. No one heard her. Over and over, Rocky's teammates disappeared into the water of the quarry, exhausting themselves in their frantic search.

"Rose," Junior called again, "hurry. Get help." His desperation sent her scrambling toward the bikes.

Up on the ridge, Coal stowed the chipmunk carcass in his backpack, strapped his bat to the handlebars, and pushed clear of the brush lining the clearing. Time to leave, but Rose was coming, would pass right by him, and he wanted to see her face.

Scrambling and clawing her way up the path, Rose fought to gain traction against the loose scree of the hillside. Her shoes, wet and slippery, fought against her. She kicked them off and kept climbing, aware of the minutes slipping away. Above, Coal listened to her pant as she tore at the slope. When she reached the top, blood trickled onto the ground from scrapes on her shins. The tiny pebbles imbedded themselves in the soles of her feet. Her hands flashed like doves in the sunlight. Coal willed his body to stillness, but his mouth widened into a jack-o-lantern grin of power and menace. Sobbing, exhausted, Rose ran to where she and Rocky had parked their bikes. She kicked at the stand to free it from the dirt. That's when she noticed the tires. She glanced over at Junior's car. His tires were also slashed.

"Rose," Coal said.

"Coal." Rose fought for calmness, her eyes red-rimmed and beseeching. "Help. Help us. It's Rocky."

The plea came out distorted, unclear, raw with anguish. Coal stared at her. Without a bike, it would take Rose fifteen minutes to reach the small bait and beer store that monitored the entrance to the Danville Creek Preserve. Coal turned away and pedaled off, his bike tires kicking up dust behind him.

Chapter Eleven

*K*elly buries her face in her hands. Now I rub her back, trying to calm the sobs wracking her body. Tuck stares, unable to voice the horror he feels. The clock ticks off another minute. I shift my weight, pull Kelly against me. Again, she resists, and this time my partner notes it.

"I'm speechless." Tuck rubs at a wet spot on the table. "What happened to the son of a bitch?"

At this, Kelly shakes off the sadness, holds up a hand to forestall my answer. "Before you tell him that, Pete, tell the rest of it."

"There's more? Holy shit, what an f-ed-up mess this kid was."

My wife grimaces as she struggles to pull the cork from a bottle of merlot. She fills her glass and takes a drink. Ignoring my raised eyebrows, she pokes me with her elbow. "Tell Tuck the rest."

~~~

Wilbur Anders finished prepping Rocky's body for embalming a few minutes before ten o'clock. Coal crouched next to the basement window of the funeral home, waiting for the undertaker to wash his hands and go home. Damned old fart. Fingering the jelly beans he discovered in his pocket, Coal ate one red, one green, one red, one orange until no more reds remained to separate the other colors. He dug a shallow hole with the toe of his boot and buried the leftovers.

At the new funeral parlor over on Delaware Street, Coal could never get this close to the bodies, but the Campion family couldn't afford the fancier place, so Rocky rested here. Bloated from his forty-eight hours underwater, the once-handsome quarterback appeared wider, puffier than he did when he was alive. The red bruise where the rock struck him was covered by makeup, but Coal knew it was there.

Through the glass he heard the telephone ring. Leaving the body, Anders crossed to another room, closing the door behind him. Coal stretched out across the grassy strip that edged the window well, leaned down into the opening, and centered the camera lens on Rocky's face. The shutter flashed once, twice. Now he had just enough time to make it to the one-hour photo lab at the pharmacy over on Thornton. Then he'd have two pictures, one to keep and one to give away.

It was after eleven by the time Coal wheeled the bike behind the garage and unwrapped the body of the chipmunk. He punched holes in the top of one of the photographs, threaded a cord through the openings, and tied the cord to the dead animal's paws. *This ought to get her attention.* He paused, nagged by the thought that Rose might not find the corpse in time, but he shrugged off the doubt. In his world, failure was not an option. Besides, he couldn't change the plan now. He estimated the steps from his house to the Stone residence. One hundred and twenty. Two minutes, tops, if he hustled, to get there and get back. He lifted his head and studied Dream Street, slumbering under the crow-dark sky. No starlight. No moon. He had time before they came for him.

At the foot of the Stone's front porch, Coal hesitated. A voice, dull, persistent, nattered at him, relaying a warning he refused to heed. Mounting one step, then another, he set each foot with care before moving forward until he reached the top. He laid the chipmunk's body on the floor, propped the photograph in its paws facing the door. That's when he heard her.

"Think I don't see you, boy?"

Coal squared his shoulders against the dark profile rising to greet him from the lawn chair tucked into the corner of the porch. The glow of a cigarette preceded Mrs. Stone as she stalked closer, something heavy in her hand. She kicked at the dead animal, sending it flying. The body thumped heavily onto a patch of grass next to the street.

"I should knock you down, pound you into nothingness."

She prodded him with the bottle. Coal clenched his hands and howled.

"Go ahead, little boy. Try it. I'll break this over your head and cut that pretty devil face of yours. Take that thing," she gestured at the chipmunk's corpse, "and go back to whatever

100

hole you crawled out of. Before the police come to lock you up."

Coal took a step back. She moved closer. "Stay away from me and mine, Coal Webster, or I'll hurt you."

Cheeks burning, trembling with hate and humiliation, Coal leaped down the steps, retrieved the chipmunk's body, and backpedaled his way home. He didn't speak. He knew other ways to get even.

Rose, crouched and eavesdropping in the front room, refused to cry. She waited until her mother passed out. Then, tucking a knife into the pocket of her jeans, she tiptoed out the back, the new clay bust of Rocky cradled in her left arm. The roses, wilting in the heat, sagged from the trellis. The sky, a bloated tic of clouds and warning, hovered over the yard. Her toe nudged a spike of gray-green thistle insinuating itself around the base of the rosebush. Shaking from sorrow and Coal's ugly words, she pressed a thumb against the largest thorn. When the skin broke, blood bubbled out in one perfect bloom.

~~~

Coal couldn't sleep with the window open. He hated the night sounds, the sigh of wind through the trees, the ebb and swell of cars passing on Grandview. The leaves outside his window pressed against the panes like visitors at an aquarium, noses flattened, mouths open, gaping at him. Despite the heat that pressed against his skin, he lowered the blind, stopping just before the bottom slat banged against the sill. He locked the door.

Holding his breath against the smell, Coal lifted the lid of the large cooler that held the envelopes, wrapped in plastic, laid flat beneath the animal bones. He spread the photographs out on the floor. Rose's face and body swam across the surface of his room. Rose, his chosen one, unaware of being observed. He touched each photo, remembering when he took it. Rose pensive. Rose laughing. Rose undressing for bed at midnight. One hundred Roses. Coal counted them, rubbing his thumb over the close-ups of her face, tracing the outline of her body with his index finger before he gathered them up. Slow and deliberate, he removed his shirt and pants, his body slick with

101

sweat in the heat of the shuttered room. Lying down, he spread the photographs over his chest, rubbing each one against his skin, kissing the one of Rose, startled, staring into the lens. Aroused, he fondled his erection, then aimed the camera and took a photo of himself. He thought about mailing the picture to Rose. Would she be flattered? Intrigued? He imagined lying next to her, stroking her thighs, her breasts, imagined her begging him to stop while she cried in the dark. Stroking himself, he pictured Rocky floating among the weeds, the underwater currents of the quarry preventing his escape from the subterranean forces of death.

Chapter Twelve

"Geezus, Pete, that's one sick kid." Tuck swallows hard, his hand shaking as he takes another drink. "But how do you know all that about him?"

Kelly folds her hands around the wine glass. "The little fucker wrote it all down, like a story. How he planned it, what he did. Mailed the journal to Rose before the police picked him up. Sent the photograph before they took him to juvie."

"So, he didn't get away with murder." Tuck wipes a hand across his mouth, trying to scrub away the bad taste of Coal Webster.

"Well, yeah, he kinda did." I twist the tab on my can until it snaps, then flick it at the empty carton in the corner. The tab pings against the cardboard top and drops inside. "He spent less than a year in detention. After the social worker visited his home and the psychologist issued her report – social behavioral disorder, mild autism, OCD, not to mention a psycho for a mother – the court felt inclined to leniency. And Coal swore the incident at the quarry was all a game that went wrong. He accused the boys of lying. Thing is, the coroner's report backed up the idea that Coal didn't kill Rocky."

"How's that possible? He hit the kid with a rock."

"Autopsy revealed Campion drowned. They couldn't prove he was unconscious when he went under."

Tuck swears under his breath. "Doesn't seem right."

Patting Tuck's arm, Kelly begins to clear the table. "Nothing about the Webster boy was ever right."

"There's more?" Standing, Tuck stows the empty bottles and cans in the recycle bin by the back door.

Kelly and I exchange a look. "Dream Street," I say, finishing my beer, "grew problems like weeds. They should have named it Nightmare Alley."

"Or Elm Street." Kelly brushes Tuck's shoulder as she stuffs the empty pizza boxes in the trash. Tuck chokes on a swallow. Beer spurts from his nose.

"Good one, Kel." He slaps the table. "I suppose the records are sealed, Webster being a juvenile? So, this Coal goes away for a while. You and Rose get a break, right?"

"You would think that, wouldn't you?" I stretch and yawn. "Let's go sit in the other room. I feel the need to put my feet up and listen to some Over the Rhine."

"Nice try, cowboy, but you're not off the hook yet. I still don't know how this helps us understand where Rose is now."

"My sister does nothing without a reason. I just need to find the connection between this," I pick up the package, "and the past."

Stifling her own yawn, Kelly rinses out the dishrag and dries her hands. I wish Tuck would leave. I need to talk to my wife. About Rose. About Fox. About the note she and I found all those years ago, crumpled up and tossed away. While I'm gathering the news clippings and putting them into the folder, a fresh downpour drums against the windows, reminding me of the flood watch in effect. If the predictions hold true, Kelly won't have to monitor Saturday school tomorrow. Maybe we can talk then. The insistent buzz of my partner's cell interrupts my internal dialogue. Tugging the phone from his pocket, Tuck leans against the doorway, blocking my way.

"Pickle? You coming?" Cradling the phone between his ear and his neck, Tuck proceeds to uh-huh his way through the call while he picks at a thumbnail. Ducking under his arm, I head into the front room. I tune up the stereo, check the CDs on the carousel, and collapse into the recliner. I set the folder, Rose's letter, and the package on the end table and fish out a coaster from the drawer. Kelly follows me in, glances at the wedding photos, then runs her hand over the mantle, checking for dust.

"Kelly?" I reach for her. "I dusted this morning."

"I can tell." She rubs her fingers on her sleeve. "It's all right, Pete. We can talk later."

When she tries to pull away, I tug her closer, pitch my words so Tuck won't hear. "Honey, I'm sorry about all this. What happened today?"

Tears spark in her eyes. "Nothing I didn't expect. Your boys swim just fine. My eggs, however, are not having any of

104

it. The doctor wants me to try a new fertility drug, says it might stimulate ovulation."

"And?"

She shrugs free. "Side effects. I'm tired. I'm going to bed."

I let go. Struggling up from the chair, I give her a hug, which she accepts but does not return. Why does everything between us have to be so complicated? All Kelly ever talked about when she was little was being a wife and a mother. Rose, on the other hand, wanted to be single and famous. And look where we were, childless and struggling to stay close. And Rose was lost in the dark.

Ducking around Tuck, Kelly pats his shoulder before slipping down the hall to our bedroom. He blows her a kiss before stuffing the phone in his pocket. I raise my eyebrows. He acknowledges my concern.

"Pickle's stuck the other side of Patterson. Deep water signs and sawhorses are blocking the road."

"Should we go get her?"

Tuck releases a breath. "She'll call back if it gets worse. But the night's not a total bust. She managed a few favors from her consulting work and guess what?"

"I'm too fucking antsy to play twenty questions, Tuck. Just tell me."

"Someone vandalized the Kaleidoscope sculpture in NYC. Removed one of the children from the circle, melted the face off, and threw it in the trash."

"Rose swore that piece was rock solid. Said she did the welds herself, made sure the seams were tight. It would take a trained eye to spot any weak joins."

Nodding, Tuck kicks off his shoes to stretch out on the couch.

"Thing is, one of the homeless who hang out in Central Park saw it happen. Said a real pretty woman with a shaved head took it apart. Said she was crying the whole time."

I blink away the burn in my eyes. My beautiful sister is out there, aching and tormented, and defacing her own statue. And, for reasons unclear, depending on me to piece together the fabric of our life on Dream Street and save her from herself. I recite her note under my breath, arrested by the sadness leaking through. *What a beautiful piece of heartache*, Over the Rhine sings in the background, *this has all turned out to be.*

"Doesn't mean Rose did it. Last time we Skyped, she still had all her hair."

"Yeah, that's an odd detail." Tuck shifts to a sitting position, cradles an untapped beer. "Let me put this together. You and Rose grow up with an abusive dad and an alcoholic mother, removed from the environment and family connections that might have protected you. Your dad dies in a terrible accident for which you both feel responsible, then some asshole of a neighborhood kid stalks her and kills her first boyfriend."

"You're batting a thousand, my friend." Waving off the offer of another beer, I lean back in the recliner. "But, wait, there's more."

"Tell on, my friend. I'm all ears and nosy toes."

"Nosy toes?" I risk a grin. It doesn't hurt as much as I think it will.

"My grandma had a way of reducing everything to a silly saying. Saved me from taking myself too seriously."

"I should be so lucky." I wiggle my nosy toes and stare at the scar on my palm. "All right, here's another Dream Street nightmare. My memories aren't as clear as my sister's, but Rose swears this is the way it happened. In fact, she wrote it all down. I've read the account so many times, I have it memorized. But no matter how many ways you parse it, I left, and left her behind, five months after we saved Kyle Parker's life."

~~~

March, 1996

Excerpt from Rose's diary:

> *Memory, I believe, serves the whims of the heart. After the incident, my brother Pete will remember almost all the details about the spring of his senior year. Almost all of them. I imagine him on rainy nights when his flight crew waits for a break in the cloud cover, sitting with the members of his squad and*

sharing the story of his big race and his broken leg, believing he is giving an accurate account of an important chapter in his life. But he will not remember how we got into Mr. Krueger's garage. He will not recall how he cut his hand nor how he broke his leg for the second time.

My memory is less selective than Pete's, my heart more hardened.

A scattering of leaves, remnants of last fall's bounty, swirled under the early spring sky. Peter stomped through them as he rounded the corner of Dream Street, his running shoes skidding as they kicked up grit from the gutter. The debris stenciled lines across his socks. Lungs burning from oxygen depletion, he dug in and sprinted toward an imaginary finish line. The promise of a scholarship pulled him on. He wanted to win next Saturday's race, needed to. Behind him, Kyle Parker labored to breathe around his asthma and poor conditioning. Kyle, who had come to stay with his grandfather in the house across the street, had never run so much as a mile in his life.

Rose sat on the porch steps and watched their progress, sketching silhouettes on the drawing pad resting on her knees. Shivering but safe, she decided she was happy.

"Almost there, Kyle." Peter's words mixed with the leaves in the gusty air, disappearing like smoke.

Grunting, Kyle kept running. Flailing his arms, he propelled himself a few more steps forward. When he reached the sidewalk, he collapsed, wheezing. He glanced at Rose, his face layered with exhaustion and embarrassment, and huddled deeper into his hooded microfleece.

"I don't know about this, Stone. I don't think I'm cut out to be a runner." Kyle avoided looking at either sibling. His eyes, runny from the cold and the wind, reflected the resignation in his voice. Pete jerked the boy upward until they faced each other. Although Kyle was only sixteen, he stood as tall as his idol. But the fire that burned in Peter Stone barely simmered in the younger boy.

107

"You have one chance here, K.P. Don't be a wuss." Peter nodded at his sister over Kyle's shoulder.

"You can do this, Kyle," Rose said. "Remember, you promised."

Pulling away from Peter's grasp and his gaze, he cut his eyes at Rose, then flicked them away. Mumbling something about having chores, he stumbled across the street, rounded the corner of the covered porch, and disappeared.

Released from his good deed for the day, Peter shrugged. "Maybe it's wrong to push him," he said. "He doesn't want to do it."

"He's a stranger here, Pete, living with a grandfather who doesn't want him. He thinks he's a burden. The old man only took him in because no one else would. I mean, his mother's dead and his father's gone. We know what that's like. We're the only friends he's made in the month and a half he's lived here."

"How do you know so much about him?"

"I pay attention, doofus. You should try it."

"Well, some boys can't be saved."

Rose turned to look down the street at the Webster house. "You're right. Some boys can't be saved."

"Yeah. And some shouldn't be." Peter's words kited away in the wind.

"Kyle's not one of them." Rose stared at her brother's feet. "Hey, what's going on with your sneakers?"

Peter lifted one foot to examine the sole of his shoe. The tread had turned shiny and slick. He checked the other foot, noticed a hole the size of a nickel.

"Damn, that's not good." His next race, the most important of the year, was three days away. Rose reached over to smooth the cowlick that escaped every time he ran.

"You need new shoes, big brother. Let's go see if Opal left any money in the cookie jar."

Peter started to follow his sister around back, stopped, returned to the front porch.

"Hey, you ever wonder why the front door's off limits? You'd think Mom expected royalty to visit. I wonder who put this beauty here."

108

Rose swung around to look where Peter pointed. The color had faded, leaving the burled oak looking grey and weathered. But the ghost of the original remained. The door was meant to grace a mansion, not a small bungalow on a forgotten cul-de-sac. Scooting closer, she ran her fingers, nails still caked with clay from her latest sculpture project, over the door.

"It is beautiful," Rose breathed. "Look. The side panels are carved like a garland of leaves. They look like the ones on Greek pillars in the books Miss Salvatore keeps on her desk."

"Your art teacher?"

Nodding, Rose ran her fingers over the stained glass inset bearing the image of an angel. Several of the lead canes sagged away from the panes. But sometimes, in the late afternoon, when the glass had been cleaned and the sun hung low on the horizon, light poured through, transforming the living room into a dusty rainbow chapel.

"Whoever made this believed in beauty," Rose said.

"Yeah, and truth and the American way. I just want to go in." Peter shoved past her and they wrestled against each other. Breaking free, Rose giggled and tried the handle. When it slid open beneath her hand, she pushed against the frame. The door opened just a crack, the warm, inside air beckoning.

"I thought Mom kept it locked."

"Hurry, Pete, before she comes back and cusses us out for letting all the cold air in."

Laughing, they hustled through the opening. A few errant leaves followed them in, settling with a sigh onto the rug that covered the floor. Rose rescued one and held it up to the light.

"I have an idea," she said. "About your shoes." She placed the leaf on her chest, scooted until the dying sun illuminated the fragile veins beneath the papery skin, watched it thump up and down in time with her Stone heart.

~~~

Mr. Krueger stood at his workbench, polishing a bayonet. The grinder whined as he lifted the blade, angling it against the stone. From the support beam above, a green-shaded single-bulb lamp spread a cone of light over the long bench where his collection of knives, swords, and other war blades lay in rigid military order. He didn't notice his grandson Kyle lurking in the garage opening, shuffling from foot to foot in a cautious dance of indecision.

Standing behind Kyle, Peter nudged him with his shoulder. Rose loitered in the driveway, pushing gravel around with her toes and trying not to worry. Her plan had to work. She fingered one of her lucky stones, a talisman guaranteed to bring them luck. Besides, she knew things about Mr. Krueger, furtive, ugly things. Kindness didn't sit easy on the old drill sergeant. Maybe that's why his children lived so far away. Maybe that's why Kyle hated living here.

"Go on," Pete urged. "Ask him now."

Lifting his shoulders, Kyle approached his grandfather and tugged on his sleeve. Switching off the grinder, Krueger set down the blade. "So?"

"Hey, Grandpa, I need to ask you something." Kyle scratched at his wrist, pulling the cuff of his sweater down to cover the scars.

"So, ask then. I'm listening."

Rose shuffled closer to the garage door and peeked inside. The old man squinted at both boys, annoyed by the interruption. Looking past them, he spotted the girl standing outside and narrowed his eyes. Rose stared back, but her knees trembled. She wanted to turn away, to forget that once he'd touched her chest and suggested she come in the house for ice cream. Lifting her chin, she ignored the warmth spreading up her neck and cheeks. Krueger blinked and, frowning, turned his back.

"I'm going to run a race Saturday, Grandpa, and I need to buy new shoes. I wonder if you can, I mean, can I have some money?" Kyle's voice faltered. He had been as brave as he dared. He wasn't asking for himself.

Otto Krueger stared at Kyle for two full minutes. Rose knew, because she counted from one thousand one to one hundred and twenty before he spoke. He peered down at Kyle, then shifted his glance to Peter's feet.

"Nothing wrong with your old shoes. Now, go away. I'm busy." He flipped the grinder on and returned to his sharpening. Dismissed, Kyle and Peter joined Rose on the drive, kicking at the gravel and avoiding each other's eyes.

"I tried, Peter. Sorry." Kyle glanced at Rose, his face flaming. "I'm sorry, Rose."

"Hey, it's okay, Kyle. It was a long shot anyway."

Before Rose could finish, Kyle darted toward the house, yanked at the handle of the screen door, and disappeared inside. Peter refused to look at his sister, his hope now swallowed up by shame and disappointment. Then, shoving his hands in his pockets, he headed down the alley toward Tallman's. It was time for work. The electric bill was due Friday.

~~~

"Pete, do you believe in miracles?' Rose scrubbed at the stained glass, trying to erase a stubborn spot of dirt on the angel's forehead. Outside, Lacey Webster walked by, dragging her bags of lint and abandoned laundry to her house by the creek. Rose stepped back so Coal's mother wouldn't see her, wouldn't raise her fist and curse Rose, the one she blamed for sending her only child to the juvenile detention center in Ross County. Despite the evidence, Lacey refused to accept Coal's culpability in the death of Rocky Campion. Although few in the neighborhood took her claims seriously, her campaign to discredit Rose and the boys continued. Pausing in front of the Stone house, Lacey turned her head and sniffed like a bird dog.

Peter looked up from the Superman comic he was reading and shook his head. Light shimmered around him. The angel's shadow rested on his chest while the room teemed with color. Looking at him, Rose giggled.

"You're all purple-y, like the glass in our kaleidoscope," she said. "I haven't looked in it in a long time. Remember what the old lady said? Quality will out. That's what she told us, and I believed her."

"What's to believe?" Peter avoided remembering that long-ago day and the toy his sister still treasured as a sign that unexpected goodness was possible. He no longer put faith in fairy tales. "Look around, dear sister. No miracles here."

"But do you think it's possible that there are, just not for people like us?" Rose tossed the wet rag into the cleaning bucket and wiped her hands on a towel. Picking up her copy of *St. Joan*, the latest assigned reading for drama class, she sat by his feet. "She heard him, you know."

"Who?"

"Joan. She heard God, and it changed her life." Rose shuffled through the pages, looking for the lines she needed, the ones that might convince him.

"Rose." Tossing the comic book on the floor, Peter shifted his weight on the couch that now served as his bed. "Believe what you want, but you are not Joan of Arc. I am not Sir Lancelot. Our mother is not the devil, just a bitch of a mom who only really cares about one thing, well, maybe two, her next drink and her next cigarette."

"You're wrong, brother. There's always hope."

Grabbing Rose's hands, he yanked her down. She pulled back. His green eyes flashed.

"Here's a miracle for you. I get a new pair of running shoes, pay all the bills, and buy us enough food for next week out of one measly check from Tallman's. Oh, and Mom gets a raise so you can buy more art supplies. Or maybe she wins the lottery and we actually buy the house instead of paying rent. Yeah. That happens, and I'll believe in miracles."

Mom doesn't win the lottery. Peter doesn't get new shoes, although he does pay the electric bill on time. And he does something else, my big brother, he wins the race. Oh, and he also performs a miracle.

~~~

It never stopped raining the night before the race. The sloppy track made for treacherous footing. To make things worse, the day began with fog. Visibility was still limited by the time Peter finished his stretches. Adjusting his windbreaker, he set off for the starting line. After placing second in the prelims, a top three finish would qualify him for state. When the loudspeaker announced the call for the 1600 meters, he stripped off his jacket, flung it at a teammate, and lined up next to Kyle.

A light drizzle continued to pepper the lanes. The gun sounded, and Kyle, playing the part of the rabbit, set a fast pace. For one lap, two, then three, he ran as hard as he could. When he faded, Peter slipped past and took command. Watching from the stands, Rose jumped up and down as the runners sped by. She pumped one fist in the air while the other cradled one of her lucky stones.

Peter sprinted forward, arms pumping, chest heaving from the effort. Several other runners tried to catch up. Glancing back, he lifted his shoulders and pushed through the pain. Approaching the finish line, he lapped the slowest runners. One of them was Kyle. Staggering from the effort, Peter stumbled forward. Startled, mouth open and gasping for air, Kyle threw his arms out to arrest his own fall. His hand hooked Peter, who stumbled on, feet slipping, arms pumping as he skidded across the grass toward the judges' stand. His right leg shot forward and slid under the bottom row of the bleachers. The momentum of the fall twisted his body around one of the steel supports. Up in the stands, Rose swore she heard the bone snap. The sound burrowed into her brain. Around her, spectators groaned. Later, Peter, too, would recall that sound, hear it over and over again, a whip cracking in the night, a rending that changed the direction of his life.

~~~

Ten days after the accident, Peter lay immobile on the couch, a coiled serpent waiting to lash out. He refused to accept Kyle's apology. His mother, slyly solicitous, waved off his protests, plying him with glasses of water and the odd plate of cookies to appease his frustration.

The doctor ordered my brother to stay off the leg. Peter didn't listen. I saw him wake up each morning, restless and angry. Today I watched him hobble across the back yard, his crutches leaving round indentations in the soft earth. I didn't tell Opal. I pretended not to see. Was that the right thing to do? I don't know. I do know this. Sometimes we need to confront our demons alone.

Rose retreated to her bedroom, determined to finish her geometry homework. She was wrestling with the volume of a cone when she glanced out the window. Juggling an oversize cardboard box, Kyle crossed the street, passed along the side of the Stone house, and disappeared in the direction her brother had gone. Abandoning the math problem, Rose headed for the back door. Through the screen, she watched Kyle set the box on top of the picnic table that crouched beside the garage. Pushing through the door, she called out. He waved her off.

"Tell Peter I can't use these anymore." Kyle pointed at the box.

When Rose stepped off the porch, he ran back the way he'd come.

Rose hesitated. Kyle meant the box for Peter. She didn't want to know what he had left behind. But curiosity proved stronger than discretion. Moving to the table, she opened the box. Glancing back to see if Kyle had returned, she lifted out the contents: a miniature wooden elephant with a wobbly trunk, a stuffed tiger, a beanie baby poodle with a frayed black collar. Digging through a stack of running magazines, she discovered several Richard Scary books and the trophy Kyle won at the spring track awards. *Most improved.* From the very bottom she pulled out a cheap gold frame holding a picture of a dark-haired young woman with Kyle's eyes. The woman wore an orange sundress and held a baby up like it was her most prized possession. Tilting the photo against the sun's glare, she jolted at the clang of a garage door closing. It reminded her of her brother's bone shattering at the track meet. A second, louder thump disturbed the morning quiet. She squeezed the frame so tight the glass shattered.

Then she was running, down the alley path, her bare feet leaving tracks in the soggy grass. She sprinted toward the creek, surprising Peter as he balanced on his good leg, tossing rocks into the water. The creek, swollen to twice its size with the runoff from the spring rains, hissed and roared. His crutches leaned out over the bank above the rushing stream.

"Pete, you have to come back. Now. Something's wrong."

"Wrong?" Picking up another rock, he rifled it across the water.

"Come. Now. It's Kyle." Without waiting for a reply, Rose darted away, arms pumping as she raced back home.

Pete hobbled along behind her. Rose's command pressed at him, grinding past his defenses, drowning out his anger at the neighbor for causing him to fall, for failing to be a friend, for being so needy when Peter needed help, too. As he huffed into the yard, Rose held up the picture of Kyle and his mother, distorted now beneath the shattered glass.

"He gave these things away. To you. And I heard a noise, Pete." She gestured toward the farmhouse. "It sounded bad."

"What kind of noise?"

"The kind that means trouble."

They stared at each other, reliving the moment when the window came crashing down on their father's head.

"Call 9-1-1. Now." Peter tried to hurdle the picnic bench that blocked his path, but the crutches impeded him. Discarding them, he shifted his weight onto his casted leg, winced, and hop-stepped around the corner of the house. Mr. Krueger's truck was gone from the driveway. Laboring to cross Dream Street, Peter heaved himself up the porch steps. He lunged for the door, pounding his fists against the wood. No one answered. He vaulted the steps, landing on his good leg first to cushion the impact, then lowering the broken one.

"Hurry!" Rose's cry rang out behind him, panic riding her words. Fear clamped down, masking the pain in his leg. "The police are on the way!"

Risking a backward glance, he saw Rose standing in the doorway, the phone cord stretched taut behind her. He closed his eyes for a second. His sister's voice buzzed in the background. Images from the past replayed in his head. Rocky's bloated face, his head resting on a satin cushion inside the casket at Armstrong's Funeral Parlor. His father's grimace of surprise, eyes closed against the death that claimed him so far from his beloved mountains. Rose yelled again. For one moment, Peter hesitated, dragging his leg over the gravel tracks that led to the garage behind the house. When he looked up, a light inside the garage went out, leaving the structure dark and brooding in the late afternoon.

"I don't know where to go." As he gasped for breath, the thud of a heavy object pulled at him. From across the street, Rose heard it too, a muffled crash inside the workshop. Dropping the phone, she leaped the steps and raced after Peter.

Shouting for Kyle, Peter ran to the double doors that opened on rollers. The doors shuddered but refused to part. Peter pushed harder, willing the hinges to give. They didn't budge. He searched the ground for something, anything, to use as a battering ram.

"Wait," Rose shouted. "I'll find something." In the vegetable garden at the back end of the property she stumbled over a small headstone, the weathered inscription barely visible: Faith, infant daughter of Samuel and Charity Krueger. 1939-1940. Clawing at the dirt, she wrestled the stone free and ran back to her brother. Balancing against the garage wall, Peter edged toward the single window. He accepted the tombstone from Rose and battered the glass. When the panes broke, he took off his shirt, wrapped his hands, and pulled out the pieces left behind. One of the shards sliced through the cotton and into his palm. Blood soaked through the wrap as he pulled himself up and over the sill, falling shoulder first onto the floor of the garage. Hoisting herself through the window, Rose followed him in.

Light barely penetrated the dim interior. Shuffling his way along, Peter stretched his arms out to ward off a collision with old man Krueger's tools. Near the center, the workbench had been wrestled from its usual position along the south wall. Crouching, he traced the scuffmarks Kyle made when he dragged it from its place. The air stirred above him. Looking up, he spotted something swaying. Kyle.

Grunting with the effort it took to shove the bench upright, Peter heaved himself onto the top. He dragged his broken leg after him. His breathing turned hoarse and labored. The pain in his leg screamed at him. Jockeying for position, he hoisted Kyle's body upward, relieving the pressure of the rope that wound around a beam and circled the boy's neck. Peter's arms burned. The cut on his hand bled, leaving smears across Kyle's shirt. Straining to keep the tension loose, Peter pleaded with the God he didn't believe in to keep the boy alive.

"Peter?" Rose called from the shadows, head cocked toward the silence around them. Death, she realized, gathering the Stones to its bosom once more. *See*, it whispered, *how powerful I am.* "The police are on the way."

"I can't hold him, Rose. Bring me something to cut the rope. Hurry."

Crouching, Rose crawled along the ground until she touched the blade of one of Mr. Krueger's bayonets. When she handed it to Peter, he lunged at the rope above Kyle's head. The blade sliced through the cord more easily than he anticipated. Kyle's body sagged. Together they tumbled off the workbench. The bayonet flew from Peter's hand, whistled past Rose, and imbedded itself in the dirt. Rose touched her cheek. Her fingers came away bloody. She pressed them against her chest, leaving a perfect imprint on the white cotton of her blouse.

The workbench wobbled like the pendulum of some crazy cuckoo clock. Before she could shout a warning, it tilted and tipped over, crashing onto her brother's broken leg. Peter screamed and passed out.

Inching over to the unmoving forms, Rose pressed her fingers against Kyle's neck. As soon as she detected a slight, irregular flutter, she turned to Peter. She patted his face until, groaning, he opened his eyes.

"My leg hurts."

"Don't you quit on me, Peter Stone." Smoothing back her brother's hair, she returned to Kyle. Loosening the rope, she eased it free. Straddling the boy's chest, she placed her hands over his sternum and started to count. Pump, breathe in, rest. Pump, breathe, rest. She bent her ear to his chest, listening for a sign. Her own heart beat a fierce challenge to the shadows for control over yet another life.

Peter woke long enough to mumble something about never running again. Then he passed out again. Faint at first, then louder, the blare of a police siren and the whoop-whoop of an ambulance filled the silence.

They rode together to the emergency room, the emergency med techs, Peter awake and Kyle, unconscious, and Rose. Tucking herself into the corner, she held Peter's hand, fingered the stone in her pocket, and stared at the pale ghost of the boy who tried to kill himself hooked up to monitors, his life hanging by the thinnest of cords.

At the hospital, at Rose's request, the boys shared a room. She dozed in a chair between them, waiting for her mother to arrive. She didn't remember getting stitches in her cheek, although the doctor said later that he placed fifty neat and tiny so she wouldn't have a scar. But she carried one anyway, a whisker-thin witness to her brother's victory. Peter needed stitches, too, for the cut in his palm. As for Kyle, the rope had burned a line around his throat, a bold red ring that faded but never really disappeared. After he recovered, his grandfather sent him back to the foster home where he had lived before.

Three months later, Rose received a postcard with no return address. The picture on the front showed a giant bonfire with a sign that read *Celebrating the Summer Solstice*. She glued it to the center of a mixed media canvas surrounded by tiny images of herself and submitted it in the county fair art show. *St. Joan in flagrante delicto*, she called it. When Miss Salvatore saw the piece, she cried.

At home, leg reset and concussion healing, Peter rested on the couch, reading his favorite Superman comics and sipping water out of a plastic cup. For days he refused to speak. Finally, to stop Rose from nagging and his mother's fretful cursing, he threw up his hands and grabbed the crutches. Rose pushed him back against the cushions, smoothed his hair, and propped a pillow under his leg.

"Stop it," he growled. "Leave me alone."

"It wasn't your fault. Hey, look at me. It wasn't your fault."

He swatted her with one of the comics. She danced away, fingers raised to frame his wild, angry face. Light leaking through the door created a halo around his head. The outline of the angel settled on his chest, a superhero emblem for a boy with shadowed eyes.

"Hey," tiptoeing behind, she tapped his head. "Stop raging. Time for me to go to work. I promised Mr. Haloub."

118

"That's my job." His voice echoed the sound of wind and leaves and fire. He exhaled, his breath moving the dust motes that danced in the light.

"It's okay, Pete," Rose told him. "I can do it for you. And Kyle's okay."

"Rose," Peter gathered up the comics and shoved them under a pillow, "by now you should know that nothing in our life is ever okay."

"You saved him, Pete." Rose grabbed his hand, traced the stitching on his palm.

"I don't think he wanted me to."

"My brother, the perpetual skeptic. Also, the great hero." Rose pinched the base of his thumb. Peter scowled.

"I'm not a skeptic. I'm a realist."

Rose let go. "Someday he'll understand. And he'll thank you."

"I don't want him to thank me. I don't want to talk about him ever again." Closing his eyes, he pretended to sleep. Pausing in the doorway, she watched the light play over her brother's face, the shadows moving across his stubbled chin. He burrowed under the blanket, frowning, struggling with his doubt.

In Paris, I sculpted my brother's image from this moment of unbelief. I entered the bust in a show, where it placed first. I called the statue Reluctant Angel.

119

Chapter Thirteen

"You never told me that. About the statue." Kelly stares at me from the hall, lower lip pouty, hair bunched on top of her head, her favorite plaid pajamas riding low on her hips. Her breasts, unbound, strain at the too-small football jersey. She looks raw, vulnerable, sexy. I want to carry her to bed and kiss away the hurt in her eyes. But Tuck's staring, too, the old sadness flaring like a lit match. I clear my throat.

"I didn't want you to know." I trace the scar that extends the heartline on my palm and wait for her to decide to trust me again. Kelly's eyes flit around the room, land on the photographs, the fireplace, my mouth, Tuck's legs. She looks away, tilts her head, turns back. Shuffling across the carpet, she flops in front of the recliner, not close enough to touch, not far enough to count as avoidance. I toy with a strand of her hair. She tugs it free, wraps it around her finger. Tuck gnaws the inside of his cheek. Then, rising, he heads for the fridge, his offer to return with more liquid refreshment trailing after him.

"Couldn't sleep?"

Leaning back, Kelly shrugs. She catches my hand, rubs it against her cheek. When I try to touch her lips, she flings it away. "I'm worried about Rose, too, you know. Do you think she's all right?"

"I don't know. If she were desperate enough, she might hurt someone else, but I swear Rose wouldn't hurt herself. Kyle Parker's near-suicide pretty much crossed that off both our lists of ways to leave the world."

"But someone might hurt her." Tuck appraises us from the doorway, his hands filled with soda now and a bag of chips. Kelly accepts the offered diet cola. She balances the can between her knees, one arm wrapped protectively around her abdomen. I lean forward, close enough to support her back. That jolt of electricity I always get when we touch leaves me aching. Tuck settles back on the couch.

121

"Yes," I agree, "someone might hurt her."

"What about money?" Tuck presses. "Does she have any? Pickle says they've tried tracing her credit cards, but no luck."

I huff at that, arrested by a memory I haven't recalled in a long time. "Money. Rose and I always found a way to the money. Despite what it cost us in the end."

Nodding, Kelly rubs a thumb over the rim of the can. The squeak fills the space between us. "My dad always said you had an uncanny knack for finding what you needed. He called you the luckiest kid on the planet."

"Luck? Coincidence?" Even a blind squirrel, Fox used to say, finds an acorn now and then. Maybe it was more than that. "Maybe Rose was my lucky stone."

Tuck rolls his shoulders, frowns at his feet. "What the hell are you two talking about?"

"Another Stone story, Tuck, maybe the best one yet. How Uncle Sam helped Peter and Rose escape the poorhouse."

Balancing the beer between his thighs, Tuck waggles his fingers at me and Kelly. "Come on, Stoner. Give me the next piece of the puzzle."

~~~

December, 1997

Snow swirled in shifting patterns against the storefront window. When the wind paused to catch its breath, a bull's eye tattooed itself in lacy flakes around the crumbled lettering that announced *Tallman's Cash and Carry*. In the reflection of the old-fashioned promise, Peter Stone, clerking during his first winter break from classes at Sinclair Community College, dipped the rag mop into the rusted metal bucket, wrung it out, and swished it slowly across the scuffed hardwood of Tallman's Grocery. The low voice of the radio announcer droned on about the approaching storm front. The clock mounted behind the cash register ticked closer to nine. Almost closing time. In the pocket of Peter's jeans, his membership card to the Lohrey Center Natatorium rustled against the brochure from the Navy Recruiting Office.

Subtle sighs behind the counter indicated Mr. Haloub had finished tidying up the register. His head bobbed up from the display of bubble gum and rainbow suckers, his dark eyes and receding hairline overpowered by the thick, round, black glasses that hugged his nose.

"All done, Peter?" Mr. Haloub asked, nodding in the direction of the mop and bucket.

"Almost." Peter lowered his head to hide the flush rising over his cheeks. He'd been daydreaming again, drawing mental pictures of an academic life at The Ohio State University. If he could save enough money to transfer there. Live off High Street in one of those plain, paint-peeling student houses. Study engineering and avionics. Breathe free.

Peter's design for the future had fractured into before and after ever since his father's death thirteen years ago. Once, his father's job at the Delphi manufacturing plant had provided a steady income and breathing room to consider big dreams. Those dreams swung now on the cusp of fading promise, helpless, like the snowflakes, before the tsunami of bills that threatened to swamp the Stone family. Ice crystals battered against the window. Peter listened to the howling, trying to forget he was now the responsible one.

Mr. Haloub touched his arm. "Peter?"

Peter jumped. The mop plopped into the bucket, scattering dirty suds across the fresh-scrubbed wood. If only he had more money. He thought about his savings, the dollars he'd collected from parking cars at football games and dee-jaying off-campus parties out at Wright State, and working for Mr. Haloub. More than a thousand dollars toward next year's room and board stashed under a loose floorboard. One hundred and fifty in crumpled ones and fives intended for Rose's art supplies. He'd hidden her share inside her shoebox collection of childhood mementos, intending to give it to her for Christmas. Doing the math again, balancing the credits and debits in his head, Peter realized it wasn't nearly enough.

"Come with me." Mr. Haloub gripped Peter's arm and escorted him toward the back room where Mrs. Haloub sat writing in the day's ledger. Mr. Haloub handed her a piece of paper with the register total inked in neat numbers. She entered the amount in the record. Peter avoided tapping his foot while Mr. Haloub emptied his pockets of the money from the day's sales. Placing the coins and bills in a purple Crown

Royal whiskey bag, Mr. Haloub accepted a deposit slip from his wife. He stuffed it inside the bag and pulled the drawstring closed. Peter wondered where he'd found the bag. The Haloubs didn't drink, and they didn't sell alcohol. Maybe, Peter mused, my mother gave it to him.

"Come with me, Mr. Peter Stone," His employer repeated. "I want to show you something."

Whenever Mr. Haloub used those words, Peter knew it meant one of two things: a new task to add to his list of chores, or an old one that needed redoing.

"I haven't finished the floor," Peter protested. "And I have to get to the pool before it closes. It's getting late." Swimming at Lohrey Center every night had become his routine since he'd broken his leg last spring, the laps a way to stay strong until the break healed completely, until he could start running again. Powering through the water released him from the cycle of worry.

Ignoring Peter's dismay, Mr. Haloub crouched down behind the counter to lift a trap door. The panel banged against the wall, revealing a narrow stairway down to a dirt-floored basement, a remnant from the eighteen-hundreds when the store had been a tavern. The Haloubs kept their deliveries there, and a safe. The best hiding places, Mr. Haloub insisted, existed underground.

Handing the moneybag to Peter, Mr. Haloub climbed down. Peter followed, running his hand over the velvety material of the money bag. The bills and coins emitted a siren song, a crooning seduction of financial security. Peter closed his ears to their promise. Money...all his problems rooted in that soil.

"Here, Peter," Mr. Haloub called, "this is how it's done." He lifted aside the Coors Beer sign that concealed the safe, spun the knob twice to the left, stopping on eight, back to the right to four and on to zero, and shoved the bag inside. Then he removed the bag and handed it to Peter. Re-locking the safe, Mr. Haloub stepped aside and motioned with one hand. "Now, you do it."

Leaving Peter to wrestle with the combination, Mr. Haloub drifted over to the stacks of paper towels and the boxes stamped *macaroni and cheese* and *beef stew*. Under the light cast by the fluorescent overheads, Peter could make out the lumpish shapes of discarded chairs, lamps, end tables, and desks waiting to be called back into service.

"What's all this furniture doing here?" Peter asked.

Mr. Haloub glanced around, his lips pursed. "Hmm, it's trade."

"Trade?" Intrigued, Peter wandered through the tangle of oak and cherry. Lifting a stained cloth, he uncovered an antique walnut secretary with panes of colored glass divided by an elaborate grid pattern. Dust, invisible in the dimness, floated off the cloth. He and Mr. Haloub sneezed in unison.

"Some people, they don't have money to pay, so they offer other things." Mr. Haloub gestured toward the various items. "Vases, silver, pieces of furniture. I offer them food and they give me these. For many, it's better than the pawnshop. They know they can always reclaim them here."

"That's a good thing to do, Mr. Haloub," Peter said, but Mr. Haloub had already turned away. Tucking the moneybag under his arm, Peter touched the old desk. He tugged at the pull-down top until it opened toward him. Two supports slid out beneath the writing surface. A memory nagged at Peter, pulling him back in time to their home in the mountains, to Mam's desk claiming the place of honor in his parents' bedroom. His grandmother's heirloom secretary, stolen long ago.

"Peter? The money?" Mr. Haloub patted Peter's arm. "Put it away now."

"How much?" Peter said.

"Peter," Mr. Haloub stared at him over his glasses. "That's not for you to know."

"No, Mr. Haloub, not that. How much would it cost to buy this desk?"

Mr. Haloub squinted through his lenses and shrugged. "That piece? I don't think you could afford that one."

Clearing his throat to hide his disappointment, Peter reached for the cloth that had protected the desk. "Should I cover it back up?"

"Later." Mr. Haloub's attention wandered to tomorrow's business. If the winter storm hit as expected, his customers would purchase all his stock. Humming, the shop owner walked beside the boxes, anticipating his profit.

Peter moved to the safe. He spun the dial once more to be certain he had mastered the combination. The existence of all that money, stashed in the dark behind a beer sign, gave way to the memory of his grandmother and the secretary his mother loved.

Upstairs, Peter returned to his mop, swishing the ropy strands faster across the boards. Gazing through the snow-flecked window, he glimpsed someone crossing under the streetlight that threw out an arc of whitened fuzz from across the street. A second figure followed the first. Dumping the mop, now flecked with dirt, into the soapy water, Peter wiped his hands on his jeans and moved closer to the window. He shaded his eyes and peered into the storm. The shadows had vanished. Shrugging off the unease prickling down his back, he slid the bolt in place and lowered the shade that announced *Closed*. Then he went to rinse out the bucket.

Sleet lashed at Peter's face and shoulders as he trudged three blocks north to the Natatorium. His tennis shoes, encased in snow, dragged at him. He stopped at every streetlight to be sure he hadn't drifted off course. Strands of Christmas lights blinked behind living room windows. White icicles, the newest trend in illumination for the season, shivered and swung in the gusts that threatened to blow him over. By the time he reached the Center, the trainer on duty was already closing up.

"Thought nobody'd be stupid enough to come out tonight." The guy unpinned his nametag before Peter could read it.

"You must be new here," Peter said. "I never miss a chance to torture myself."

Pulling on a scarlet and grey ski cap, the guy grinned,. "Yeah, they told me to watch out for you. Peter Stone, right?"

"Affirmative."

"You got your key?"

Peter patted his pockets. "Damn, all I have is my ID card. I left the key at home. Good thing you were here."

The guy cocked an eyebrow, jingled the keys in his hand, then tossed them over.

"Thanks." Peter stashed them into the zippered pocket on his jacket. "I'll lock up when I leave."

"If I were you, I wouldn't stay too long. Forecast says there's a blizzard coming."

"I know," Peter said. "I'll just do my laps and go. I don't live far."

"They told me you were hardcore. Have a good one." The guy flashed him another grin as he shoved his way through the door, his gym bag banging against the glass. A gust of snow curled in, depositing a small white drift on the welcome mat.

The pool shimmered in the moist air, heavy with the odor of chlorine. The smell hung heavy in the locker room, causing Peter to cough and blink his eyes. He hung his jacket and cap to dry over one of the heat registers, stripped to his trunks, and dove into the lap lane. The water welcomed him, curling around his body with each stroke. Stretching his arms, rotating his head to stroke, breathe, stroke, Peter tried to lose himself in the cadence of the swim, but worry wouldn't release its hold. The knowledge of the money in Mr. Haloub's safe, the discovery of the antique desk that surely belonged to him and his family, the bills stalking like lions, it all refused to slip away. He had only completed half his laps when he heard footsteps. Treading water, he drifted nearer to the steps that swanned out of the far end of the pool.

"Who's there?" he called, staring into the darkened hallway that led to the front door.

Rose, head swathed in a layer of wool scarf, collar pulled close around her neck, stepped out of the shadows. Teeth chattering, she uncovered her head, took off her mittens, and clapped her hands to restore their circulation.

"Brutal." Rose avoided looking at him. "You're a masochist."

"Do you even know what that means?"

"I know. And you are."

"What are you doing here, Rose?"

"Guess what?" She shrugged out of her coat and waved toward the entry door. "Kyle's here."

Down the hall, Peter glimpsed a second muffled shape. The figure shook, doglike, spraying droplets of snow and ice across the tiles. He lifted one gloved hand to wave and croaked out from beneath his muffler, "Hi, Pete."

Peter floated on his back, shifting his gaze from Kyle to Rose. "You stalking me?"

Rose flashed him a grin, one he recognized, the sorry-but smile that passed for apology. "We walked around in the dark as long as we could. Thought you'd be done sooner."

"Don't blame Rose, Pete. It was my idea." Moving to the edge of the pool, Kyle extended a hand to help Peter out of the water.

Ignoring the offer, Peter heaved himself up, wrapped a towel around his hips, and headed for the locker room. He didn't want to talk to Kyle. Old man Krueger's crazy grandson could just go back to whatever place they put him in when he tried to hang himself last year. Kyle followed him. So did Rose. When they reached the doorway, Peter paused.

"You can't come in here, Rose."

"Peter." Rose's warning echoed through the empty room. Peter looked at Kyle.

"When did they let you out?"

"That's rude." Grabbing Peter's arm, Rose spun him around to face her. "He wasn't in anyplace. Mr. Krueger had a stroke, and Kyle's the only one left to help."

"Lucky for Mr. Krueger."

Rose swallowed hard. "Kyle's better."

"Whatever," Peter said. "I still don't know what you're doing here. How'd you get in?"

Rose held up Peter's key. "Forget something?"

Peter shrugged. The pool used to be his haven. Now he had no place to hide. He needed to lash out at someone. Then he looked at Rose, saw the bruise blooming over her left eye, saw how she held herself to stop the trembling. Kyle stepped closer, bracing her with his body.

"What happened?" Ice formed in his chest, ran nails over his bare skin as Rose stomped in circles. Her boots shed snow that pooled and melted, leaving a hazard of slickness on the tiles.

"Nothing. Everything." Rose picked at snow crystals clinging to her mittens. "I don't know."

"Rose?" Pete grabbed her and held on despite her efforts to wiggle free. Shifting her gaze from the floor, she covered up the proof of their mother's rage with one edge of her scarf.

"She found the money," Rose said. "I tried to stop her, but she found it, and she took it. She even got the bills you hid in my memory box."

Dropping onto a bench, Peter buried his head in his hands. The ghost of loss hovered in his words. "It's gone? All of it?"

Kneeling, Rose took his hands and squeezed. "Every cent," she whispered. "Damn her."

~~~

Drifts a foot high crouched along the front yard. Squinting against the cold, Peter imagined they were the humps of prehistoric animals waiting to snare the unwary. Rose said goodnight to Kyle, rising to give him a quick kiss on the cheek before trudging up the driveway. Her back morphed into a dark smudge swallowed up by the darker shadow of the house. Peter stood on the sidewalk and stared at Dream Street. The snow hallowed all the ugliness, covered the peeling paint and uneven concrete, hid the loneliness and loss that visited, unwelcome and unexpected, the most normal of families. If any family could be said to be normal. Turning toward the dead-end side, Peter inspected every house on the block. They all looked shrouded and clean, their flaws erased by the shawl of whiteness. Even the Webster's funhouse of scary family secrets that had given rise to Coal Webster. Weird Coal and his tormented quest to captivate Rose had led to the death of Rocky Campion. Even that place, under cover of the storm, sported a clean, benign look. But the name? Dream Street? How many bright and shining plans of his sleeping neighbors had fallen, like his, under the indifferent blade of life?

Inside, the furnace struggled against the cold creeping under the door and around the windows. Ice frosted the corners of the glass panes. Peter scraped at one over the kitchen sink until the frosty coating began to melt beneath his fingers. Rose wandered in, her chenille bathrobe knotted over a worn pair of flannel pajamas, the cheery penguin pattern sad and mopey in the dull glow of the overhead bulb. She opened the refrigerator and stared at the bare shelves. Suddenly thirsty, she poured herself a glass of water. Leaning against the sink, she waited until Peter removed his coat and shoes. Then she asked the question.

"What are we going to do, Peter?" She fisted a hand over her heart to hold back the anger.

"I don't know, Rose. What do you think we should do?"

"Get the hell out. Now. And take me with you." Finishing her drink, she set the glass down so hard it cracked, sending a shock wave through the room. Shards of glass tinkled against the worn ceramic, trickled into the sink.

"You're graduating early. You've got a scholarship. Didn't Miss Salvatore set it up for you? You can't run now." Reaching into his pocket, he pulled out his natatorium pass. The recruiting brochure, crumpled and damp, that he'd picked up at the post office tumbled free. Before his sister could recover it, he stuffed it back in his jeans.

Rose lifted her hand to the top of the refrigerator and scrabbled for the mail Opal had shoved out of sight. She lifted down the envelopes, three of them, each stamped *Second Notice, Third Notice, Final Notice* and tossed them on the table. They slithered across the surface, plopping over the edge and onto a chair. He picked them up.

"What am I supposed to do with these?"

"This is how our mother deals with things." Rose pointed at the stamps. "Look at the postmarks."

Peter squinted at the dates, the last already a week old. He pulled the letters out, read the greetings, ran his eyes over the figures. Rose peered over his shoulder, tapping a finger at the deadline printed in the last paragraph.

"We have two weeks?" He struggled not to betray his disgust and resignation. "I can't earn that much in two weeks."

"You might have, if she hadn't taken it all."

"Where is she?" Peter asked.

130

"At Carl's. The bar doesn't close until two." Rose sat down and folded her hands in her lap. "We're going to be evicted."

"I'll get another job." Peter's words settled like lead in the small chamber of their failure to save themselves from this final insult. Unbidden, the image of the purple bag pressed against Peter's despair. In his back pocket, the Navy recruiter flashed a grin. *See the World. Earn your degree.*

"Got a coin, Rose?" Peter stretched to cover a yawn. It was almost midnight. Maybe Opal wouldn't have time to spend all the money.

"Why do you need a coin?" She rummaged in the junk drawer, her search accompanied by the brassy sound of orphaned keys knocking against each other.

"To make up my mind." Snatching up the notices, Peter headed for the living room. "To make up my goddamn mind."

Peter heard his mother stumbling up the steps before she opened the door, her grunts and curses erupting in long bursts as she fumbled with the lock. Illuminated by the shaft of light slicing into the night, Peter watched her rock against the kitchen table. Raising one hand to her lips, she whispered, "Shush." Then Opal Stone, half frozen from her walk from the bar and totally pickled from drinking, slipped, fell to her knees, and sprawled across the kitchen floor.

"I need a drink," she said, giggling, as she pulled herself onto a chair.

The stuff of dark comedy, or darker tragedy. Peter closed his eyes, trying to remember his mother the way she was before. Before they left the mountains. Before his father died. She had always been a hard woman, but never cruel, and never drunk.

"Mama?" Rose's call drifted above the furnace growl, the word cracking, whip-like, in the dark.

"Come help your mother, Rose." Opal stretched out over the table, one hand grasping the edge, the other rooting in her pocket.

"Leave her," Peter said, blocking Rose's path. "Did you spend it all, Mama? Did you drink away the house along with all your self-respect?"

Opal raised her head, closing one eye at a time until her son came into focus. Peter shoved a chair out of the way and knelt down beside her.

"I. I," Opal hiccupped, groped in the pocket of her coat. "I bought lottery tickets. We're gonna be rich. But I saved some."

"How much did you save, Mama?" Rose sidled closer, hands clenched in the folds of her robe. Opal pulled out the remaining bills and flung them across the floor. Bending to retrieve the money, Rose smoothed each one, added them up. Her voice rattled like dry leaves.

"There's barely two hundred left." She hovered over the table, wrinkling her nose at the smell rolling off the drunken woman. "What'd you do with all that money?"

Opal looked up. Dismissing Rose, she fastened her gaze on Peter. She batted at his face, swiped a finger across his cheek. "Peter'll get some more. He always does."

Handing the money to her brother, Rose returned to the bedroom. Opal wiped her mouth on the sleeve of her coat, leaned back on her elbows, and, lowering herself to the floor, passed out. Unable to sort his anger from his compassion, Peter stuffed the bills in his backpack and left her there.

The following day, the storm closed all the schools and most of the businesses in town. No one answered the phone at the rental company. Peter tried calling the bank, the one where Mr. Haloub did business, but the snowfall had prevented many people, including the manager, from coming to work. The forecast for blizzard conditions later that afternoon, he was told, would keep them all away until Monday. He was still sitting with the phone next to his ear when it rang, startling him into falling off the chair.

"Peter?" Mr. Haloub sounded stuffed up, his voice croaking like a bullfrog through a long tube. "I'm not well today, and the doctor has ordered Mrs. Haloub to bed as well. She, um, had some difficulty last night, and the baby is still three months away."

"I'm sorry to hear that, sir." Peter switched the phone to his other ear, wondering what his employer wanted.

Mr. Haloub's voice trailed off as a bout of coughing took over. "Peter?"

"I'm still here, Mr. Haloub," His voice sounded lame, but he knew Mr. Haloub wouldn't notice, not today. He had no thought for anyone but the baby now. Peter's head ached.

"Can you come in? I would consider it a great kindness."

Peter measured Mr. Haloub's request against the urgency of his own situation. Wouldn't he feel better working than sitting around worrying? And he needed the money. Opal hadn't awakened, nor would she until late afternoon.

"Rose?" Peter dragged his coat off the furnace grate and searched for a scarf to wrap around his neck.

"I'm going to see Kyle," Rose said, stuffing her hands into mittens. "I hid the money, someplace she won't ever think to look."

"You going to tell me?"

Shaking her head, avoiding eye contact, Rose shrugged into her coat.

"No, seriously, where?" Peter handed her a knit cap, zipped up his own coat, searched for gloves that didn't have holes in the fingertips.

Rose grinned, adding a ray of hope to the gloom of their day. "Someplace she'll never look. Trust me. You going to work?"

"Yeah," he said. "What else is there to do?"

The trek over to Tallman's proved more difficult than he anticipated. The wind had carved the snow into dunes, then polished them to a hard sheen. Breaking through the crusty mounds cost him time. He could see Mr. Haloub watching through the *Cash and Carry* window. The drift in front of the store had been mashed into a slippery stew by the feet of the customers who already crowded the shop. They milled around the shelves, commenting on the length of the storm and the strength of their wallets. It crossed Peter's mind that maybe he should bag some groceries for himself and Rose. Opal could starve.

"Finally, you are here." Mr. Haloub opened his arms at Peter's arrival. The customers turned to greet him, then turned back to their scavenging. "I leave it to you, Peter Stone, to mind the shop. You can close up early. Remember to put the money in the safe when you close," Mr. Haloub whispered. "We'll deposit it tomorrow."

Covering his mouth to cough again, he shuffled his way through the swinging doors that lead to the living quarters. Peter thought of the first day he'd come to ask for a job. His employer, recently immigrated from Lebanon, had been eager to establish himself in his new country. But he was a cautious man, a clever man. He had interviewed and turned down many boys before Peter stepped in front of him.

"You are an honest boy, Mr. Peter Stone?" Mr. Haloub had asked. "You are a hard worker?"

To each question Peter had answered yes. His age presented a problem, Mr. Haloub stated. A minor detail, Peter argued. Mr. Haloub excused himself and went into the back room. Peter listened as he debated with Mrs. Haloub in a language Peter didn't understand. When Mr. Haloub returned to the front of the store, he was frowning. Peter made one last appeal.

"I need this job, Mr. Haloub. I need to take care of my mother."

That had been enough to change the man's mind. As soon as Peter relinquished his claim on the scholarship to the magnet school, the Haloubs had taken him on, taken him in, treated him almost like family. Rose too, had become a favorite of theirs, welcomed and fussed over whenever she stopped by. But even the Haloubs' goodness couldn't conjure away the specter of homelessness. Peter tried to forget about the letter threatening eviction, but worry nagged as he waited on the morning's customers.

By two o'clock, dark, moisture-laden clouds settled over the town. The temperature dropped below twenty degrees. Tallman's, empty now of customers and most of its goods, braced for more bad weather. It was time to close. He checked the weather report, then lugged out the mop and bucket to swab up the grit and melted snow the clients had left behind. If any last-minute shoppers banged on the locked door, he would let them in. *But then I'll have to clean the floor again,* he thought. *I hate mopping.*

Just as Mr. Haloub had predicted, the day had proven profitable. The shelves, depleted by the weather warnings and the natural inclination of nervous neighbors to prepare for a worst-case scenario, would need to be re-stocked before tomorrow. Peter paused in his assessment to open the cash register. Laying a piece of butcher paper on the counter, he counted and separated the bills, arranging them to face the same way, stacking the ones in groups of ten, the coins in piles that equaled a dollar. When he finished, two thousand, three hundred and four dollars and thirteen cents, plus twenty IOUs, lined the shiny paper. Half of it was enough for their rent and insurance, although it wouldn't cover the utility bill.

Peter rested his hand on top of the money. Who would know? And he could pay it back. His fingers twitched. The George Washingtons winked at him, offering to barter the trust of the Haloubs for a few more months in the only place he and Rose called home. The mountains they came from were lost to them. The desk cowering in the cellar, the sole remaining piece of their heritage, remained in alien hands. Wasn't he owed something for all that loss?

Outside, driven by the wind, a grind of sleety pellets battered against the door. Inside, the empty shop held its breath. Glancing at the curtain separating the back of the house from the store, Peter counted out five hundred dollars, folded the wad, and stuffed it in his back pocket. He craned his head to see if the bulge showed. Folding the paper over the remaining bills and coins, he used tape to seal the package. Then he tugged open the trap door, releasing the musty smell of earth and damp. He had descended halfway when he heard Mrs. Haloub.

"Mr. Peter, are you there?" Her veiled head peered over the counter, her eyes shy and tired. "Mr. Haloub asked me to speak with you."

Peter backed up the steps, the package clutched in his left hand. He waited near the top, mute with fear and shame.

Placing an envelope on the counter, Mrs. Haloub patted it with ringed fingers. "We wish to honor your custom of Christmas, Mr. Peter. You have been a good worker and a good friend to us. Please accept this small measure of our

135

regard." Before Peter could respond, Mrs. Haloub backed away and waddled slowly toward the living quarters at the back of the building.

Caught in the backwash of her gratitude, Peter slipped and bumped down the stairs, clutching the money before it could spill free. Shaken, he crouched at the bottom, waiting for the thumping in his chest to settle. He stood, conscious of the roll in his pocket, listening for sounds of Mrs. Haloub coming back. When she didn't, he released the breath he'd been holding and looked around.

Boxes in need of recycling littered the floor. Mr. Haloub must have been in a hurry when he filled the shelves the night before. The accumulated furniture loomed around him, accusing but silent. He tiptoed over to the desk, lifted the covering, recalled his grandmother sitting at it to write her grocery list. Some days she would offer advice, opine about life and honor and the code of the hills. Reaching for the finial, he lifted it down, ran a finger over the letters carved into its base. *stone* Replacing the fixture, he traced the wooden insets that decorated the glass. Each pane shimmered in the light from above, shifting like the shards of glass in that kaleidoscope he and Rose cherished. Dropping to his knees, he unwrapped the stack, careful to remove each piece of tape so he could reseal the package. Removing the wad from his pocket, he laid the money on top, re-wrapped it, and moved to the safe.

Back upstairs, Peter stared at the counter. The envelope lay where Mrs. Haloub had placed it. Embarrassed after his aborted attempt to rob his benefactors, he stuffed it in the pocket where the money had rested. Moving to the swinging doors, he called Mrs. Haloub's name. He had to shout three times before she appeared, her eyes quizzical now and apprehensive. "Is something the matter?" she said.

Peter cleared his throat, drummed his fingers against his leg as he fingered the envelope. "Mrs. Haloub, before I go, may I use the phone? We don't have one anymore."

Mrs. Haloub bobbed her head, pointed toward the wall, and backed out of the room.

"Thank you," Peter called after her, "for everything." He unfolded the brochure the recruiter had given him, dialed the number listed. He didn't expect anyone to answer, but someone did.

"Navy Recruiting Station. Commander Strong speaking."

"My name is Peter Stone," Peter said. "If I enlist now, how soon can I leave?"

"How old are you, son?" Lt. Strong asked.

"Nineteen. Sir," Peter said.

"Do you have any responsibilities you can't leave?" Strong rustled papers as he spoke.

Peter thought about Rose. She could take over for him here at Tallman's. He thought about the Haloubs. They'd be glad to have his sister's help, and they'd respect his decision. He thought about his mother, sprawled and snoring in the bedroom on Dream Street. He didn't imagine she'd do more than snort at his decision. Money was tight, but whatever the Haloubs had given him would help tide them over. He could send his pay to Rose to help with the bills.

"No." He waited for the recruiter to give him instructions. When to report. Where to go. Wrote it all down on the back of an order sheet. Then he shrugged into his coat, pulled on his boots, and headed into the storm. The shape of his world had just expanded. He didn't waste time considering what had shrunk behind him.

Chapter Fourteen

"You enlisted?" The question leaks out of Tuck like air from a balloon.

"He didn't see any other options." Kelly squeezes my calf, withdraws her hand. Tuck cuts his eyes away. The cat clock in the kitchen twitches its tail as the hour chimes. Ten o'clock. My phone rings, cutting through the moment like a scythe. Tuck's grimace indicates he would have handled everything differently. Kelly scoots sideways as I answer.

"Peter Stone?" An androgynous voice worries its way down the line. I acknowledge the greeting and wait for the next question.

"Detective Alice Munroe, State Police assigned to OBCI."

"The Bureau of Criminal Investigation?"

"Yes, sir. I understand you're with the Hopewell P.D.?"

"Yes." Beneath the formality, I detect incredulity. She's already suspicious. "Do you have information regarding my sister?"

"Are you alone, sir?" Munroe scrapes her chair across the floor. The screech sounds in my ear like a crow cawing. She wants to be cagey? Fuck that.

"No. My partner and my wife are here."

"What about Rose, Detective?" Definitely sneering. I swallow against the urge to sneer back, choose diplomacy instead.

"Rose?"

Detective Munroe's voice mellows as she switches tactics. "Is your sister with you, Detective Stone?"

"With me?" I glance up. Kelly stands by the fireplace, her arms wrapped protectively around her. Her eyes glisten. She licks her lips, cocks her head. I accept her concern with a nod, return my attention to the unpleasant voice on the phone. "Why would you think Rose was here?"

"We have a turnpike cashier report that a woman matching your sister's description exited I-80 at Route 76."

139

The shuffle of papers is followed by throat-clearing. "And additional sightings of her heading south on I-71."

"Are you certain it's Rose?"

"Nothing certain but death and taxes, right, Stone?"

Great, an old-time comedian. I withhold agreement. Munroe sighs. "The witness IDs are pretty consistent," she goes on. "They all said they recognized her from the wedding photos in those supermarket tabloids."

"Yeah, gossip mags are great for making a positive ID." I put her on speaker phone so Tuck and Kelly can hear. "When were these statements taken?"

"Time stamp on the ticket indicates she passed through two days ago at two p.m. State troopers found the car she was driving abandoned at the rest stop just south of the outlet stores near the I-76 exit. Unless she hitched a ride or was abducted, someone picked her up."

"Rose is too smart to let her guard down. She'd never accept a ride from a stranger."

"All right. Let's assume someone picked her up. Where would your sister go?"

"I don't know, Munroe, but she didn't come here."

"Mind if we make sure of that?"

I grit my teeth. Anger crowds my lungs, making it hard to breathe. "Are you sending an officer to my home?"

"Better than that, Detective. I'm coming myself." She ends the call without saying good-bye. I stare at the phone, wondering what new ring of hell I've entered. The idea of Rose catching a ride with some trucker or traveling salesman refuses to settle. No way she would ever open herself to violation again. Yet she's gone. Snatched by a pervert or rescued by a friend?

"Pete? What if it isn't Rose? What if they're mistaken?" Kelly steps closer. Tuck shadows her movements. We stand in a tight circle, connected by bonds so tangled I'm not sure we can ever free ourselves.

"They have a sighting?" My partner raises his drink and takes a long swallow.

I nod and wander into the kitchen. Opening and closing cabinet doors, I play for time. I try to make sense of what the investigator has shared, searching for that elusive piece of the puzzle that will explain all my sister's actions. Nothing comes to mind.

"Pete?" Tuck calls to me. Shaking off despair, I return to the living room and relate what Munroe told me. Tuck rubs his chin.

"Why do you think Rose wouldn't accept an offer of a ride? She strikes me as a pretty daring woman."

Kelly, fists clenched, backs Tuck against the wall. "You know nothing, Tuck. After what happened to Rose, she would never go anywhere with anyone she didn't know or trust. Which is just about everybody."

"Whoa." Tuck holds up his hands, surrendering to my wife's fierce scowl. "What are you talking about?"

I slip between them and fall into the recliner. "I really don't want to go through this again."

Kelly settles in front of me. Snagging an afghan, she leans against the recliner, her shoulders wedged between my calves. With a sharp intake of breath, she pulls the blanket tighter.

"You don't have to tell this part, Pete," she says. "I will."

~~~

June, 1998

Last fall's leaves crunched under Rose's scuffed sneakers. The spongy layers had shifted in the runoff from the spring rains, covering the tracks she and Peter's feet had left in the hard clay soil just before he reported for training. Already she missed him. Taking a deep breath, she inhaled the familiar earthy smell of fecundity and rot. Loss gnawed a hole in the wall around her heart, leaving just enough room for sadness to squeeze through. Soon she would be leaving, too.

Glancing over her shoulder, she studied Kyle. His breathing, still ragged from the morning run, carried down the street. His hair, damp with sweat, stuck up in clumps around her ears. He had filled out, his chest taut with muscle, marking the transition from boy to man. She wanted to run her hands over the tanned and muscular frame, to trace the lines on his face, then sculpt him in clay. Kyle grinned when she caught his eye.

141

"You miss Peter, don't you?" Kyle's deep bass startled her. He reached for her sleeve to slow her pace. "Rose? Talk to me."

Rose jogged ahead, dragging him along. She did miss her brother. Kelly, with whom she used to share late-night confidences, was wrapped up in her own family drama. Peter was the one who shared all the Stone family secrets, the only one who understood her need to leave this place. But Peter had already escaped. And Kyle stood beside her, his presence a new factor in an unsolved equation. Desire, to be held, to be cherished, pushed against the loneliness.

"You don't know anything, Kyle Parker, so just shut up. Six months on Dream Street doesn't make you an expert." Wrenching free, she sprinted toward the creek.

"I miss him, too, Rose. C'mon, don't be mad, okay? You know I'm here for you." Kyle hustled to catch up.

"You don't understand." Scrubbing at her face, she stopped running. "I'm not mad at you."

Wrapping his arms around her, Kyle met her stare. "You don't have to go."

"It's all arranged. The scholarship, the plane ticket. I even have a place to stay, with Miss Salvatore's aunt and uncle in Queens. The Haloubs bought me a suitcase. Everyone's expecting me to do great things. Everyone but Mama."

"You can stay here, you know, go to school at the community college." Kyle leaned in to kiss her. "You can marry me."

Rose pushed free, fisted her hands. "What did you say?"

The woods grew quiet. Only the murmur of the creek interrupted the stillness. Kyle ticked off the arguments on his fingers. "While I was in the hospital, I finished my credits. I'm a high school graduate. I have a job at the assembly plant. Pay's good. I have benefits. They even have a tuition reimbursement plan for spouses. That may not sound like much."

"It sounds," Rose said, "great, Kyle, really. All your ducks in a row, just like my parents, right before our life fell apart."

Kyle grabbed her hands, squeezed to still their trembling. "We're not them, Rose, and I'm not going to die."

"We lost the house," Rose said. "Peter bought us a few more months at Christmas, but it didn't last. We have to move out next week."

Taking her by the hand, Kyle led her to the edge of the creek. Squatting, he searched for rocks, then tossed them one by one into the water. "You can stay with Mr. Wentworth."

Rose shook her head. "Kelly's moving back in, at least, that's what she told Peter. And that's where he's going to stay when he comes home on leave. She and my brother, well, they're a thing now."

"Yeah, but your brother won't be back for a while."

Rose plopped down beside him, rested her head on her knees. Dredging up a pebble of her own, she used it to scratch at the dirt.

"Are we a thing, Rose?" Kyle stared at the water. She felt the warmth of him where their shoulders touched, the new strength. When he took her hand, she blushed, but she didn't look up.

"Do you know what Peter and I called this spot when we were kids?" Rose tossed her stone toward the swirl in the middle of the creek, watched it skip twice and disappear. "The heart of the world. Silly, huh. Back then, though, I guess it was."

Furtive rustlings disturbed the brush behind them. Along the far bank, a heron stilt-walked the shallows, squawking at their human intrusion, and winged off. In the meadow beyond the trees, where the city was planning a housing development, birdsong floated above the grass and thistles. Squeezing her eyes shut, Rose listened hard to the life beating around her.

"What do you do," she whispered, "when you lose your heart?"

"Stay or go, Rose." Kyle skipped two more stones into the stream. "It won't change how I feel."

"I don't know what to do." Her words fluttered like moth wings. The bird song stopped. Startled by a sharp whistle, Kyle rocketed to his feet.

"What's that?"

Rose, still on the ground, released a handful of pebbles into the water.

"That," she brushed her hands on her jeans, "is Opal calling me home."

Pivoting to face her, he tapped the end of her nose. "Race you."

Slapping his hand away, Rose darted up and took off down the path, gliding in and out of sunlight. Her hair bounced from side to side as she ran, measuring the seconds and the beating of her heart. Kyle raced behind her, their two figures slipping with ease past the trees crouching over the path.

Opal Stone stood in the garage, smoothing a pile of old tablecloths that emitted a musty odor. Leaning over to catch her breath, Rose's laughter faded beneath her mother's disapproval.

"Need you to carry out the rest of the boxes, Rose." Opal wandered to the card table where the pots and pans nested.

"Mama, you shouldn't sell those." Rose pointed at a large kettle and the roasting pan. "How'll you cook?"

"No place to cook in Pearl's basement." Opal fished her cigarettes out of her pocket. She shook one from the pack and put it to her lips. "No one to cook for. I hate menthol."

Rose bit her lip to keep from incurring more of her mother's displeasure. Kyle shifted closer, placed a hand on her back.

"I'll be around if you need me," he said, attempting to wink. "Tomorrow?"

Rose giggled when both his eyes squeezed shut. She watched as he loped through the yard and crossed the street. Opal watched, too, cutting her eyes away when Rose turned back to her.

"There's one good thing about all this." Opal drew a deeper breath, releasing it along with a stream of smoke. "Least we'll be gone before that devil comes back."

Rose stiffened. "What devil, mama?"

Opal pressed her hands to the small of her back and groaned. "That Webster kid. Course his mother's a devil, too, and her still living at the end of the street. Damn, I miss real tobacco."

"What are you talking about? Coal? He's locked up until he turns eighteen, isn't he?"

Opal picked at her lip. "Heard he was getting released from some halfway house near Columbus. Bad news for everyone, that."

Rose choked back the questions boiling up. Opal loved to gossip. She believed in UFOs and alien abductions. She must be mistaken about Coal Webster. It couldn't be true.

"Let's get this over with." Turning her back, Rose rescued the garage sale sign from the cracked concrete and headed for the porch. Her shoulders sagged beneath the gravity of loss. Among the few things her mother counted as valuable, this house topped the list. She had fought to get it, and now even that small victory was gone. Planting the sign in the yard, she returned to her mother.

She wanted to offer Opal some words of consolation, to share the grief she recognized as kin to her own, but even the kindest words bounced off the hard shell of her mother's back. Twisting a strand of hair behind her ear, Rose surveyed the back yard. The weathered picnic table they'd always planned to repaint still occupied the larger portion of the lawn. The stalks of dead tomato plants drooped. The herb garden that she and Peter had cultivated was choked with weeds, and not the edible kind. Even the rose bush that spread its canes under the kitchen window and up the back trellis had failed to quicken this year. She hurried past the dead branches and into the house.

In her room, the curtains were gone. Her books, childhood albums, and bedding rested in the trunk her cousin, Little Butch, had given her. Before she flew to New York, Big Butch and Pearl would take it to UPS for shipping. Rose pulled her comforter out of the trunk and lay down on the worn floorboards. She refused to think about Coal Webster. He couldn't be coming back. They didn't let murderers out, did they?

Propping her head on her hands, Rose squinted at the dust that layered the space under her bed. Way back in the corner, hidden from view until now, she spied a shiny white pebble. Stretching her arm beneath the box springs, she pressed with her fingertips until the lucky stone yielded and popped free. Clutching it to her chest, she curled up, humming syllables that made as much sense as this uncoupling of all that was familiar. The house folded its arms around her as she slept.

Thursday morning two bargain hunters eager to pick through the remnants of a family's life knocked on the door before seven a.m. While her mother spoke with them, Rose showered, pulled on an old pair of stretch pants and a tank top, and bolted out the back. Kyle was waiting in the alley. The day threatened rain. Along the path, the areas usually rayed with sunshine lay in shadow. The damp and weedy dirt sprouted mysterious mushroom rings.

"I dare you to eat one of those." Rose pointed at an orange cone with brown spots along the edges.

"My mother didn't raise no fools." Laughing, Kyle shook his head and his index finger at the same time.

Rose paused, her face blank with memory. "My father used to say that," she said, "once upon a time."

"I'm sorry, Rose." Kyle laced his fingers through hers as they stepped around the mushrooms. "Do you miss him?"

"No. Not really. I miss the idea of a father, of someone to care for my family, of what might have been and never will. Tell me, Kyle, how do you make the past a figment of some storyteller's imagination? Because if I knew how to do that, I would."

Pulling her to a stop, he wrapped his arms around her. "A wise man once told me to let the past go, that living in the now was all that matters."

"Who said that?"

"Peter. Said he learned it from Fox."

"Ah, wise men indeed. It's just so hard to do."

The water in the creek chuckled as it flowed over the rocks, amused by its secret knowledge of the way of things. They shared the same perch, staring into the stream, until Kyle leaned closer and kissed her. Inside Rose, the wild urge stirred, desire flickering like flames beneath her skin.

"Kyle," she touched his cheek, the rasp of whiskers sending her nerves a message. "I think I know what I want to do."

In the woods, that furtive, sustained rustling they heard the day before returned. They listened, tension curling them toward each other. Kyle tightened his embrace. Touching a finger to her lips, he whispered, "What was that?"

"Someone's coming." Gripped by a panic she couldn't explain, Rose pushed to her knees. Behind them, a branch snapped.

"Who comes here besides us?" Kyle scrambled up.

"I think it's Coal." Staring into the dense cover, Rose focused on the stillness.

"That Webster freak? Not possible." Kyle searched the ground for rocks. "He's still in jail, right?"

"Not."

Rose recognized the voice before she saw him. Coal Webster, taller, heavier, hair buzzed and sporting a goatee, stepped free of the honeysuckle and wild forsythia. He shook off the leaves clinging to his hair and moved forward to block the path. His hands, clasped behind him, fiddled with something. "Who's this, Rose?"

Kyle faced Coal, hands loose at his sides, head cocked in defiance.

"No one you need to meet." Rose recalled Coal's laughter when the police brought him to her door, asking if he was the boy she'd seen at the quarry, if he was the one who launched the rock that caused Rocky Campion to drown. Remembered Coal's words as they hauled him away: *It's not over between us.*

"C'mon." Rose grabbed Kyle's elbow and shoved him toward the path. "There's no heart beating here anymore."

Coal brought his hands around. His old baseball bat, painted now in a pattern of gang symbols, rested lightly in his palms. "Too late to run, Rose. You're not going anywhere."

Rose willed Kyle to keep walking. She glanced back, couldn't resist a taunt. "Why'd they let you out, Coal? Did your mama persuade them to give back her little boy?"

"Words don't mean shit. This is all the talk I need."
Rushing forward, Coal raised the bat and swung. The wood
smashed into Kyle's elbow. Grabbing the shattered arm, he
slumped to the ground. Coal stepped closer. He rested the bat
on Kyle's forehead, tapped it twice. "Come with me, Rose, or
I'll finish the job."

Dropping to her knees, Rose smoothed the hair off Kyle's
forehead, then glared up at Coal. "You have to promise you
won't hurt him."

"You come with me," Coal held out his hand, "and I
won't."

"Promise. Damn you, promise me!" When Coal nodded,
she allowed him to yank her up and drag her through the
woods. The layer of old leaves muffled their footsteps along
the trail he had forged from his backyard to the stream. When
they emerged from the trees, he shoved Rose forward. Before
she could dart free, he slipped a chain over her head. When
the links settled around her neck, he pulled it taut. Gagging,
she tugged at the chain as she staggered on. When they
reached the back of the Webster house, the doors to the storm
cellar lay open on the ground. Coal ushered her toward the
opening. She stumbled down the first two steps.

"Have a nice chat with my daddy." Securing the end of the
chain to a ring set into the wall just inside the darkened
shelter, Coal lifted one of the heavy doors and banged it
closed. The hinges leaked flakes of rust. Grabbing her chin, he
forced her to kneel as he cupped his crotch with his free hand.
"One more thing. I never forgot you, Rose, and I never will.
Never."

When Coal slammed the outer door, closing her in, Rose
cowered on the steps. Her mind jabbered at her to run, to
scream, to pee her pants. Pressing her ear to the metal, she
listened for Coal's footsteps on the sandy path that ended at
the back of the house. Instead, they rustled through the weeds.
He was heading back to the creek, back to Kyle. Rose forced
deep breaths of the stuffy air. Tugging on the chain, she tried
to pry apart the links, but Coal had added a padlock her
trembling fingers couldn't free. Extending a hand to protect
herself from whatever might be hanging from the ceiling, she

inched down the flight of stairs toward the floor of the shelter. She detected the odor of garbage, the smell of rotting flowers. She even recognized the scent of patchouli. *Patchouli*, she thought. *I'm going crazy already.*

When she reached the bottom, the cloying smell grew stronger. Slapping off cobwebs, she spread her arms wider and shuffled forward, searching the dark for obstacles. Perhaps she could find a discarded garden tool or a piece of wood, something to use as a weapon. She set aside the image of Kyle lying on the ground, wounded and alone, at the mercy of Coal.

She had almost reached the farthest extension of the chain when she bumped against what felt like a small table. She ran her hands over the surface, her fingers assessing what her eyes couldn't see. She touched a square of cardboard that opened to reveal three slender strips of paper. Matches. Bringing the pack close to her face, she removed the first one and scraped it against the table. It refused to light. Cursing, she tugged the second one free. When she struck it, the tip broke off and skittered away into the dark. Trembling, struggling to control her breathing, she knelt and scored the third and final match over the concrete floor. The match flared to life.

In the flickering light, Rose scanned the shelter. No sign of standing water, no clumps of dust or dirt. Someone came here on a regular basis. The match sputtered. She glanced across the table, straight into the face of a mummified dead man. Screaming, she jumped back. The match dropped to the floor, hissed, and went out. Backtracking to the steps, Rose crawled to the top. Huddling there, she waited in the dark in the company of a corpse.

With no way to tell time, she counted heartbeats, rocked to the chant of nursery rhymes, changed position when her muscles cramped. Despite the discomfort, she dozed off. When a hand touched her shoulder, she yelped and jerked away, bumping her head on the overhead doors. The chain cut at her neck. Coal, holding a flashlight, stood two steps below. She considered flinging herself at him. The chain might strangle her, but if she could knock him out, it would be worth it.

"Don't try it." Coal held up the chain he'd liberated from the ring. "Come on. My mother's gone to work."

She didn't want to ask, but he led her right past the table. Under the beam of the flashlight, the mummy observed them in silence.

"Coal?" She cleared her throat and tried again. "Coal? Who is that?"

"My father. My mother likes to look at him sometimes. When I was little, she used to bring me down here, too." He snorted. "We never had much to say to each other."

When they reached the far wall lined with shelving, Coal pushed the end of the unit. The partition swung inward, revealing a passageway from the storm cellar to the regular basement. Tugging Rose after him, he threaded a path through the mounds of clothing and boxes, the bins filled with empty cans and labels. They mounted a set of stairs and stepped out into the kitchen. Rose noticed a litter box.

"Where's the cat?" she said, hoping to distract Coal. He didn't answer. "Coal, what did you do to the cat?"

Coal halted, raised his eyes to hers. "I don't need her anymore. I found you."

Rose strained against the chain, panic rising. Pulled along by the threat of choking, she stumbled after Coal as he passed through the clutter in the front room, climbed a second set of stairs. At the top, he glanced to the left, hesitating.

"I'd like to take you in my mother's room, Rose. The bed's nicer. But I think we better use mine."

"Coal, you can't do this. Please, don't do this." Rose recognized the fear in her voice. She knew Coal heard it, too.

He faced her then, drew her to him with both hands, tightening the chain until she was afraid to move, afraid she would strangle herself before he could do it. Bending close, he pressed his lips to hers. She pushed against him, but each time she drew back, the pressure on her throat increased.

"Don't fight me, Rose. You can't win." He traced her lips with his tongue, forced her mouth open and explored it. The perfume of his aftershave clogged her nostrils. He tasted of beer and marijuana. Releasing her, he sucked his bottom lip, smoothed a hand down her neck, over her breasts, and held it tight against her crotch. "Rose." He said her name like a prayer, but his eyes smoldered. She didn't want to beg, clamped her teeth around the words that fought for release. Inside, she screamed.

Kicking the door closed, he laid her down, then fastened the chain to the bedpost. He taped her arms together above her head. The walls crowded in, water stains drifting down in long, brown waves. She closed her eyes so she wouldn't see him touch her. When he had stripped off her clothes, Coal started to remove his own.

"You can force me, but you can never have me. And I hate you. I will always hate you." When Coal refused to answer, she went someplace else in her mind.

The water swirled as the crawdad fought to escape. She set it back in the creek, humming the itsy-bitsy spider song while it slipped, swift and sure, under the rocks that protected the heart of its world. Rose slipped down with it, into the cool, welcoming darkness. The rush of the stream was all the lullaby she needed.

He lay on top of her, his semen mingling with the blood that trickled down the inside of her thighs, staining the sheet, proving her virginity and his power. Raising himself above her, he stared until she looked away. Leaning closer, he stroked her hair, whispered her name. Rose refused to open her eyes. She focused on the creek, imagined the water swirling around her, washing away the shame. He might kill her, but she would not beg. After a while, she felt him harden again.

During the night, Coal brought a basin of water and washed her. When she asked, he allowed her to urinate in a can, then chained her back to the bed. He offered her granola bars and an apple. He kissed her mouth and her breasts and her belly above her pubic hair, and then he urged her to come. Rose did not respond. She returned to the stream, swam away from the musky odors and Coal's breath in her ear, his groaning when he emptied himself inside her. She replayed the few happy memories she could recall, the days she and Peter spent at the creek. And then she remembered. A small thing, really, just that one time years ago, when Peter and

Kelly had been alone in Fox's house. She'd seen her brother running from Fox's yard carrying something wrapped in cloth. Kelly, checking over her shoulder, followed him into the alley, urged him to hurry. When they could no longer see her, she followed their trail to a hollow tree on the south side of the meadow. She hid among the honeysuckle until Peter and Kelly left. Then, she went to the oak, reached in to see what her brother had placed there. That's where she found Fox's gun. And the crumpled note, in Fox's handwriting, asking them to forgive him. A suicide note from a man who never followed through. A reprieve for Fox, a gift for her. Rose smiled. *When I get out of here, I'll kill him.*

Coal sat naked beside her, munching raisins. "We're together now, Rose, and everything will be all right."

"You're not right. You never will be." Rose stretched against her bindings. Her body ached.

"I love you, Rose." Coal rubbed a hand down her calf, stretched out beside her, traced a circle around her nipple. Rose returned her gaze to the ceiling, slipped back under the water, ignored Coal's fingers pressing between her legs. When the door slammed open, Rose thought she was dreaming.

Lacey Webster, strands of black and grey hair caught in a loose bun, pounded her foot on the floor. A leather strap dangled from her hands. "What is she doing here, Coal? What have you done?"

Jumping off the bed, Coal cradled his genitals with one hand as he stretched the other out to ward her off.

"You shouldn't be here, Mother. Go away!"

"You? You brought her here?" Lacey swung the strap in front of her, cracked it against the wall. "You forced her?"

"I take what I want. You taught me that." Coal clenched his fists. "And I keep what is mine."

"No! You're no better than your father. No better than Norman. Just like him." Lacey glanced at Rose, chained and helpless on the bed. Lashing at her son, Lacey forced him to retreat. Ripping the tape from Rose's hands, she scrabbled at the chain and the padlock that held it.

"Where's the key?" When Coal didn't answer, she swung the strap harder. The leather bit into his thigh, wrapped around his leg, sliced open the skin. Blood leaked from the cut. "Where's the key?"

Coal reached for his jeans. Wrestling the key from the front pocket, he tossed it at his mother. Sobbing, Lacey fumbled with the lock. When it snapped open, she grabbed Rose and dragged her off the bed. "Go, wicked girl. Enticer. Seducer. He was my good boy until you came along."

Dizzy and stiff, Rose stumbled from the room. She paused to orient herself, then groped down the hall to the stairs. Coal shouted her name. Staggering through the trash that filled the Webster house, Rose focused on the gun, nestled and waiting for her in that hollow tree. She ignored the sounds of struggle from the room above. She had almost reached the creek when she heard someone call her name.

Along the dark path, the wind stirred the leaves. The trees swayed, restless and upset. When she tripped, she mistook the body for a tree root rising up to block her way. Falling to her knees, she ran her hands over the unyielding form until the outline of his face told her it was Kyle. His skin was so cold. She pressed her fingers against his neck. A weak pulse beat there. Behind her, she heard Coal Webster thrashing through the brush.

Panic filled her, and rage. Leaving Kyle, she slid down the embankment, splashed through the water, and struck out across the field. Light flared behind her. Looking back, Rose glimpsed a plume of fire rising above the trees, Dream Street flaming up like the entrance to the underworld. She tripped, pitched forward, clawed her way through the wildflowers and thistles that ripped at her skin. Rising again, she ran, sensing pursuit. Breathing, ragged like hers, huffed closer.

"Rose! Run!" The command rang out around her. Kyle? Coal?

When she reached the tree, she stumbled again, gashing her knee on a loose piece of bark. Dragging herself up, she whimpered, her words punctuated by the sucking sound of her lungs gasping for air.

"Please. Let there be at least one bullet. Please." Rose stuck her hand in the hollow. At first, she grasped only air. She stood on her toes, reached deeper. Her fingers snagged the end of the cloth. Jumping, she managed to wrap a hand around the weapon. She fell, landing on her back. Tugging the gun from the wrapping, she fumbled to check the safety just like Fox had shown them so long ago. She braced her back against the oak, aimed, and pulled the trigger. The blast reverberated around the field. Blood sprayed, stippling her pale skin and the bark of the savior tree.

~~~

Clutching the hospital gown around her, Rose stepped out of the room. Visiting hours had ended, but the nurse allowed her to stay until the drugs kicked in and Kyle, in and out of lucidity, fell asleep. Returning to her room, she changed into the jeans and sweatshirt Kelly had dropped off. Stuffed the hospital toiletries into a draw-string bag. Eased her way down the corridor. In the patient lounge, she took down the framed copy of the Gibran poem hanging above the sofa, removed the print, and tucked it in her pocket. She didn't feel guilty. The poem spoke to her, each word a comfort and a direction. *For life goes not backward nor tarries with yesterday.* Each step she took moved her closer to tomorrow. The house on Dream Street was lost now, a flyer announcing the sheriff's sale mounted to the mailbox out front. Peter had come and gone, his three-day pass enough to see her through the interrogations and examinations. Kyle's future still balanced on fate's scale. Lacey Webster's body remained at the morgue, waiting for transport to a crematory. Charged as an adult, Coal remained in custody at the Montgomery County Jail.

Ahead, the nurse's station loomed. Two heads, one bright, one dark, bent over paperwork. The lights lining the hall threw off small circles of illumination. She hopped from one to the other, playing a child's game of mother-may-I. Before she ordered the elevator, she peeked into Room 127 one more time. Kyle slept on, unaware that Rose Stone had decided to leave him behind, too.

Chapter Fifteen

he fire dances over the ceramic logs. Kelly knits her fingers together, covers her mouth. Tuck fiddles with the tab on his can of beer.

"Jesus." His soft expletive rustles the air.

I scrub my eyes with my knuckles. We spend a full minute avoiding each other's gaze.

"Jesus." Tuck repeats. Draining the rest of his beer, he crushes the can between his hands. "Rose killed Lacey Webster?"

"Woman had an axe, Tuck. She was carrying a god-damn axe, had it raised above her head. To Coal's credit, if you can give the asshole any at all, he tried to warn Rose. It was his voice telling her to run." I shake my head, overwhelmed by my sister's ordeal all over again. "I should have been there."

"They didn't suggest charging her, did they?" Tuck moves to the front window, pulls the curtain aside.

"It was clearly self-defense. They caught the Webster kid after he torched the house to hide the evidence. Firemen managed to put it out before the entire structure burned down. Found his father's mummified body in the storm cellar." Kelly stands, stretches, yawns loudly. "I really do need to go to bed. You guys staying up?"

"Still raining like a son of a bitch." Tuck leans his forehead against the glass, shades his eyes. Before he can say more, lights flash on and off in the street. "We have company."

I step to his side. My phone announces an incoming text. Munroe. At the same moment, Tuck's cell rings. I listen to the rumor of Pickle's voice. She sounds rattled, but I can't make out the words. When Tuck turns around, his face is one massive scowl.

"I have to go," he says. "I have to get Hannah."

If he's using her given name, I know it's serious. I half-turn toward Kelly. She nudges me off, waves Tuck toward the door.

"Go. I'll be fine. I'll put on some coffee." Stifling another yawn, she heads into the kitchen, her words floating after her. "Guess I'll have to entertain that damn policewoman while you're gone."

Something in her tone twists my heart. When Kelly swears, I know she's more angry than sad, and an angry Wentworth takes charge of things. The doorbell rings, then a fist pounds the door. I greet Munroe with a handshake and an apology.

"Munroe, my partner, Tucker Cornell. We're heading out to rescue a colleague. My wife," I gesture toward Kelly, who has returned to the living room, "will keep you company until we get back."

Munroe shakes out her umbrella, looks for a place to put the dripping thing. Her eyes, the color of a purple sky, scan the room. Kelly takes the umbrella and her raincoat. Rubbing her hands against the damp, Munroe heads straight for the fire.

"Sorry for the late call. My supervisor never misses a chance to piss off the public."

Tuck's doing his antsy dance at the door. I spare a moment to re-evaluate our visitor. Not her choice to be here, far from home base in the middle of a hundred-year rainstorm. Maybe her earlier tone was a result of work and not some-deep seated need to earn points by making me feel small.

"Rose isn't here, but I promise we'll see what we can do to help you find her when Tuck and I get back."

Her look turns suspicious. "This colleague wouldn't be my missing person?"

Tuck raises an eyebrow and snorts. "Hannah Pierce is a forensic scientist and professor who assists our department on difficult cases. Maybe she'll agree to help you, too. Sounds like you could use the assist."

Before Munroe can reply, my partner bolts for the driveway. I grab a jacket and hat from the closet and follow him into the storm. I pause at the car, remembering how the creek at the bottom of Dream Street used to top the embankment and spill over the road during spring storms.

156

Maybe we should check on Fox after we pick up Hannah. Tuck jostles me back to the moment.

"Get in, Pete. Time's passing."

I settle in the passenger side, fiddle with my phone. I want to call Fox, but I can't let Tuck hear our conversation. *Relax, Peter*, I hear Wentworth saying. *I'll call you when I need you.* I lean back, tell myself to trust the man who's always been straight with me.

The streets are mostly deserted. Only the occasional driver flashes lights at us as we navigate the rising waters along the side streets and out onto the main thoroughfare. Sawhorses block a number of low-lying spots in the road. Visibility has decreased to a mere car-length ahead.

"So, what's going on between you two?" I punch the home button on the dashboard computer, search for a weather station. Tuck slows further as we fishtail through a low spot on the roadway. He flashes me a quick look, runs a hand through his hair.

"I fucked up, Pete. Thought Hannah was on the same page as me. Asked her to move in to my place."

When he slows for a red light, I wait for more. Nothing. I hesitate before pushing on.

"And? What happened?"

"She said no."

The minutes pass. I fiddle some more with the radio, finally give it up. "She still called you, Tuck, when she needed help."

"Yeah, but—" He leans over and pops open the glove box, pulls out a velvet-covered box. "What am I going to do with this?"

I ease the box open, stare at the diamond nestled inside. "Maybe you should have given this to her first."

Bigger sigh. "Yeah."

"It's not too late, Tuck." When he doesn't respond, I replace the box and stare out the window into the storm. "Where is Pickle anyway?"

"Parked on the berm across from the pharmacy at Woodman and Patterson. There was a bad accident at the intersection, so the roads are mostly blocked off. All the side streets are already underwater."

"How do you plan to get to her?"

Reaching over the seat back, Tuck drags up the corner of a tarp.

"What good's that going to do?"

"There's a flashlight under the seat." Tuck hunches over the steering wheel, his Land Rover slipping sideways in the current of water rushing across the road. "Got an inflatable under the tarp, and a pump in the back. We were going rafting this weekend."

"And you didn't check the weather report?"

"No, smart-ass, we didn't count on your sister still being gone."

I have to give him that one. I could protest that he's the one who decided to get involved, but I don't. Tuck's basically a good man. I'm not going to give him any more grief. "So, what's the plan, exactly?"

"Hey, I'm just the driver. You're the former Navy seal. You tell me."

I finger the tarp. I have no real gear, I'm not dressed for a water rescue, but my partner has faith in me, a woman's life is perhaps at stake, and Rose would tell me to go for it. Fine. Pull out that Stone heart and save Hannah. I nod, although I'm pretty certain Tuck doesn't see me. Rolling down the window, I hold out my hand, estimate the temperature. It's getting colder. Maybe close to freezing. In a little while, we'll have ice to contend with. I lean down to remove my shoes.

"Don't suppose you have a wet suit in the back?"

Tuck shoots me a grin. "Look in the dry bag."

I lean over my seat to sort through the jumble of bags and boxes in the back. When I locate the dry bag, I unzip it to find a long-sleeved insulated top and shorts made from the same material. Better than nothing. I also discover a pair of soft-soled slip-ons good for kayaking. Tuck's feet are a size larger than mine. I pull out a roll of duct tape and strap the water shoes to my feet. Tuck slows as he approaches the intersection. Down the road several vehicles huddle together at the north end of the pharmacy parking lot. A police light strobes the night.

"How many can fit in your craft?"

"It's a one-seater. Hannah has her own," Tuck says, "but you can walk beside it, right?"

I don't bother to enumerate the many things wrong with that statement. No lights, unseen floating objects, critters in the water, chemical pollution. I open my door, go around back, and drag out the inflatable. Attaching the nozzle, I begin the inflation. Tuck calls Pickle on his cell. His steady voice seems to calm her. Squinting into the downpour, I notice the lights of several cars in the lot flashing on and off, on and off. An alarm blares. As soon as the compressor hiccups, I detach the connection and shake water out of my face. Then I cross to the flooded roadway and hoist myself in. The inflatable rocks wildly as it bumps against the base of a Yield sign. I narrowly miss banging my head on the metal pole. Tuck slogs through the water, hands me a paddle and I stroke my way toward the opposite lane and the lone car stranded among the rising flood. The torrent of water cascading down my back reminds me to hurry.

Chapter Sixteen

Refilling her own mug, Kelly offers to top off Agent Munroe's cup. The woman has planted herself in front of the fire to stare at the wedding photo on the mantel.

"This your wedding?" she asks. Kelly acknowledges her with a nod. "How long ago?"

"Two and a half years."

"So, this is Rose." Munroe taps the photo with the tip of a well-manicured finger. Without taking her eyes from the picture, she accepts the refill, sips cautiously at the hot liquid.

"Yes, that's Peter's sister. But you already knew that."

Alert to the accusation in Kelly's voice, Munroe turns to face her. "We only have one clear shot of her from the dedication of her sculpture four years ago. In the commercial she was shooting, her face is shadowed by a welding mask. Your sister-in-law was reclusive. It's almost like she didn't want to be recognized."

Settling onto the couch, Kelly rubs a hand over the welted fabric. "Rose had good reason to hide from photographers. You should understand that, but then again, maybe you haven't done your homework."

Munroe perches on the edge of the recliner. Cradling her mug, she leans forward. "Please, call me Alicia. And I admit I don't know enough about Rose. There are juvenile records that were sealed, names redacted, legal protections in place to prevent anyone from finding out what happened to her. Can you tell me?"

"Surely you've guessed. Rose was held prisoner by a psychopath and brutally raped when she was still in high school. The boy pled guilty, so there was no trial. He was almost fifteen, tried as an adult but sent to juvie until he turned eighteen. We lost track of him after they moved him into the regular prisoner population. I can only hope someone took care of him in prison."

161

Alicia Munroe lowers her eyes. "What do you mean, Mrs. Stone?"

"Coal Webster deserved to die, Alicia. Maybe someone in the system took care of that and saved us all a ton of problems."

Munroe starts at the mention of Coal's name. "What did you say? Webster? Coal Webster?"

Swallowing the bile rising in her throat, Kelly watches the woman's hands shake. "You know him."

Munroe tightens her grip on the mug. She takes a second careful sip, then wipes her mouth with the back of a hand. "Christ save us," she says, standing to pace in front of the fire. "A convict by the name of Coal Webster escaped from Chillicothe Correctional a little over two weeks ago. Are we talking about the same guy?"

Setting her cup on the end table, Kelly crosses to Munroe, grabs her arm. Coffee splashes onto the carpet. "When? Tell me exactly when."

"April third. Two days before Rose went missing."

Kelly covers her mouth, sinks to her knees. "Oh, God, no."

The front door bangs open, the doorknob thumping against the wall. Tuck and Pickle carry Peter between them. He's wrapped in a blanket but shivering and his lips are blue. Scrambling up, Kelly rushes from the room, returning with an armful of towels. While Pickle shakes free of her coat, Pete drops the blanket, snatches a towel, and staggers toward the bathroom. The sound of running water is punctuated by Kelly's commands to take off the wet clothing. Pickle sets down an attaché case swathed in plastic. Sniffing at Kelly's coffee, she gulps down half the cup before nodding at the woman.

"Munroe, is it?"

"Alicia, BCI special investigator. And you are?"

"Hannah Pierce. Professor. From the look on Kelly's face, I'm guessing you told her about the Webster fiasco."

"How do you figure that?"

"Because I just received the reports from one of my contacts in Columbus. It's criminal that no one alerted the family to this man's escape. I've dealt with a number of monsters in my career, Alicia. Coal Webster is one of the worst. No remorse. No conscience. Believes he's entitled to whatever he wants. And now he's out there somewhere. Do you believe he has Rose Stone?"

Munroe scrubs at her forehead and swallows hard. "Didn't until now. I sincerely hope not. Uncaged, monsters have a habit of repeating their offenses. If Webster has Rose..."

Munroe's words trailed off. Pickle steps to the fireplace, rubbing her hands to warm them. Crouching, she stares into the artificial flames before she speaks again. Tuck steps closer, massages her neck, says what they're all thinking.

"She might already be dead."

Chapter Seventeen

*F*lash flood warnings scroll in repetitive lines across the top of the TV screen. Kelly clomps down from upstairs, her arms filled with blankets and sheets.

"Tuck," she orders, "you and Hannah take the upstairs room. Agent Munroe, I'll make up the daybed in the nurs––, uh, the downstairs spare room."

"I appreciate the offer, really." The investigator has resumed her formal tone, putting us all on notice that she's here for an investigation, not a sleepover. "But I plan to head back tonight. I like to sleep in my own bed when I can."

I shake off the chill of my evening's water adventure and gesture at the screen. "Where's home?"

"I'm based out of the Springfield office, but my home is west of Columbus, in Plain City."

I shake my head. "The closest entrance to Route 35 is three miles up Wilmington Pike, which is now impassable. Sorry, Munroe, but it looks like you're safer if you stay here."

Tuck gives me a three-fingered salute as he steers Hannah toward the stairs. She rears back in protest. He puts a finger to her lips, whispers something in her ear. She shoots me a quick glance, nods to Munroe, and allows my partner to escort her from the room. The agent joins me in front of the fire, her brows knit with anxiety, her hands clasped around a small notebook.

"My family's waiting. They expected me an hour ago."

"Hazards of the job," I say. I study her body posture, the neat crease in her trousers, the way the collar of her blouse chafes the side of her neck. "How long you worked for OBCI?"

"Two months," she replies, her answer halfway between a laugh and a groan. "Worked Patrol for six years prior, then asked to transfer. Thought as an investigator I'd be home more for my kids."

"How many?" I keep my voice low, so Kelly won't hear.

165

Munroe rolls her shoulders, cracks her neck. "Four. My two, hubby's two. And a surprise." She places a hand over her belly.

"Ah," I say, accepting the confidence, understanding her reluctance to overnight in a strange place. "Congrats."

Shifting her shoulders, Alicia Munroe smiles ruefully. Tapping the notebook against her palm, she leans her head toward the hall, the question hanging in the air between us.

"To the left, second door down."

Kelly steps back into view, carrying more towels. Munroe nods her thanks, but declines the invitation.

"I'll just use the facilities, then be on my way.' She taps her notebook again, and moves toward the bathroom. "I'll put in a request to my boss. If he agrees, you, Cornell, Pierce, the FBI agents assigned to the case out of Cleveland and I will form a task force. More resources, more manpower should go a long way to finding your sister."

I watch her walk away, the slump of her shoulders a measure of her emotions. When she returns, I help her out to her car. The rain has turned to sleet. The snow cracks under our boots as we walk.

"You should stay."

She slides onto the seat, punches in co-ordinates on the GPS, and shrugs. "I'll be back tomorrow."

I stand on the porch and watch as her taillights disappear into the storm. Inside, Kelly waits for me to turn off the lights. I check the weather report one more time before entering our bedroom. We undress in the dark, careful not to touch, then slip beneath the covers. When I turn toward her, she places her hands on my face, slides them down my chest, rests one delicate palm over my heart.

"I want to make it better, Kel. Tell me how."

She traces circles around my navel, presses a kiss against the skin. "Oh, Peter, you and your stone heart. Don't you know you don't have to heal everyone? You just have to love them."

I gather her close, startled and aroused by the press of her naked body against mine. I can't deny my need for her. Her hand slips lower, closes around my erection.

166

"Forget about Rose, Peter. Forget about making a baby. Tonight, I just need you. Please. Make me believe nothing else exists except you and me and this heat between us."

I lift her hips, slide a pillow beneath her, move my hands over her skin. My lips trace a path from her mouth to the softness between her legs. She presses me to her, stifling the moans that threaten to spring free. I shift above her, guide myself inside, biting back my own response. She is warm and wet and tight and mine, the only woman I have ever wanted, and I revel in the way we join together. She clutches at my hips, urging me on in terse whispers. I brace my knees inside her legs and draw out the pleasure with slow, sure, steady strokes until, breathless and gasping, I empty myself as she climaxes around me. Afterward, I lie still, waiting for my heart to stop thundering. Normally, she reaches for tissues, pads to the bathroom before settling to sleep. Tonight, she doesn't move when I hand her the box.

"Kelly?" I touch her cheek. "Are you okay?"

She grabs my hand, pulls it to her lips. "I think I'll just lie here a while, let your boys do their thing. Who knows? Maybe tonight one of them will reach the goal."

I hear no sarcasm in her words, no sense of loss, only a strange and wondrous possibility. I fall asleep to the sound of her breathing, my arm snugged tight across her belly. If Kelly can still hope, who am I to give in to despair?

~~~

Sometime during the night, the sleet eases back to rain, then stops. When I wake, she is gone from our bed. I hear her stirring in the kitchen, fixing breakfast for our guests. Country music plays softly. I don't need to be there to know she's tapping a foot as she grinds the coffee, stirs the eggs. I pull on a t-shirt and sweat pants and stumble through my morning ritual. When I come out of the bedroom, Tuck is setting the table. Hannah is pounding out messages on her cell. The smell of bacon frying makes my stomach rumble.

"Sit," Kelly commands, waving a spatula at our hungry faces. "Eat."

"Where's Munroe?" Tuck leans over the chair to snag a piece of bacon.

167

"Went back." I spoon eggs onto my plate. "I don't think she's keen on being away from home."

"Professional hazard," Hannah says, stowing her phone in a pocket.

While we eat, I explain how she wants us to form an official task force assigned to the disappearance of Rose Stone.

"Screw that," Tuck says. "We don't need BCI to find your sister, Pete." Nodding, Hannah abandons the remainder of her meal to open her laptop.

"Give me a minute to pull up the Webster files." Tuck and I exchange glances. At last, we're on the same page.

"Well, all right," Tucks presses his lips together, but I can tell he's pleased. "Cornell and Stone are on the case."

The women groan.

"Well, all right, all right, all right," Tucks drawls, doing his best McConaughey impression. "Cornell and Stone, working alone, will solve the case with style and grace." Everyone groans. I shake my head, carry my plate to the sink, but inside, I feel more hopeful. Maybe we can find Rose before Webster does. When my wife smiles, I give her a hug.

"Where are you going now?" Kelly wiggles free of my embrace, pats my cheek, and sets a pitcher of orange juice on the table.

"Tuck and I have to go into the station for a while. I still have a few days leave left, but it won't hurt to work a shift today. I'm sure last night's floods left us with a backlog of calls to answer, loose ends to take care of in ongoing cases. Tuck, give me a minute to change and we'll head out."

Tuck stares hard at me, Kelly, and Hannah, then takes the steps two at a time. I hear him clomping around in the upstairs bath. Kelly tugs me aside.

"You going to be okay?"

I kiss her nose, run my hands over her hips and ease her closer. She blushes and waves me off.

"Something wrong?" I force the words to come out light and not accusatory. She arches one eyebrow, nods toward the phone on the counter.

"It's Fox," she says.

"Have you heard from him this morning?"

168

"No." She bites her lip. "Not in days. Not since we had that talk. This is not like him, Pete. And I have a feeling the creek has flooded. Whether it will rise as far as the house, I don't know. Can you go over there later today, check things out?"

I make the promise, then hurry to dress and grab my gun. Tuck joins me and we head for our cars, leaving Kelly and Hannah to work the phones and do the research. All the way to Hopewell, I puzzle over Rose and Coal and now Fox, gone without a trace.

Chapter Eighteen

The glass façade of the Hopewell Police Station reflects the watery state of the parking lot and the roadway beyond. Tuck pulls in beside me and we sprint through the ankle-deep puddles, bang our way into the foyer. I shake off the feeling of disconnect being back at work produces. The day shift duty officer beeps us in. After checking my messages, typing up old reports, and shuffling through folders, I head down to the briefing room. Janeece Terl greets me with a bob of her braided head. Henry Clayton, former forensic tech now serving as community relations officer corners me before I can sit down.

"You just passing through," he says, "or you back for good?"

I raise one eyebrow, wink. "Thought you guys might need some help, but I still have some leave time."

"That's big of you, Stone." He punches my shoulder. "I hear you performed a water rescue last night."

Tuck leans over my shoulder, laughs. "Once a SEAL, always a SEAL, no, H?" My partner claps me on the back, then heads for the restroom. Ducking my head, I reshuffle the papers on my end of the table, wondering how many families were flooded out last night. Janeece calls us to order, runs through the assignments for the day, but my mind is busy cataloguing the clues, connecting the dots of Rose's journey. Cleveland, New York, back to Ohio, then south. I can't shake the feeling I should have examined the package she sent more closely. Abandoning the list of calls to make, I trace the lines in my palm as I consider all the memories clinging like leaves to the tree of our past. One of those contains the clue I need to find my sister.

A rumble in the hall announces the arrival of the chief. Janeece cedes the podium to the boss. He steps up, grasps the corners of the stand, and clears his throat. The room settles like a flock of pigeons.

"Good morning. Last night's storm left a helluva a mess to clean up. Jackknifed semi on I-75, power outages in three subdivisions, several water rescues." He nods in my direction. "So, people, we've got our hands full today. Terl's given you your assignments, but I want to apprise you of an APB that just came from the State Patrol. It appears that the two convicts who escaped Chillicothe Correctional earlier this month headed into Shawnee State Park. The local authorities apprehended James Anthony Cordred three days ago. Coal Webster, however," the chief looks at me as he announces the name, "is still on the run. There is a suggestion from OBCI that we form a task force to address the situation."

Several officers turn my way. Janeece shifts from foot to foot. They're all remembering that my sister is gone and that this Webster was the one who violated her all those years ago. Cradling my head in my hand, I fiddle with my pen. The past rises like last night's fog, engulfing me in yet another awkward situation. The chief waits for the undercurrent of whispers to dissipate, returns to me.

"You want to say anything, Stone?" He rests his bulk on the podium and waits for me to respond. Tuck and I exchange glances.

"If it's all the same, sir," I stand, "my partner and I would rather work that on our own time."

The chief clears his throat. "Yes, well, by the book, officers, by the book."

The phone in my pocket vibrates. Kelly. I thumb on the message.

Have you talked to my dad yet?

Shit. Only two hours in and I'm already the recipient of everyone's angst. The other officers file out, flashing me curious or questioning glances.

"A moment more, officers." Terl's request interrupts the exodus. Everyone hustles back, finds their seats again. She clicks on a PowerPoint, scrolls through a series of photographs. A headshot of Rose. The vandalized sculpture in New York. A photograph of Coal Webster, smirking at the camera. "Apologies, Pete, but I think they should see this.

172

Recent photo of Coal Webster, a former resident of our sister community Kettering, and an escaped felon. As a juvenile, he allegedly killed one young man, and he was convicted of kidnapping and rape when he was only fourteen. He is a dangerous sociopath. It's not outside the realm of possibility that he'll go to ground somewhere around here. Keep a sharp eye out for anomalies. Follow up any possible sightings, no matter how bizarre or strange they seem. I repeat, this man is dangerous. Let's hope he's not armed. And, to borrow a very old phrase that still resonates, be careful out there. Chief?"

"Terl's right, officers. Be careful out there. Dismissed."

I gather my papers and follow Tuck back to the squad room. Before he can tell me where we're going, I press the speed dial to Fox's phone and wait through the rings. No answer. When voice mail kicks in, I leave a message for him to call me back, then listen as Tuck runs down the plan for the day.

The morning hurries on. Gloomy skies give way to a slow drizzle until, finally, the sun leaks through a rip in the cloud cover. I dial Fox's number every hour, listen for the click, leave a message. At four o'clock, instead of the answering machine, someone picks up after three rings.

"Fox?" I hold my breath.

"Peter?" Fox gasps my name, coughs, clears his throat. "I'm ready."

Before the gentle click of disconnection, I detect the hiss of the oxygen tube. That settles it. I text Kelly. **Spoke to Fox. He's home. It's time**. The whoosh reassures me that the message has been sent. Then I erase it. Tuck taps his pen, gives me the Cornell stare. I start to speak, then shrug him off. It's none of his concern, and I don't want him involved in this business.

"Detective? Do you think you'll catch the guy?" The father of the family we're interviewing about a break-in runs his hands through his hair, paces the upended living room. The rest of the family huddles together on the ripped-up couch, stunned by the violation of their space, and I know I can't go to Fox now. But tonight, after dinner, I'll head over. Alone.

Chapter Nineteen

Alicia Munroe calls to say that all available agents have been dispatched to the site of a multiple shooting near Hillsboro and she won't be back until tomorrow. Dinner is a listless exchange of theories and suppositions. Tuck and Pickle grumble about restricted access to certain databases to which only BCI has passwords. Kelly eats in silence, then explodes in a flurry of 'I'll just take that out of your way' and 'don't mind me, I'm just part of the wait staff.' I try a joke, attempting to defuse tension, then throw up my hands and head for the garage. Kelly and Soldier follow me out.

"I'm falling apart here, Peter. Do you have to leave now?"

"Kel." I finish tying my laces and pull on my windbreaker before drawing her close, "We promised. I have to go."

She stills in my arms, molds her body to mine, and presses a hand to my cheek. "Why do you have to be the one?"

"There's no one else he trusts. Do you want to do this?"

She shakes her head, blinks back tears. "Fine. You're right. But take Soldier with you."

The dog sniffs her feet when she calls him from the back yard. Handing me the leash, she squeezes my hand. "Please tell me you're going to be all right."

"Don't worry about me. Just follow the plan." We check our watches, set the timers. I kiss her, then reluctantly let go, afraid, as always, she won't be here when I get back. I toss the leash on top of the recycle bin. I won't need it tonight.

The stars pop out as I run, shining like lucky stones all the way to Dream Street. As we jog, I check behind me. The sidewalks are empty, the street as well. Leftover patches of ice reflect the dimpled sky. Soldier trots beside me, silent and alert. When we reach the intersection of Grandview and Dream, I crouch on the last patch of concrete before the asphalt begins. Weak light rays from the windows of the house on the corner, pools around my feet. Soldier pads up, noses the ground, a dark shadow against the darker night. Arrested by memory, I stare into the inkwell of my childhood. Fog creeps up from the stream at the end of the lane, meanders over the yards, gathers around the solitary light pole. Tendrils obscure the street sign to the left of the road. I check my watch. I have one hour before Kelly makes her call.

A wheezing compact with a single working headlight rattles past, eclipsing my shadow, splashing water over my running shoes. Soldier sniffs the leaves and discarded fast food containers that clog the gutter. Two more cars pass the mouth of the cul-de-sac, turning the street into a series of old movie frames. The sounds of their passing echo, then disappear, into the black hole that is the place where I grew up.

"Why does he always ask so much of you?" Kelly's words, flung into the evening air a month ago, claw at me. "You don't owe him anything more."

But I do. And it's time to pay my debt. With a low whistle, I call the dog to heel, check the perimeter one final time. Grandview Avenue stands empty now. Soldier and I slip across the road, avoiding the windows of the Pendleton house. Beyond the peaked roof, I can just make out the tumble of grapevines in the small square of backyard before the alley takes over.

Soldier walks point, returns to lick my hand. I pat his head before snapping him back to attention. The cluster of modest bungalows rests, silent tombstones awaiting final epitaphs. I wonder what mark the engraver will finally carve on my family's old shack.

When the rental company evicted us, my mother moved in with Aunt Pearl and Uncle Butch, but that arrangement didn't last long. She worked her way through a series of loser boyfriends and dead-beat roommates. Now she lives in an aging, subsidized apartment in the Oregon District. She drinks herself to sleep each night, usually too confused to give me more than a puzzled greeting when I call. Nothing different from when I was a kid. We Stones are all adrift on the current of bad luck and lost dreams. My father, a victim of his own violent tendencies. My mother, buried in addiction. Rose, my brave, sad sister, disappeared into silence, into the fog of the past. Wiping a hand across my lips, I scrub away the new Pete. The child I was climbs out of memory, puzzled by the man I have become.

The rattle and crash of a garbage can startles me. Soldier growls. Not everything sleeps on Dream Street. I crouch again. The hedge that borders the front yard of the property on the corner makes a good shield. At my command, Soldier lies down beside me. We wait, quiet and apprehensive, but no porch lights switch on, no voices swear into the ebony-fogged stillness.

My heart beats a drum roll and I remind myself once more that this is just a duty call. Still, I pat my jacket, checking that the painkillers and placebos are snugged inside. Clutching at the left pocket once more, I stand. Soldier inches forward. I count to twenty, take a deep breath, and move on.

Fronds from the honey locust tree litter the driveway. A breeze lifts the fur on Soldier's back. I smooth it down, guide the dog toward the porch.

"Three steps up, swing glider to the left and no doorbell." Fox reminded me when we last went over the plan, the day before Rose went missing. As though I would forget. As though I couldn't find the way. The street is dark and no moon keeps watch overhead. But the new contacts I wear provide perfect night vision, and something else, a sense of the possible. Now the reticent boy who daydreamed his way through childhood morphs back into a man with a purpose. I recheck the time. Stepping carefully to avoid the squeaky floorboard at the top, I signal Soldier to stop. *I owe you, old man.* I knock lightly on the frame, then try the knob. When the door unlatches, Soldier and I step inside.

The living room lies in shadow. Through the arch that leads to the kitchen, I glimpse a flicker, liquid as mercury and just as elusive. The wraith that greets me whispers, the sound faint and gravelly around the vibrator held to the hole in his throat.

"Peter." Fox pauses to draw in air. "Thank. You. For coming."

Soldier whines, the hairs on his back rising again. I comfort him with a pat and order him back outside. He circles the porch three times before settling. I close the door and move to Fox's side.

The cloy of dust and the faint but unmistakable odor of Fox's aftershave welcome me into my past. In the gloom, I can't see his eyes, although I recognize the wheeze as the old man strains to draw breath into his failing lungs. The cancer that claimed his larynx has moved on to more fertile ground. Despite the surgery, it has expanded its territory to Fox's lungs, a pincer maneuver guaranteed to bring victory within a few short weeks.

I stand under the arch, uncertain of my next move. Fox shuffles by, lowers himself into the old armchair with the gray and red striped afghan draped over the back. A Buckeyes fan to the end. I nod at the memory of watching games with Fox, my boy-self stretched out on the faded carpet, the man balancing a beer and a ham sandwich as he waves a cigarette at the screen, cajoling and cursing through each season. The good times before the bad times began again. Such a brief respite. I swallow sadness and close the distance between us.

"Why didn't you answer our calls? Where've you been these past few days? Kelly's really worried. So am I."

Fox ignores my questions. "Did. You. Bring them?"

Startled by his intensity, I reach in my pocket, crumpling the plastic around the square of cardboard that protects the pills. Kelly's voice rings clear inside my head.

"Are you sure, Pete? Remember the last time he asked you for a favor?"

She meant to caution me, to let me know it was okay to bail. Unable to let go of the belief Fox abandoned her, she uses her resentment like a shield against loving him. I understand, but I can't share her feeling. This man saved me and Rose. While I hesitate, the furnace kicks into its cycle. Although the April temperature has risen from last night's freeze into the lower sixties, warm air blows through the floor grate, swirls around my ankles. Once Fox would have scoffed at the idea of paying for heat any time after spring began. He thought like that, a rigid adherent to the principle of things.

"Why. Did you. Steal my gun?" Fox growls the words around the voice amplifier, fracturing my memories into shrapnel that impale themselves in my brain. Above my left temple a twinge promises to become a full-blown headache. Fox croaks out his question a second time, the words more demanding, but I detect no defeat, only the curiosity of a man unafraid of death. Going down for the count, Fox is determined to face it alone.

"I didn't. Kelly found your note. She asked me to take the gun. To put it somewhere safe. She was trying to protect you." I squat down next to the coffee table, shuffle the piles of *Sports Illustrated* and *Modern Woodworking*. Copies squirt out from the stack, cascading onto the floor, but Fox doesn't admonish me like he once did. My answer has shocked him into silence.

"She was afraid," I tell him. Kelly's voice floats down the hollow tube of memory, her laughter muted as she shies away from our first attempt at sex, her call down the stairs while she hunts for a handkerchief in her father's dresser, the anxiety in her cry as she carries the note and the gun from the bedroom. But I can't reveal these private moments to Fox, refuse to share how Kelly gave me the great gift of herself when I needed it most. I definitely won't explain how her image of Fox warped around the discovery that her father kept a loaded weapon after he swore he'd never have one in the house. That discovery eroded her faith in all Fox's pronouncements. When he accused me of taking the weapon, the rift strained our friendship, severed the tie that bound Fox and Kelly. I say nothing, waiting for Fox to process the truth.

In one of the bedrooms, a clock ticks, reminding me of the timeline I have constructed. Fifteen minutes have already passed, and we have barely begun.

"You should have believed me." Stepping over the tubing attached to the oxygen, I wander into the kitchen. The counter has been wiped clean of crumbs and responsibility, an empty slate for the next owner to inscribe.

"It was not hers, or yours, to take." Fox creeps up behind me, his glide already part of the shadow world, noiseless, without substance. "How. Did Rose. End up. With the gun?"

"I think it was meant for her all along." I stare out the darkened kitchen window, fighting back the image of Rose, naked and bleeding, finding the gun in the hollow where I hid it, lifting it free, and firing the shot that left crazy Lacey Webster bleeding out in the field at the end of Dream Street. The shadow of the silver maple in the backyard broods along the fence line. I contemplate burying my clenched fist in the wall behind Fox's pale face. *You should have believed me, old man.*

Tears I don't know I own escape to channel themselves along the contours of my cheeks. I brush them away with my thumbs. Fox's hand lifts to rest between my shoulder blades.

"If I had the gun, Peter, I wouldn't need the pills."

Stalling, I open the refrigerator door and inventory the sad contents of the old man's lost appetite: a half-eaten Healthy Conscience dinner, a quart of soymilk, two eggs, an opened tin of tuna. Assorted condiments crowd the top rack next to two bottles of Blue Ale IPA. Lifting them out, I offer one to Fox. He cocks his head, considering. When I close the door, an appointment card from the oncologist slips out of a realtor's magnet and skids under the fridge. When I bend to retrieve it, Fox waves me off.

"No. Use. Saving it." Grabbing the bottle, he twists the cap free, tosses it on the floor. "No miracles. For grunts. Like me. I deserve. My own shot. You know. Neither you. Nor Kelly. Had the right."

"We're always skirting the edges, you and me, Fox."

"Do. You. Dream, Peter?" Fox picks at the label on the bottle.

"Did you hear what I said, old man? We never seem to get to the point."

"I do. I dream. About this house." He stops to draw a lengthy breath. "How it used to be. When you. And Kelly. And Rose were here. You and Rose. Like my own. Kids. Everyone helping. Everyone. When. Did. We all get. So angry? So angry." His voice stalls, segues into a cough.

"I don't have much time." I lift my beer, salute him, and pull out a chair. The legs screech across the floor. The lighted candle that occupies the center leaf of the new dinette set, the one Kelly sent last Christmas, smells of pine.

Fox chugs a mouthful of beer, swishes it around. Tilting his head back, he lets the liquid ease down the back of his throat. A small dribble rolls out of the trach opening and nestles in the hollow at the base of his throat.

"I might. Tell you. Something, Peter. Something important." Fox clutches his chest before he speaks again. "First. I need. To know. When. I asked you. About the gun. You never. Answered me. Not then, not now."

"Fox, I promised Kelly. I hid it in that old maple, the one by the spruce trees on the other side of the creek. No one saw me. I didn't tell Kelly where I hid it until later. And I never told Rose."

"Bullshit, Pete. Bullshit. I know you. Told Rose. How else. Could she have. Found it? Then you lied. To me. All these years. I been waiting. For you to explain. And you give me. The same. Old story."

"Because there isn't anything else to say." I upend the beer and swallow hard.

"I should have. Asked Rose," Fox says. He pauses to breathe. "That last time. She was here."

"What last time?" I push my chair back and rise, my shadow creeping over the shrunken flesh of my former mentor. "When did you see Rose?"

Fox doesn't answer. He sets his bottle down on the table. Condensation forms a small pool that reflects the candle and our sadness in equal measure. I stare at the shimmer of the water as Fox moves to the stairs. When I turn to follow him, he holds out his hand. His eyes plead with me.

I glance at my watch. Only thirty minutes left, and now it all hangs on my next move. I put my hands into the pockets of my jacket, weigh the futures nestled there, and make a choice. Drawing out a packet, I free the tablets and clench them in my fist.

"If I. Were a dog. You'd put me down. Hold me. Till I passed." Fox pauses, his gaze wandering and unfocussed, before he speaks again. "Rose understood. The hard choices. Peter. You and Kelly never. Wanted to."

"You're more than a hard choice to me, Fox." I stifle the explanation that threatens to burst out of me and settle like a

181

shroud over the frail shell of the only man who ever treated me like a son. Opening my fist, I drop the pills onto Fox's palm.

"The answer. Is here. Pete," Fox says. "It's been here. All along. Rose called. I went and got her. I brought her. Home." Fox turns then and trudges up the steps, one hand trailing along the handrail, the other clutching the pills against his laboring chest. The oxygen tube trails behind. I rest a hand on his back, supporting him as we climb. The landing looms as far away as the moon.

At the top of the stairs, Fox angles to the right, heads into Kelly's old bedroom. He switches on the bedside lamp and reaches under the pillow. Drawing out a clutch of papers tied with a blue velvet ribbon, he hands them over. Rose's precise handwriting marches across the top page, just like it did in her note to me.

"She's sick, Pete. Sick as me. She wants to die. At home." Fox moves to the window, stares into the night. "But first. She has to. Finish it."

Outside, the maple whispers. Up the alley, a trash can bangs again.

"Finish what, Fox?" I'm not sure he hears me. Without acknowledging the question, he retreats into the bathroom. I tuck the packet of letters into the inside pocket of my jacket, listen to the water running into a glass and the clink as the old man finishes drinking. When he returns to the hall, he's smiling. We stumble toward the bedroom. Removing the portable oxygen and the cannula, I turn back the covers and lift him into bed.

"Tuck me. In, son. Take. The letters. Then go." Fox lifts a hand to my face, grimacing as pain pounds a nail through his chest. "Find her. She's waiting. For both. Of you."

I glance at the clock on the dresser. Kneeling, I wrap my arms around him, the *I love you* barely a whisper around the tightness in my throat.

"Thank you." Fox sighs. "You're. A good man. Peter. A good son. I'm proud. To have. Known you." When his eyes flutter closed, I let go.

Downstairs, I rinse the bottles, wiping them clean of fingerprints, and stow them in the recycling bin by the back door. Then I blow out the candle. I try not to imagine Fox breathing, first in ragged gasps, then in sighs that dissipate into stillness.

On the porch, Soldier greets me with a sniff and a yawn. Checking that the street is still shuttered, I slip around the house to gaze at the tree brooding in the yard, the one Fox, Rose, and I planted a year after my father died. I blink against the flicker of movement, imagine the gauzy outline of a figure above the ground. Patting at the clutch of envelopes, reassured by their solidity and the promise they make to unlock the mystery of Rose, I offer a prayer to whatever god is listening. To take Fox Wentworth home for good. To let me find my sister. When I'm certain there's no more to be gained by standing in the dark, I jog back to the sidewalk and down to the guardrail at the end of Dream Street. Just as I hop over, I hear the sirens. Kelly hasn't let us down.

On the far side of the field, I locate the tree with the hollow core, the one where, at Kelly's request, I hid Fox's gun, believing as she did that the man we both loved would take his own life. The tree remains, but the field is gone, divided into staked-off lots awaiting new construction. I lay my hand against the bark, blessing the place where Rose found the courage to shoot the mother of the man who raped her, who tried to kill her to cover that awful deed. In the carved-out space above the first low-hanging branch, I unwrap the placebos and shove them deep into the spongy mass at the core of the tree. By the time the police car turns down Dream Street, Soldier and I are halfway home.

Chapter Twenty

"Where've you been?" Tuck greets me at the door, arms folded, mouth set in a thin line. Pickle looks up from the computer, her frown a rebuke. Brushing past him, I nod to Kelly, strip off my fleece, and toss it on a chair. Soldier nudges my legs, then laps noisily at his water bowl before settling in the corner.

"Needed a run to clear my head."

"Yeah?" My partner stalks after me. "A run in the middle of an investigation?"

"Back off, Tuck. I'm going to take a shower. After that, we can talk about the case." My breath catches at calling my sister's disappearance a case. How the hell did I get to be such a callous bastard? I bump against the chair. The letters in the pocket of my jacket thump against the seat. Grabbing the fleece, I hurry into the bedroom, stash the packet under a pillow, and shed my clothes. While I'm shampooing the odor of pine from my hair, I work out an explanation, hoping it's good enough to satisfy everyone. Kelly will back me up. She can vouch for my evening runs, my need to burn away the anger and the fear.

When I come out, my wife is sitting on the bed, the letters clutched to her chest.

"Did my father give these to you?"

I wrap my arms around her and hold on. When she's done crying, I wipe her tears away with my thumbs.

"He told me he helped Rose, but he wouldn't say where she is, just that she wanted to go home. Do you want to read them first?"

"I don't know, but Tuck and Hannah are waiting." She glances at the clock on the dresser, "The call will be coming soon."

"All right." I take the letters and stuff them back under the pillow. "I'll deal with our friends. Take all the time you need."

185

When I return to the kitchen, Soldier trots over. He sniffs my crotch, yawns, and farts before accepting a treat. Tuck and Pickle are huddled together at the table, pretending to be engrossed in paperwork, but I feel the tension bleeding into the air. Sitting, I open my laptop, scroll through the emails and updates from the station. Ten minutes tick by, punctuated by the rustle of papers and a few heavy sighs. Someone's phone chimes and, as if on cue, we all look up.

"Peter." Hannah leans one arm over the back of her chair, fiddles with the pencil in her hand. "We need a direction. There's been no sign of your sister since the last video cam shot at the rest stop. Webster's still in the wind somewhere between Pike County and the Ohio River. The sheriff in Portsmouth reported a possible sighting two days ago, nothing since then. Is it conceivable that Coal found your sister, abducted her, that somehow all this is more than coincidence?"

I shake my head. Watch as my wife pads barefoot from the bedroom to stand at my shoulder. "I don't see how. That's a lot of distance to cover on foot."

Tuck slaps the table. "Hold on, Pete. You know they're connected. Your sister goes missing. This Coal Webster's on the loose. I can't figure how or why, but my gut tells me he's got her. If you know anything, you need to tell us now."

I look at Kelly. She raises an eyebrow, waits for my response. When I nod, she reaches over and squeezes my shoulder. Then she pulls out the letters Fox gave me.

"I found these." Kelly places the bundle on the table next to Rose's package. "They were hidden in an empty flower pot at my dad's house when I stopped there yesterday. I didn't know if they were important, and, with everything that's been going on, I forgot. I didn't have a chance to read them. But, I think—."

Pickle goes to Kelly, wraps an arm around her. "But what, Kel? You can tell us anything."

Kelly takes a deep breath. "I'm pretty sure Rose sent them."

Pickle reaches for the letters. I beat her to it. Untying the ribbon, I shuffle through the envelopes. Each one bears Fox's address. The oldest is dated January, 2006. The most recent is stamped April 5, the day before my sister went missing.

Tuck frowns. "Pete," he hands him a pair of gloves and an evidence bag. "Let's read through them now, see if they can explain what drove your sister to run away."

Before anyone can respond, Kelly's phone rings, breaking the night in two. When my wife answers, I huddle over my notes, fold my arms so no one can tell I'm nervous.

"Yes? Yes, this is Kelly Stone." She squares her shoulders. In a heartbeat, a look passes between us. I'm calmer now. She blinks twice, nodding at the invisible caller. "Yes, I did request a wellness check on my father."

I read the tremor in her voice, stand up. There's a longer pause. She holds a hand to her mouth. Her knees buckle. Now I can move. I grab her elbows, prop her body against mine.

"Kelly? What's wrong?"

She's still nodding at the phone. Tears well in her eyes, slide down her cheeks. She looks up, the phone crushed between us. "It's Fox. He's gone. My father is dead."

She collapses to the floor. The phone chatters on. I slide down with her. We kneel, holding each other, faces buried so no one can tell the news isn't a surprise. Tuck and Hannah close their laptops and shuffle papers as we stand, clutching each other for support, and wander out of the kitchen. Surprisingly, Hannah follows.

"I can go with you, drive you wherever," she offers.

Kelly waves her off. I scrub my face, run a hand over my head. "No need, but thanks. He, Fox, he's been ill for some time. We've been expecting this, but it's..." I stop rambling as sadness snatches the breath from my lungs.

"It's never easy to lose a parent." Hannah places a hand on my back. Her sympathy is genuine, but the words don't ring true. I think of my father, head lolling, fists unclenched. See my mother's blank stare as she ignored our need for her. Will I miss her when she's gone?

"Thank you, Hannah." Kelly accepts the hug she offers. "My father had arrangements."

I chime in with the name of the funeral home, the location of his will. "We won't have much to do tonight. You guys should stay here and work."

"What about the letters?" Hannah holds up the stack and that blue ribbon, the one that sparks a memory of Kelly at eight, the strip of velvet tied around her ponytail. It's the same ribbon she wove around her corsage for senior prom, the one Tuck took her to. She dried the flowers, stowed them in a box, then threw the keepsake away after we started dating. My sister must have rescued the ribbon from the trash. Not the first time we used junk to mark chapters in our lives.

I accept the letters, weigh their possibility before handing them to Kelly. She shoves the packet in her purse. Catching Tuck's eye, I give him a thumbs up. "Do what you can, buddy. We'll read these together when I get back."

Hannah slides up beside him, scrunches her nose to keep the tears at bay. "We'll be here. Call if you need anything."

Soldier scoots between her legs, lifts his ears, and barks once. I bend to scratch his muzzle, then order him to stay. Kelly leans against me. Her hands press at my waist. I feel her trembling. Inside her bag, the letters crinkle and sigh.

"Yeah," I say, "I'll call you."

~~~

The man at Anderson's is calm, efficient, discreet. He asks if we want to see a photo of the body or make the identification in person. Kelly chooses the second option. He escorts us down a short flight of stairs. We trail behind him down a long, narrow corridor. The walls are painted in muted colors, the carpet dulls our footsteps. The decorations whisper tasteful and soothing. I shudder at the vise of time closing in around us. What if there's an autopsy? But, no, Fox is already here, his medical history revealing a clear progression of advanced-stage lung cancer. No reason to suspect foul play. He was on a cocktail of drugs, so no need to even conduct a tox screen. Kelly takes my hand just as the man whose nametag is a blur opens the door. I hang back, let my wife balance her sorrow against the resentment that has defined her adult relationship with Fox Wentworth. The loss threatens to break me. The only man I ever thought of as a father has joined the one who made me in that unknown and unknowable darkness.

When the director unveils the corpse, I step closer.

"How small he looks in death." Kelly touches his face, recoils, leans in to kiss his brow.

"He's not in pain anymore, Kel."

"Mrs. Stone, is this your father, Fox Wentworth?" The undertaker stands in the doorway, hands folded over his stomach.

"Yes." Kelly straightens her shoulders, turns away. "Let's finalize the arrangements."

An hour and a half later, the celebration of life for my father-in-law is settled. I send a text to Tuck, telling him we're on our way. Then I drive home, blinking into the lights of oncoming cars, anxious to bury my sorrow in work. When we arrive, Tuck greets us at the door. Hannah's already in the car. Soldier races toward me, his tail scribing welcome symbols in the air.

"You're leaving?"

He pulls me close, thumps my back, turns to hug Kelly. "We want to give you some space. Be back first thing tomorrow."

He slips past my grateful smile. Kelly carries in the insulated bag of fried chicken and sides supplied by Mr. Carney, I remembered his name the third time he said it. Setting the food on the table, bare now of folders and laptops, I rage against my inability to save the ones I love the most. Death comes, Rose said once, not like a thief but a conqueror. *Yeah*, I breathe, *and I'm once more defeated*. On the counter, the package waits, its secrets still hidden.

The silence mocks me. I clench my fists and turn. "You hungry?"

Kelly shrugs out of her raincoat and tosses it in the corner, my usually-tidy wife's unconscious act indicative of her distraction. I set out plates, napkins, silverware, and we sit down to eat, using food to fill the hollows inside. When she finishes, she shoves the plate away, settles back in the chair. The letters lie next to my plate.

"Read to me," she says.

"Really?"

"Really."

Pushing aside the half-empty food containers, I set aside the ribbon and check the dates again. I start at the oldest postmark, one month after her marriage to Mason.

> Dear Fox, Kelly tells me you have throat cancer.
> Strange, isn't it, how our lives have always entwined?
> Well, now you and I have another bond. I have cancer,
> too.

Kelly's hand flutters to her neck. "No," she whispers, her already-tear stained face crumpling. "No."

Wiping my mouth, I swallow hard, and keep reading. Two hours later, I finish Rose's last letter. Mute with sorrow, Kelly and I stare at each other across the table. Then I rise to get the package. My fingers fumble as I tear at the wrapping, but I already know what's inside. When the box falls open, among a sea of foam peanuts, the kaleidoscope nests, waiting for me.

"What are you going to do?" Kelly says.

I pull my cell from my pocket, dialing even as I speak. "Call Mason."

Chapter Twenty-One

As the temperature climbs, the fog continues to creep in on Sandberg's little cat feet, layering everything in mystery. I stand at the front window, sipping coffee from my favorite mug while I contemplate the possibility that my sister, holed up and waiting to die, is doing the same. I've made the calls. Tuck messages me that he's stopping at the deli for sandwiches. Hannah inches up the driveway, the headlights on her Subaru indistinct as a sonogram. Once inside, she joins me at the window, accepts a cup from Kelly, and fingers the tab on the folder she holds close to her chest.

"You call Munroe?' Hannah says. I shake my head as Mason Carruthers's limo pulls up in front of the house. The man hops out, yells orders to his driver, and hurries up the front walk. I meet him at the door.

"Where is she?" My brother-in-law grabs my shoulders and shakes until I fling him off.

"I'll tell you when we're all here."

"Who's we?" He paces the room, scrubbing at his hair, biting his nails. He flicks angry glances at me before striding to Kelly and giving her a hug. He lumbers back to me just as Tuck barrels in. We nod to each other. He tugs Hannah in after him.

"What's that?" I point at the paper she clutches to her chest.

"It's an update." She coughs, reluctance written all over her face, "on Coal Webster."

Mason cocks his head. "And you are?"

Hannah bristles at his tone. Before she can erupt, I introduce her. "Professor Hannah Pierce, head of the criminal justice program at Sinclair Community College currently serving as a consultant on Rose's case. And this is my partner at HPD, Tuck Cornell. We're all trying to find Rose."

"Damn you, Peter! What if she's hurt or what if that maniac–." Mason jams a fist against his mouth to stop the words from spilling free.

"Mason." Kelly rejoins us, holds out yet another mug. "They're doing everything they can."

Rose's husband collapses into the recliner, brooding, his eyes centered on Soldier, who stands, ears cocked, next to the TV. When Mason waggles his fingers, the dog pads over, insinuates his muzzle between Mason's hand and the chair arm, and waits for the petting to begin. Outside, the fog looms thicker, taunting our need to get going. A new set of headlights weaves down the street, moves past the house. In my head, I run through the letters, shuffling the clues, hoping I've placed the pieces of the puzzle correctly, unsure of the next step. Should I bring them all with me – Mason, Tuck, Hannah? Rose wanted me to find her. Just me.

"We just going to stand around staring at each other?' Mason rises to confront me. "After what you told me last night, we should call in the fucking army." Shoving him ahead, I lead everyone into the dining room. We settle around the table, unable to avoid staring at the letters and the box holding the kaleidoscope. Tuck settles his formidable gaze on me.

"I realize this is a difficult time for you and Kelly, Pete. We're all sorry for your loss. But Rose's life hangs in the balance here, so I need to know your plan."

"Wait." Hannah holds up a hand. "Where's Munroe?"

I look around the table. "We're doing this without her. Rose wants me to find her. And that's what I'm going to do."

Tuck whistles. "She's gonna be pissed, partner."

"Tough shit. Are you in or not?"

One by one, they nod. Kelly stands beside me, arms folded, her face unreadable. We stare at each other, let the consequence of the decision settle in our hearts.

"It's what Fox would have wanted, too." When she lowers her eyes, I take a deep breath and pick up the letters.

"Last night I read through my sister's letters three times." I place them back beside the box and pick up a yellow-lined tablet. Scooting my chair over, I put a hand on Mason's arm, pin him to his seat with a look. "I made notes of what I found.

192

Number one. Rose has ovarian cancer. Her doctors tried to convince her to undergo chemo, radiation, but she refused. She and Fox planned to live out the remainder of their time doing what they wanted to do. Neither wanted to lose their hair, to watch the world from a hospital bed, to die chained to an IV tube."

Mason pounds his fist on his thigh, his voice thick with grief. "She never told me. Why?"

"The second thing Rose wrote about was disappointing you, Mase. She realized some time ago that you loved her, but you loved your career more. You wanted a traditional wife, one who would stay home, pose for pictures, play the adoring spouse. She believed she could never be what you wanted her to be. In the end, she cared for you, deeply, but she refused to be a burden, refused to rob you of your dream."

"That's bullshit, Stone." Mason slams out of his chair, kicks it across the floor. Soldier rises, growling. I settle the dog. Running a hand through his hair, Mason punches the wall. Cradling his hand, he winces, then hooks a foot around the chair, pulls it upright and slumps into it. "Show me where she says that."

I lift the letters and wave them at him. "Later, Mase, you can read them all. Third, while Rose was corresponding with Fox, plotting out their final adventure, she came across a news item regarding famous prison escapes. At the end of the article, she read a line about the most recent breakout. Two prisoners from Chillicothe Correctional convinced a food worker to smuggle them out. The details you all can read for yourself, but the important thing is one of those who escaped was Coal Webster."

"Aw, no." Tuck does his own version of a rabid Khrushchev, slapping the table with both hands as he rockets to his feet. "You've got to be shitting me."

"He's not." Hannah calms him down, opens the folder she's been holding, and scans the contents. "I'm surmising that our cunning little psychopath kept track of Rose, followed her career as an artist. Using prison contacts, he discovered where she was living and began sending letters. Am I right, Peter?"

I nod and tap the packet. Hannah keeps talking. "It seems clear that Webster never let go of his obsession with her. When Rose learned about his escape, she decided to take charge of her life once again."

"You can't mean she met up with him?" Kelly's horror resonates with all of us as she inches closer to me.

"Maybe." I glance at the tablet in my hand. "She and Fox had a plan. What it was isn't clear because they didn't write it down. What I do know is she called your dad, Kel, the same night she was spotted on the video cam on the Turnpike. I believe it was Fox who picked her up at the rest stop."

"And did what?" Sorting through the folder, Hannah pulls out a single sheet of paper. "The police reports have Rose Stone at the rest stop last Tuesday, Coal Webster at the Ohio River the same night. Where were they going?"

Picking up the kaleidoscope, I roll it between my palms, then hold it up to peer through the lens. The stones Rose reconfigured so long ago still sparkle, the message clear in my mind. The jagged brown, green and purple shards of glass rearrange themselves into mountains. I hear her telling me to put it to my eye, see the image sketched inside.

"Home," I say, closing my hands around the scope. "She's going home."

"I don't understand." Mason slumps against the wall, his bravado replaced by the bleakness ahead of him, the lost opportunities behind. "You said you checked Fox's place. She's not there."

I place a hand on his shoulder, lock eyes with the others.

"Tell them," Kelly says, "what you think."

I go into the living room, pick up the wedding photo, and return to the group. Staring into the past, I consider all that led us to that one bright day. "She's gone back to the first place we called home, to the real heart of our world. She's gone to the cabin in Tennessee."

"What about Webster?" Tuck approaches, tension carving lines in his forehead.

I let the fear settle before I speak. "He's gone there, too."

Chapter Twenty-Two

We opt to take two cars. Mason insists on accompanying us. At first Tuck refuses to consider it, but my brother-in-law is a pushy bastard, and a well-connected one. Against my better judgment, I support his request. We may need his resources when we get there.

"Hannah, when we reach the turnoff, you're going to stay by the vehicles. Mase," I push at his chest, "if we spot Webster, do not approach him. He's dangerous, unpredictable."

"He hurt Rose once." Mason paces up and down the sidewalk. "I won't let him hurt her again."

"You don't know him. I do. You think I want you going to jail because of him? Any of you?"

"I have a permit." Mason taps the back pocket of his jeans, opens his jacket to show me the 9mm in a shoulder holster, "and I know how to use it."

Tuck slides up close, nose to nose, squints at him. "You take that out and I arrest you, understand? The only reason you're coming along is Stone vouches for you. So, toe the line or all our heads roll. Pete?"

I stare down Mason. When he drops his eyes, I breathe easier. "He won't interfere."

"Not sure this is the right decision." Hannah checks the time. "Think we should alert the locals?"

Grabbing her elbow, I walk her away from the others.

"Promise me you won't do that yet. Please, Pickle." She startles at my use of her pet name.

"You're in deep shit if this thing goes wrong, Pete. You know that, don't you? Besides, they can help."

I shake my head. My mind's ping-ponging between concern for Rose and the danger Coal Webster represents. "No. If Webster's there, if he's somehow got Rose and they confront him, who knows what he might do?"

"Okay." She eases out of my grip. "I won't do anything. Yet. Thing is, it's out of your jurisdiction. We can't just bull our way in. Professional courtesy, co-operation, you remember those, don't you?"

I do, and she's right. I ought to accept the restrictions of an out-of-town operation. But Rose is my sister. She left the clues for me. I let her down once and it almost cost her everything. I can't let that happen again. The front door bangs open. Kelly hurries over, hands me a pack filled with water bottles and energy snacks. Soldier trots behind her. I kneel to give him a hug, breathe in his doggy smell. He heads for the car. I head him off, tell him to stay and watch after Kelly. He whines, sniffs my hair, burrows his nose against my neck.

"You should take him," Kelly says.

I bury my hands in his fur. "No. He's had his share of danger. I want him to stay with you."

"You're a good man, Peter Stone." Kelly wraps her arms around me, kisses both cheeks. "Stay safe."

"Let's do this." Mason tugs me to the car. When I look back, my wife stands in the doorway holding onto the dog's collar while one arm wraps around her waist, protective and strong. A gust of wind lifts her hair, blurring the plea in her eyes that shares space with the effort not to cry.

The four lanes on I-75 leading into Cincinnati crawl with traffic. Instead of lifting, the fog thickens, cutting visibility to two car lengths. Tuck and Hannah follow close behind, their presence a comforting reminder I'm not entirely on my own. Closer to the river, traffic creeps toward the bridge over the Ohio River. Hannah and Mason message each other as we cross into Kentucky. It takes three hours to reach the airport turnoff, but we're not going there. Another forty-five minutes farther south and the morning rush begins to dissipate.

"How long till we hit Lexington?" Mason fiddles with the radio, intercepts a report of a pileup in the right lane.

"Normally, you can make it there from our house in two hours. Not today."

He echoes my last words, drums his fingers on the dash. A cop with a flashlight is directing the traffic onto a side road, but I can see a way to advance ahead if I use the shoulder. I stop, wait for him to approach.

"Officer." I flash my badge. "We're on a tight schedule. Have an escaped convict to pick up. My partner's in the next car back."

He shines the light on my face and ID, then asks for the registration and license, does the same with Tuck. Finally, he waves us through. His light strobes through the haze, warns other vehicles from following us. We ease through the scattered wreckage, bump along the berm, and balance on the edge before easing around the barrier on the south side of the accident. While I navigate, Mason takes out Rose's letters, shuffles through them. I'm glad I hid the last one in my pocket, the one I didn't read to Kelly. I concentrate on the road while I mouth the words of my sister's final cryptic instruction. DO NOT SHARE Rose commanded, the order scrawled over the sealed flap. My heart stutters, settles back into rhythm. Mason taps my arm.

"When we reach Lexington, where do we go?"

Reaching for the map between us, I motion for him to spread open it. He flattens it across his lap and I lean over to trace the blue highway line. "We need to go all the way to Jellico, then take 160 to LaFollette, then go north on 63. Into the heart of the wilderness." All those forgotten names from my childhood spark in my mind. Eagan. Morley. White Oak. Habersham. Duff. None of them describe our place, but all of them lie close, a scatter of rural hamlets stewing in the juice of neglect and poverty. It's a wonder Rose remembered how to get there. But then, I could be wrong. Maybe Rose didn't head back to our hills. Maybe she flew someplace far away, the French Riviera, the Brazilian coast. I close my eyes for a moment, consider the possibility I am wrong, that all this hurry is for nothing.

We're halfway to Lexington before the fog lifts. When it does, the sun spreads a welcome over the blossoming countryside. Swaths of spring green, dotted with redbud and dogwood, flirt on the hillsides. We pull into a gas station for a restroom break and a time check. When Mason takes over the driving, I search for a country station on the radio. The lilt of mountain speech makes my chest ache. I didn't realize how much I missed the cadence of my childhood, echoed now only in raspy conversations between my mother and Aunt Pearl. As my brother-in-law speeds on, I feel like I'm drifting back in time, remembering the swoosh of the tires as that old station wagon carried us north, away from all the safety I had ever known. My father belonged in these mountains, where his temptation to violence found an outlet in hunting, chopping wood, building furniture. In the city, he was just one more lost soul, unable to grip the earth with his toes, the trees with his hands. Rose and I became his pounding rock. Mama simply flew away with the crows.

Following the southern route of the highway, we stop again to fill up before we turn onto the backroads. At the service station, Mason paces like a caged thing. Hannah consults her laptop. Tuck pesters his phone. I lean against the car, staring at the hills, conjuring up a scenario where my sister lives on and Coal Webster returns to prison.

When we reach the exit for Route 160, Tucks pulls ahead and flags us down.

"What's our next move?" he wants to know. I worry my lower lip, anxious to get going. But Tuck is insistent.

"Stone," he hooks two fingers in his belt, "where exactly is this cabin?"

"It's been a long time since I've lived here, maybe too long. I can tell you where I think it is." I smooth the map over the hood of his car and draw a circle north of Norris Lake. "We may need to go in on foot."

"Why's that?" Mason looks over my shoulder.

I indicate the contour lines with a wave of my hand. "The cabin has a sweeping view of all approaches. All we had was one dirt road going up the mountain then. Narrow, steep, exposed. If Rose or Webster or both are there, they'll hear us coming."

I hide my concern with a cough. Tuck rests a hand on my back. "So, if we're not driving up, what we are going to do?"

Mason and Hannah crowd closer. "How close can we get by car?" she asks.

I rub my mouth, trying to remember how it was when Rose and I wandered the forest. "There used to be a roadside rest between LaFollette and Speedwell. Just a table and a lookout. If it's still there, we can park on the shoulder, head northeast through the valley."

"If it's still there." Tuck picks up the map, looks us over. "You all coming?"

"Damn straight." Mason squares his shoulders. "No way you're leaving me behind."

Hannah shakes her head. "I'll stay with the cars at the rest stop and monitor your progress. One of you, check in every half hour. I can call for backup if you need it."

"Not much cell coverage in there." I check my phone as I speak.

Hannah opens her briefcase, hands me and Tuck each a radio. "These will allow us to stay in contact. I have one, too."

Mason pouts. Tuck gives her a fierce embrace. I mouth a thank you. We set the frequency, test them, and clamber back into the cars. As the road winds on, I channel all the ancestral Stones, ask their forgiveness for my neglect, and beg their help. Maybe they hear me. Maybe they don't. A gust of wind buffets us as we climb higher, into the stone heart of the mountains.

Chapter Twenty-Three

Another forty minutes go by until we reach the rest stop. Although Mason protests, Tuck insists we put on Kevlar vests and ID jackets. We move out along a deer trail that tapers to nothing about two hundred yards in. The deeper we go into the back country, the more anxious I grow. The terrain is rugged, seamed with rain-carved ruts, dotted with old wells and abandoned cabins. Every mile, I use my compass to correct our course, consult the map, draw on long-buried memories to keep us on track. Two miles in, Mason is gasping for breath. Calling a halt, I wait for him to hydrate, then pass around the granola bars Kelly packed. Tuck reports back to Hannah for the fourth time.

"How much further?" Mason wipes his forehead, resettles the ball cap he's wearing. The reluctant sun has decided to turn coquette. It struts across the land, heating the moisture-laden air. We trudge on. Another hour passes. It's too early for mosquitos, but midges swarm in patches of sunlight, swarm our eyes and ears. I pull out a travel-size bottle of deet, spray my hands and hat, then offer it to the others. Unused to the terrain, Mason lags behind. *He shouldn't be here.* Then I hear Kelly's voice in my ear. *Don't be so overprotective, Stone. He's Rose's husband. He deserves to be there.* I think about Rose, about all the emotional terrain she has traveled, and bow my head. When the sun moves west, Tuck shifts to my side.

"How much longer?"

Mason and I stop walking. He and Tuck suck in water, while I check the map.

"We're more than halfway there." Tuck gestures for us to move on but I call him back. "Hold up. I've been thinking, about my sister and the cabin. I know it's been a long time, but my father was obsessed with protecting our land. He left some precautions in place when we came north."

Mason swears softly. Tuck grunts.

"Now you tell us?" My partner chews his bottom lip. "What kind of precautions?"

"My father hunted these hills. He laid out traps. I suspect most are still out here." I shrug an apology. I'm still not positive Rose is here, but if she has come back, she won't be helpless. Sick or not, dying or not, she'll be ready. "When we get close, tread carefully."

"What the hell does that mean, Pete?" Mason pokes me in the chest. I stumble, right myself, and push back.

"It means Rose isn't helpless. She'll check for the traps, make sure they're set. Then she'll wait in the shadows. And she's probably armed."

"Armed?" Mason stamps in circles, worrying his hair into spikes. "She doesn't even know how to shoot."

"How little you know about her. My mother taught us how to shoot before we were ten years old. Rose killed Coal Webster's mother with a single shot. She won't hesitate to shoot again."

My brother-in-law leans against one of the poplars gracing the bank of a marshy stream we plan to cross. His eyes glaze over, his mouth tightens. The Rose he thought he married has faded like an old photograph. He doesn't want to believe me, so he looks at Tuck for confirmation. My partner raises an eyebrow, nods slowly.

"Rose Stone is a force of nature, Mr. Carruthers."

"Well, then," Mason interrupts, "we better get moving."

We trudge on, crashing through the brush like a herd of wildebeests. We've just topped another ridge when the crack of a single gunshot, distant but echoing, rings through the woods.

Lifting my head, I sniff, test the wind. All I smell is damp earth. The trees stand hushed and brooding. Even the birds have stilled, except for a woodpecker somewhere in the deadwood off to my right. The staccato beat matches my pulse. I take two strides before Tuck catches up, holds me back. Mason points to the northeast. We form a line, me, Tuck and Mason bringing up the rear. I follow another animal trail down into a deep valley. When we straggle up the other side, I spy a field of wild raspberry canes stretching skyward behind a shack fallen in on itself. Only the stones of the fireplace remain upright.

"Wait." I close my eyes, separate the memories crowding back. Is this where Aunt Pearl took me to pick berries? If so, the cabin lies east only half a mile away. "Let me go first."

Tuck blocks the path. "Pete," he scrubs his upper lip, "you sure?"

Another woodpecker tattoos a tree opposite the collapsed cabin. I search my memories, recalling all the times Rose and I wandered these broken hills. When I close my eyes, the way to the cabin unspools like the image in the kaleidoscope, all greens and purples, and slipping into place.

"Yes." I move to the front of the line. "Just remember. Step carefully."

Tuck and Mason sort through a tangle of fallen branches until they each find a stick worth carrying.

"Hey, Pete." Tuck swats at a spider web above his head. "I should have asked this earlier. There any snakes in these woods?"

He's trying to ease the tension, but I can't relax. If I'm wrong, I've wasted everyone's time for nothing. My sister might still be running from Webster or be a captive once more in some other hideaway. If I'm right, that gunshot may mean one of them is already dead.

Mason slides up next to Tuck. "I heard there's all kinds of snakes in this place. While the rattlers may hiss at you, it's the human ones who will strike."

"Amen," I mutter. The others attempt to step quietly, but one city boy and one rock star tromping a path through the spring vegetation in the backcountry don't exactly equal stealth. As we near the ridge where the cabin sits, I raise my hand, signal a stop.

"I'll go first. Tuck?"

"I got your back, partner." Gesturing to the south, Tuck yanks Mason's sleeve and my brother-in-law reluctantly follows him. I step forward, toeing my boot beneath the leaf cover as I approach. I'm not certain how Rose might have boobytrapped the place, but in my stone-cold survivor's heart, I know she did.

The forest gives way to a band of honeysuckle draped over a rusting stretch of barbed wire. I peel a section from a post and edge my way past the boundary. Three hundred yards farther on, I spy it, the cabin where our story started. It, too, has fallen on hard times. Although the walls still stand, most of the logs have weathered to a moss-stippled gray. The chimney leans. The windows sag against the sashes. The once-weed-free front and side yards lie strangled by brambles and thistle.

I creep forward when, a hundred yards out, my boot thunks against something hidden beneath a stand of ferns. I can't tell if it's a bear trap or a snare for catching rabbits, but it doesn't matter. My sister set it for Coal. The trap rattles when I brush by, but it doesn't spring shut. I'm twenty yards closer and three traps in when I see a pair of legs, then a torso, lying face down amid the spring-green stalks. One leg lies at a ninety-degree angle, knee bent, ankle caught in a steel vise. One hand clutches a machete.

"Rose!" I start forward. "Rose?" My radio crackles. Hannah's voice spits a warning.

"Peter? We've got company. I —" Before she can say more, a man snatches the radio, drawls at me over the distance.

"Mr. Stone? Sheriff Bill Yoakam here. Your Ms. Pierce says you're tracking an escaped convict. Would've been nice, son, to tell me 'fore you went in there."

I hesitate, uncertain what to say. The figure on the ground groans but doesn't rise. I edge closer until I can see the head, shaven and inked with tattoos. It turns toward me, a sneer peeking out of the pain. Coal.

Chapter Twenty-four

"Stone?" Yoakam shouts at me over the radio. I lurch away from Webster, crouch, and peer through the weeds. "Tuck?"

"Over here." He steps from behind a tangle of forsythia my mother planted years ago.

"Mason?" Looking left, I see my brother-in-law slip free from the shadow of the cabin. His gun is drawn. Both men begin to approach, but I wave them off. I edge closer to Webster. He lifts his head, turns toward the cabin. Blood trickles from a cut on his forehead, but his eyes are clear. He flops to his right and lunges to his knees, dragging the trap with him, the iron wedded to his ankle.

"Peter Stone. The boy who wanted to fly." He wipes the blood with the back of his hand, rattles a step closer. "Come to rescue Rose?"

"No." I circle to the left, inch my hand toward the gun still riding my hip. "I came for you."

"What if I don't want to go? At least, not before tasting your sister again." When he laughs, a bubble of blood explodes from his nose. He must be hurt somewhere I can't see. I keep moving, try to draw him away from the cabin.

"Where is Rose?"

"On the porch, dumbass. Waiting for me."

I glance toward the cabin. A cloud passes overhead, shrinking the sunlight, shadowing Coal's face. I'm reminded of the angel on our door, the way the light poured through the stained glass, coloring the room. How my sister read about Joan of Arc saving the people of France. Back then, I was quick to dismiss her belief in what was good and right. Would I do the same today? Before I can shift my attention back to Webster, he raises the machete and leaps toward me. I catch a glimpse of him and lose my balance. Staggering, I drop to one knee and fumble with the strap on the holster. Webster keeps coming. The machete swings down.

"Peter." My sister's command carries across the clearing. "Lie down."

I dig my heels into the ground and propel myself backward, a human crawdad searching for a rock to hide under. Rose yells my name again. I lie still, unmoving, as a bullet burrows into Webster's head. My ears ring. My mouth tastes like steam and sulphur.

"I told you, Peter." My sister's voice carries in the heated air, faint yet full of triumph. "I'd never let him hurt us again."

Rising to my knees, I face the cabin. Framed by the door, Rose stands on the porch, tall and stern as that avenging angel from our past. My personal Joan of Arc. She sets the rifle down, then lowers herself to the floor. I check Webster for a pulse, move closer. The cancer has ravaged her. The skin on her face is stretched thin, like gauze on a lampshade, but even mortality can't erase her beauty. Mason sprints toward her, calls her name. I race past him, mount the steps to kneel beside her.

"Rose. You didn't have to do this alone."

Grabbing my hand, my sister rolls her eyes.

"Stop trying to run my life, big brother." She looks beyond me. "You brought Mason."

"He loves you, Rose. He wouldn't stay away."

"I know." She fumbles in the pocket of her overcoat. "But this has never been his fight."

I want to argue, but in my heart, I know she's right. Rose sits taller, touches my cheek. "Don't tell him everything, Pete. Just find her."

"Find who?"

She presses a paper against my palm and folds my fingers over it. When Mason reaches the porch, he shoves me aside, takes her hands, and buries his face in her lap. She cups his chin and sighs. When he gathers my sister into an embrace and begins to rock, I join Tuck in the yard. Some reunions deserve to be held in private.

Tuck contacts Hannah and the sheriff, then hands the radio to me. I remind them to be careful on their approach and to advise the county coroner. With a bridge washed out due to the recent storms, they're at least an hour away. While we wait, I wander the overgrown clearing, unsettled by the thought that I never expected to return here, and now I'm certain I never will again. Tuck shadows me.

"Anything I can do?" he finally says.

"Call Munroe. Tell her we found Rose. And let her know Coal Webster's dead. And call Hannah. She deserves to hear from you."

"What about Kelly?"

"You take care of yours, Cornell, and I'll take care of mine."

Tuck moves off in search of a signal so he can make his call. I check my own phone, send a message as soon as three bars appear, then head around back, still kicking the undergrowth for traps. Clever girl, my sister, resetting all the traps, but then, she always was.

When I'm certain I'm alone, I unfold the note she gave me. Written in her bold hand is a name and address. *Bridget Stone St. Rose's 263 Brookfield Avenue Oswego New York*. There's a phone number, too. Perhaps this explains what Rose was doing in New York before she came down here. But now is not the time to solve this last piece of the puzzle.

When Yoakam's men arrive, they spend the remaining daylight hours locating and collecting the traps Rose set to catch her stalker. As soon as the sheriff gives the all-clear, an ambulance bulls up the lane to collect my sister. Although she protests, this time Mason and I insist. When she finally agrees to leave, Mason rides with her. I imagine he'll arrange for better transportation once they reach Lexington. He calls me over just before the EMTs close the doors. Rose struggles to sit up on the gurney and hugs me tighter than she ever has.

"How's Fox?"

"Gone, the way he wanted to go."

"Did you help him?" There is no disapproval in her whispered question. When I nod, she pulls me close again.

"I love you, brother. Promise me you'll make this come out right?"

Because I have no choice, because I want to prove my heart is as strong as hers, I make that promise. Then I tender one of my own.

"Promise you won't leave without saying goodbye?"

Smiling, she taps my chest with one skeletal finger.

"You do know I'll never be truly gone, don't you, Pete? I live inside that heart of yours, in the kaleidoscope, in your memories. It's up to you to guard the past."

I feel the tremors in her, recognize how hard she's fighting not to give up. Mason moves closer, uses his body to support hers. The doors close, and they're gone. As the ambulance sways down the hill, I picture my sister's crawdad limbs struggling to find the heart of the world and realize she already has.

Before they reach the city, she slips into a coma. I make it to the hospital at midnight, take her hand in mine, and retell all our stories, the ones I shared with Tuck and Hannah, the ones we lived. When morning lightens the eastern sky, she wakes. Her eyes light up and she smiles.

"Do good things," she whispers. With Mason and I beside her, Rose Stone Carruthers slips away, heading for the heart of the world.

Chapter Twenty-five

A week after Rose passes, Kelly and I scatter Fox's ashes in the creek at the bottom of Dream Street. Mason mourns alone for fourteen days before arranging a funeral for his beloved Rose. He insists on burying her in the sculpture garden at their estate on the Lake Erie shore near Oswego. I leave it to Kelly to oversee the after-burial dinner while I make a call to the number Rose left me. A stern, no-nonsense voice answers the call.

"St. Rose's Orphanage. Marilyn Sutter speaking."

It takes me a moment to process what she says. Orphanage. I explain who I am. The woman's voice softens.

"We've been expecting your call, Mr. Stone. Bridget has been waiting a long time for you."

Like the kaleidoscope glass slipping into place, I put the pieces together, fight the stab of recognition that cuts through me.

"Mr. Stone? Are you there?"

I stutter a reply and set up an appointment for the following day. As soon as Mason disappears into his studio, I pull Kelly aside and ask her to walk with me through the garden. Flowers cover the earth where Rose lies. Around her, formal paths lead to ten statues, one a mini-replica of the Central Park installation, one a larger version of the Opal statue that won my sister the scholarship and set her on her journey. I tuck Kelly's hand close against my side, afraid if I let go, she, too, might slip away. Sorrow grows with the twilight creeping over the shoreline.

"I think Rose had one more secret, Kel."

"Another one?" She looks out at the water. Her hand trembles in mine. "I'm so tired of secrets."

"This one's different. I hope you'll find it as amazing as I do."

My wife purses her lips before she speaks. Seems like hesitation is the by-product of every decision these days. "Just tell me, Pete," she says. So I do.

The next day we drive into Oswego, follow the bodiless voice on our GPS to Brookfield Avenue. The receptionist hands us over to the woman in charge. Her badge reads Ms. Sutter, General Manager, clarifying her status at the institution. Inviting us into her office, she opens a folder, lays it on the desk in front of us. I stare at the photograph paperclipped to the inside. Then I read the birth certificate.

Bridget Rose Stone. Birth date: February 14, 1999. Kelly leans closer, traces the date, does the same calculation I do.

"Coal Webster's child." She fishes a tissue from the box on Sutter's desk, wipes her eyes. I set the certificate aside and read through the anecdotal notes.

Unable to care for the child at this time, the mother requests placement in the care of the nuns at Mother Mary's, our home for unwed mothers. She has arranged for monthly payments to cover the cost of the child's clothing and incidentals. The mother insists she is not abandoning the child.

"I thought this was St. Rose's Orphanage."

Sutter gazes at a plaque on the wall. "A number of years ago, your sister provided an endowment to the home with the express desire that the name and the purpose be changed. It was the least we could do."

"And these are your notes?"

She shakes her head. "No. I wasn't here at that time. Sister Elizabeth did the initial intake. As you can see, as your sister's circumstances improved, she increased the funds for Bridget's care and education. She mailed gifts on birthdays and holidays, it's all listed in the folder, with letters explaining, if not the circumstances of the girl's birth, the family she hoped would one day come to claim her. When Rose married Mr. Carruthers, it was with the understanding that she and her husband would buy an estate near the town, an estate in Rose's name only so her child would have an inheritance. Mr. Carruthers was not to know about the child."

Kelly clenches her fists. "Why keep this a secret?"

210

I work through the possibilities, arrive at the only one that makes any sense. "She was afraid Webster would find out. Afraid he would make some kind of claim."

"But she left the child an inheritance, so the girl would never be homeless the way you and she were." Sutter taps the deposition. "It's all there in Sister's hand."

I read through the file a second time, amazed at my sister's foresight. Ms. Sutter waits until I finish. Then she gathers the papers, tamps them into a neat pile, and slides them back in the folder.

"Now," she clears her throat, "Rose wished for you and your wife to care for the child. All that's needed is a commitment. If you formally adopt the girl, as Rose wished, Bridget will have a forever home. And as you can see, your sister left enough money to cover all expenses until she's grown."

"What does that mean?" Kelly places a hand on the folder to prevent Ms. Sutter from taking it back.

Ms. Sutter slides a new folder across the desk, points to a figure on the first page of the document. "Rose had an insurance policy in your name, Peter. She wanted the child to be loved. It would be a great disappointment if you cannot take her."

I shake my head. After all Rose went through, she had this extra sorrow to bear. Kelly rises from her chair. Before I can respond, she reaches across the desk and grabs Ms. Sutter's hand.

"Can we see her?"

"Kelly." I pull her back. The weight of possibility presses against my fear. This revelation, this demand, could break us. I choose my words carefully. "You don't have to do this. We can keep trying."

"Of course. We will keep trying, but, Peter," she raises her face to mine, "we can have this child, Rose's child, now. I want to see her, Peter."

"It's his child, too. Can you forget that?"

"Rose loved the child all this time." Marilyn Sutter folds her hands over the adoption papers. "She named you both in her will, and the attorney drew up the papers. If Rose could overlook the circumstances of her child's birth, surely you can do the same."

Kelly brushes away my hand, stands, and hurries to the door. Her eyes are bright with unshed tears and her hands tremble where they clutch her purse. "Take us to see her. Now. Please."

We follow the matron down the hall to an art classroom. Seven girls are huddled around a long table, their smocks daubed with paint and clay. They all look up as we enter. At the far end, a slender girl with Coal Webster's hair and my sister's elfin features lifts her head.

Kelly covers her mouth, as taken as I am by the resemblance to the Rose of our childhood. Standing, the girl shifts her gaze from the teacher to Ms. Sutter to me. I take two steps closer, kneel down, and fold her clay-caked hands in mine.

"Hello, Bridget." I take a deep breath, aware that Kelly has joined me, that our gazes are now fixed on this child. "I'm your uncle, Peter. This is my wife, Kelly. We've come to take you home."

Chapter Twenty-Six

I don't know what my mother is doing this morning, but I can make a pretty good guess. Opal Stone waits, the shot glass sitting on the table beside her, for the doorbell to ring. My message on the answering machine has roused her too early. Unsettled by my request, she rises to wander from the bathroom to the bedroom. She shakes her head often, desperate to clear it of her most frequent dream. She floats the bedspread over the tousled sheets, but the images persist. She and Estill are climbing their mountain, selecting a spot for the home they will certain sure build right after Estill finds work. The wind sings its way up from the valley, carrying a mournful tune across the summer sky. Swift gusts push her dress halfway up her thighs. Rose and I hover in the background, holding hands and tongues. Around us mountain flowers bloom and tease. Even the insect noises come back true in her dream. So she tells me, every time I visit.

"Ma?" On the machine, I sound half apologetic and half belligerent. "You up? I have to see you. It's about Rose." I hang up. Opal replays the conversation, trying to decipher what time I might arrive. It's already half past ten. She needs time to gather her defenses, to prepare for battle.

"What I need," she murmurs to the curtains fluttering at the window, "is a stone heart."

When the doorbell sounds, she jumps, knocking over the glass. Sweet Kentucky bourbon spreads its perfume through the room. My mother swallows hard, dips a finger in the spill, and licks it clean. A knock at the back startles her. Which should she answer first? She shuffles through the kitchen and yanks open the door.

"Hey, Opal." Sybil Olsen from Apartment 3 leans against the wall, her fingers flipping a box of cigarettes end over end. "Want to take a smoke break?"

"Can't." Opal lifts her hand to her lips before she remembers she hasn't lit one yet. "Got a visitor coming."

"A visitor?" Sybil rocks back and forth, puts a hand out to steady herself.

"My son's coming over this morning." Opal backs away, points her thumb toward the front of the apartment. "In fact, I think he's here now."

Sybil turns around, waving over her shoulder. "Didn't know you had a son," she says. "Lucky you."

I let myself in, toss the key on the card table set up with puzzle pieces, a thousand fragments of a blue-grass horse farm. I lean against the wall, debating the wisdom of this final visit.

Back in her recliner, a gift from her sister Pearl when she first moved to the rent-subsidized apartment, Opal smooths the corduroy armrests and raises the glass. Refilled and sparkling, the liquid filters amber shadows across her face. "Lucky me," she says.

"Hi, Mom."

Opal lets out a shout, then pours a new glass and knocks it back. The third shot spreads through her, numbing all the sharp edges of memory. When it reaches her toes, she'll be home free. "What the hell are you doing here so early? Ain't you got to work?"

I apologize for startling her. "I'm kind of on a leave of absence right now."

"In trouble, ain't you. I should've seen that coming."

I ignore the barb and hand over the mail. Whatever happens with the department is none of her business. "Figured you might want this."

She rifles through the stack and tosses it on the rug. I pretend not to see the second-notice stamp on the utility bill, or the way her hand shakes, the new slump to her shoulders, the new lines around her mouth. Scanning the room, I note the TV off-balance on the wooden tray table, the heat register stretched beneath the single window. I'm searching for proof that I and this woman belong together. "Still no pictures, huh, Ma?"

Opal shrugs off the accusation. Tossing her hair back, she stares straight at me.

214

"Your eyes are the color of the sea," she hiccups, "sea green eyes, just like your father's."

I hold her gaze long enough to see sorrow spear its way through her defenses. Inhaling, she fists a hand over her stomach.

"Ma?" I resist touching her. "How you doing today?"

She waves me off. Reaching for grandma's quilt, she arranges it over her lap. The wedding ring pattern, faded from years of washing, reminds me of all that has leached out of her life. For a while, we sit in silence, regarding each other across a gulf of unexplored feeling, until she can't resist the urge to ask.

"You said you had news about Rose."

I fiddle with one of the puzzle pieces, then toss it back on the table. "Not that you asked, but Kelly's expecting. The doctor says everything's going well." I point at her. "You're going to be a grandma. For the second time."

"I'm too young to be a grandma," Opal spits out the usual retort, but she can't stifle the stir of pride. A demand slips out. "I want them to call me Mam, like what you and Rose called my mother."

The request surprises me. "Maybe," I say. "That's for the grandchildren to decide."

My mother frowns. I ignore the smell of whiskey drifting on the breeze that pushes through the open window. Reaching into my pocket, I pull out the packet of letters tied with blue velvet, set them on the edge of the sofa, and lean forward. The envelopes shift and slide into Opal's lap.

"Fox had these." I swallow against the grief. "They're from Rose."

"Fox Wentworth? I hate that man." Picking at her lower lip, Opal flicks a shred of tobacco onto the rug. Eyes narrowed, she curses under her breath. "Always trying to show me up."

I rub a hand over my mouth, erase the sting of her jealousy. "He took care of Rose, Ma," I pause. "He loved her."

"I loved her," my mother says, but there is a pleading quality to the statement, like she needs my affirmation to make it true. I refuse to play that game.

"Like him or not, Fox is dead. Your spite can't hurt him now."

"So. Whyn't he mail these to me, then?" Opal threads folds of the quilt through her fingers, over and back, over and back. She licks her lips, stares with longing at the glass by her hand, but she doesn't pick it up.

"Rose asked him not to. She was dying, Ma. She wrote them while she was dying." I choke on the words.

Opal grits her teeth, places her fist over her heart.

"Did you hear me? She was dying, Ma."

"And now she's dead, and I didn't even get to say goodbye." Opal bends forward and rocks through the sobs tearing out of her. When the moment passes, she sits up and waves toward the bottle.

"Have a drink, son. It'll dull the pain. For a little while."

The invitation floats in the air. I clear my throat and stare hard at my mother, who might have saved Rose, saved me. Then I set the letters on the table and tap them with a finger.

"I don't want the pain to go away, Ma. I want to remember Rose forever." Rising, I go into the kitchen, pluck a glass from the cupboard. Then I lift the bottle and pour a shot for each of us. When Opal lifts hers, I mimic the motion.

"To Rose," I say. We drink, my mother and I, for the first and last time together. Silence hovers around us, oozing from the discolored walls and the plain brown rug. Rose's shadow flickers in and out of the light from the window. My mother rests a hand on the packet, then holds it out.

"My eyes," Opal said, sipping, "they ain't what they used to be. So you go on. Read one to me."

Releasing the ribbon, I open the top envelope, unfold the sheet of paper, and begin.

Peter,

I don't deserve to live. For my sins of commission. For my sins of omission. For the lives that are gone, because of me, and for the one that isn't. For all the thoughts and secret longings, I accepted my fate long ago. But not like this. Not this soon. Poetic justice, perhaps, after all I am a rose, a brief bloom and many thorns. Rose Harmony Stone Carruthers, the little girl

216

who could, until she couldn't anymore. But, then, you know me, don't you, Peter? I am writing this for you, and for Mama, even though she'll just shrug and say I told you so. I'm writing this for Fox, too, if he chooses to read it, although he won't.

He'll say he's not family, that he has no right to know. He was good to us, wasn't he? See how I repaid him? Came back to die, to kill one more time, knowing he *wouldn't refuse me, knowing he wouldn't say no if I asked. So, imagine that we are there, you and I, on the bank of the creek where we spent so many hours hiding from Dad, hiding from Mama, hiding from the world and sharing our impossible, soaring dreams. Hiding at the stone heart of the world.*

"Why'd she say that?" Opal twists the sleeve of her blouse. "I deserve to die."

"She felt responsible, Ma, for all that happened." I lean back against the sofa cushion. The cording cuts into my neck.

"Well, she was, wasn't she?" Opal taps her foot, the heel of the slipper flapping free. "How'd she die?"

Instead of answering, I return to the letter.

Forgive me. The drugs have kicked in and I'm rambling, but I want you to know it isn't the cancer that's killing me. The doctors urged me to seek treatment. Radiation and chemo and the slow roasting death of desperation? Nope. Not my style. So, cancer's the agent, but it's guilt that's my undoing. Isn't that right, Mama? Guilt and the loss of all that makes us strong. I've lost everything that kept me whole even on Dream Street, that blighted dead-end thorn of a place that fastened its hooks early on and never let me go.

"She can't put that on me." Opal buries her face in the corner of the quilt, unleashing all the grief she had denied. "Your father and I, we did the best we knew. I told her to go back."

"You told her to go back?" My hand trembles. I lean toward Opal, shoving the letter at her chest. "When did you see her? Ma, did you know where she was?"

Opal worms her way beneath my arm and dashes to the window, a fist still clenched tight against her chest. She swipes at the wisps of gray hair escaping from her ponytail.

"You're just like her, always pushing. What do you want from me?" Bracing herself against the sash, she rocks from side to side.

"All those weeks of searching, all those days of fear and pain, did you know where she was?"

Opal stops rocking. The secret she's fighting to protect refuses to stay hidden. The words squeak out. "I promised not to tell."

I move closer, shake her hard. "When?"

She pushes me away. "She came here. Probably Fox brought her. About a week after she disappeared. Stood outside the building, waiting, until I stepped out for a smoke." Her words slip loose like chips of granite. "She wanted to stay with me."

"God damn it. She came to you and you told her to go back? Back to what?"

"To Mason. To her world. She made her bed." Opal shrugs off my scorn. She shoves her way back to the recliner and reaches for her glass. Grabbing her arm, I snatch the glass and hurl it against the window. The panes shatter in one loud burst. Slivers fly out, littering the carpet.

I close my eyes, remembering what else Rose wrote.

> *You know that Coal raped me. What you don't know is he left his seed inside my body, already planted and growing despite the doctor's assurances. By the time I started classes in the fall, I knew. I covered it up well until the last month. Then I simply went away. The Sisters of Charity didn't judge or lecture. They helped me, and they provided a home that wanted what I didn't. So, ask Mama. Is it possible to die from guilt? From being a bad mother? Did my shame erupt from inside, like black spot on rose petals,*

to pay me back for all the deaths? Daddy. Rocky.
Lacey Webster. To pay me back for abandoning my
child?

I refold the letter and place it back in the envelope. Opal
deserved to hear this.

"What about my window?" my mother asks. But I am
done with her. Retrieving the letters, I move toward the door.
Ma snorts. "I have to use the washroom."

I rub my eyes. "You have to use the washroom?" While I
stare at my mother, a rush of sunlight floods through the
broken window, throwing the room into high relief.

Tripping over the quilt, Ma navigates around the chair
and shuffles away. Inside the bathroom, she turns on the
faucet. Over the sound of running water, I hear her sobs.

I'm almost out the door when she returns. She grabs my
wrist, sinks her nails into my skin.

"Tell me then," she says. "Tell me what you came to say."

I free myself from her grip, glance at the stove, rust and
grease staining the burners. I survey my mother's face. When
I look at her feet, swimming inside the mules she wears, I
recall the statute Rose sculpted, the one that won the contest.

"Ma, where are Rose's statues, the ones she made in high
school?"

My mother turns her back, body rigid and unyielding.
"She gave them to me," she says. "They're mine."

"Where are they?" I spin her around to face me. "Damn
you, where are they?"

She drifts toward the bedroom. Shoving past her, I open
the closet, shuffle through the litter of linens and old shoes.
My mother follows me.

"No, Peter." She claws at my back, wraps her arms around
my waist, and pulls. "I got nothing left of her but those statues.
They're mine."

I stagger free. Supporting myself against the doorjamb, I
reach up and sweep all the boxes off the top shelf. They tumble
across the bed and bounce onto the floor. Sweaters, purses,
old photos spray out. The heaviest box bangs against the
nightstand and cracks open. The statue of me that Rose called

Reluctant Angel rolls to a stop at my feet. Earthbound, the one of Opal with her feet mired in mud, slaps against the wall and splits in half just below the figure's waist.

Breathing hard, I gather up my statue and cradle it next to the letters. "This is all I want from you. It's more than you gave Rose. God, why didn't you fight for us as much as you fought against us? Huh, Ma?"

We stare at each other, years of longing compressed into a heartbeat of sadness that pounds between us. I look away first. Bending over, my mother lifts the two halves of the statue and brings them together. Holding them to her chest, she falls to her knees, gasping for air. When she lays her head on the bed, humming a ballad my father wrote, I remember the mountain dream, how the air filled with birdsong, and the wind rose above the hills in the company of sorrow.

Chapter Twenty-Seven

Setting aside Rose's letter, the one I read at least once a day, I pull down the top of the antique walnut desk. My heart fills with gladness. Mam's legacy, the sole remnant of my time on the mountain, sits here in our dining room. Mr. and Mrs. Haloub gave it to us when Kelly and I got married. I can't resist running my hands over the smooth surface. I tease free the finial and gaze at the letters incised in its base. *stone*

We have both journeyed a long way to this place, this home that belongs to me and Kelly and Bridget and, now, our unborn child. I intend that it will always belong to us. But it is Rose's memory that I must attend to today. I pick up the package she mailed the day she disappeared. I have waited to re-examine it, certain I know all it contains, afraid to be wrong.

Soldier whines to go outside. I watch him circle the yard, reassuring himself that all is well. He sniffs at the trees Kelly and I have planted, one for Fox, one for Rocky, one for Rose, and moves on to the fence at the back of the property. Done with his business, the shepherd returns. Sensing my disquiet, he winds himself around my legs until I bend to pet him. Then he lies down, gifting me with his presence as I consider Rose's final communication.

Fox is gone, and a portion of Rose's ashes rest with him. Kelly and I decided, after much negotiation for Mason's permission, to scatter them in the creek at the end of Dream Street. If there is such a thing as reincarnation, they'll come back as father and daughter. They'd both like that.

"So, Soldier," I tell him, "now I know all the answers I'll ever know. Or do I?" He looks up at me, yawns, and puts his head down again. I use my pocketknife to tease free more of the packing tape. The brown paper wrapping comes loose, but not without a fight. Like Rose, the package resists revealing its secrets. Careful to preserve the hand-written address, the calligraphy as beautiful as the woman who drew it, I remove the outer layer and examine the words on the inside wrapping.

For my brother, Peter Stone, whose soul dwells in the house of tomorrow.

Then I touch the kaleidoscope. Rose has polished and preserved it, but something about the toy is different. When I lift it out, the barrel rests heavy in my palm. In the space where it lay, I find a leather pouch decorated with papier-mâché leaves. I set the kaleidoscope aside and search the package again. Among the leaves, I uncover a tiny arrow inset in a miniature bow aimed at the stem of an oak leaf. I scratch at the thin brown stem. The leaf springs upright, like a sail caught in the breeze. Unaided, the leaves explode upward, unfurling in a long ribbon that hangs suspended from the wrapping. Beneath the leaves, secured by painter's tape, the coiled bills our mother stole and Rose recovered lie safe and waiting. Unable to stop myself, grateful that Kelly has gone out and can't witness my departure from stoic endurance, I clutch the kaleidoscope to my chest and allow a sob to escape. I had forgotten. All these years, despite her own need, Rose kept the money safe, just as she'd promised.

Retrieving the bills that have fallen to the floor, I see that the pouch is engraved as well, the words marching around the drawstring opening.

Her name is Bridget. She lives in Oswego. She is safe and loved.

Bridget Hope Stone. My niece. Rose's daughter. If I failed to solve the riddle of Rose's disappearance, she had a backup plan.

I recall the verses Rose quoted when I told her Kelly and I were getting married.

"Remember, Pete, if you have children, what Gibran wrote." Her voice cracked with a huskiness I mistook for a cold. "Your children are not your children, they are the sons and daughters of life's longing for itself. Seek not to make them like you."

"Rose," I told her then, "you're supposed to be happy for us."

She didn't respond. When I prodded her, she said, "I wish we'd known that growing up."

I remember something else Rose said, words spoken in the bedroom of our house on Dream Street. *Put your eye to the glass, Peter.* Lifting the kaleidoscope as she urged me so long ago, I put it to my eye and turn the scope. Inside, among the slivers of pink and green and amethyst-colored glass, I spy something I missed. It is a picture of Rose's daughter. In the photo, she is laughing, her hair so much like Coal's, but her mouth and nose and eyes the steady, uncompromising features of Rose. The image twists and wavers, unveiling itself only to drift away the moment I turn my hand.

A Word To My Readers

*I*t has been a long journey with Rose and Peter. These characters have lived in my heart until they demanded to be set free. I hope you like them as much as I do. Although several place names actually exist, I have taken some liberties with their locations. This is, after all, a fictional tale set in a fictional version of a real city.

Writing this novel has been a joy enhanced by all who have accompanied me in the process. My sincere thanks to the editors who chose to publish four of the chapters as stand-alone stories. My love and enduring gratitude to my writing angels who kept telling me to finish this story: Rosalie Yoakam (deceased), Joanne Huist Smith, and Kristi McBride Purnhagen. Deep thanks and appreciation to my first readers, poet extraordinaire Myrna Stone and editor Donna Laugle, who gifted this novel writer and novice poet with their fine comments; and to my brother Walter Mackin, who told me the story broke his heart and who created the artwork that represents Rose at the creek bed with her sand drawing. I send special writer love to my grandchildren – Michelle, Mara, and Mateo – who think I'm good at telling stories and have started to write their own.

I also give special thanks to Shirrel Rhoades and the group at Key West Mystery Fest who support my writing and who selected this novel for the WHODUNIT Award in 2019. My publisher, Absolutely Amazing Books, has an expressed mission to give voice to writers who might not otherwise have one. I am deeply grateful.

Acknowledgements

Grateful acknowledgement is made to the editors of the following publications where chapters from this novel, in slightly altered form, first appeared:

FLIGHTS and ACROSS THE SPECTRUM: "The Weight of Possibility" 2003

OASIS Journal 2005: "Halfway Home"

Plymouth Writers Group Anthology ACTS OF EMANCIPATION: "To Touch the Heart of the World" 2005

Plymouth Writers Group anthology POINTS OF CONNECTION: "Rose in Waiting" 2008

Deep appreciation and thanks to Linford Dettwiler and Karin Bergquist of Over the Rhine for permission to use a line from "Latter Days" on the Good Dog, Bad Dog album.

About the Author

J.E. Irvin is a career educator and award-winning author. Her stories have appeared in both print and online journals and magazines, including *Alfred Hitchcock Mystery Magazine* and *Spark a creative anthology*. Avid canoeists, Irvin and her husband live in Springboro, Ohio, on the edge of a nature park.

ABSOLUTELY AMA⚡ING eBOOKS

AbsolutelyAmazingEbooks.com
or AA-eBooks.com

Made in the
USA
Lexington, KY